Prai[se]

"If a novel can be measured [by the] ness of its characterization, [and the] prose, then *The Poser*, Jacob Rubin's smart and absorbing debut, claims its power early and rarely surrenders it. . . . I hear echoes of Steven Millhauser and Tom McCarthy. . . . But the sensibility with which [Rubin] shapes his story is highly individual: probing, witty, yet hiding at its center a strangely iron compassion."

—Kevin Brockmeier, *The New York Times Book Review*

"A masterful debut . . . [a] meditation on the nature of identity delivered with vaudeville verve . . . *The Poser*, as it follows Giovanni from triumph to perilous triumph, seduces you with its fanciful prose, its larger-than-life characters, and its fun-house-mirror take on a land of opportunity where appearance often trumps reality. It's also one heck of a way for Rubin to announce his own presence on the literary stage." —*The Washington Post*

"Precise and inventive writing . . . *The Poser* is an exciting debut, and I recommend it for its noirish beats. It is also richly, darkly funny. The novel is set in a fictional country that resembles America in the 1940s and '50s, and Rubin has exquisitely created this world; it is easy to get lost in it. . . . At its heart [*The Poser*] offers a deeply sensitive exploration into matters of identity and authenticity." —Associated Press

"*Zelig* with a dash of *Being There*."
—*New York Magazine*, Approval Matrix (highbrow/brilliant)

"Rubin writes with unbridled inventiveness, a vaudeville show on paper. . . . There's a hint of Woody Allen's film *Zelig* here, and a picaresque quality that finally tips over into darkly comic horror. . . . Rubin, who's worked as a stand-up comedian, knows about performance, and the ways it can both trap and liberate. . . . The novel's last pages . . . open out into a surprisingly tender ending."

—*The Cleveland Plain Dealer*

"To map Rubin's lineage, one would have to draw improbable links between the rueful comedy of Sam Lipsyte, the strange, tender inventions of John Crowley, and the off-historical tales of Steven Millhauser. . . . Rubin isn't afraid of majestic, trippy metaphors à la Denis Johnson."　　　　　　　　—Alexander Benaim, Bookforum.com

"Startlingly fresh . . . Uniquely hyper-energized and metaphorical prose."　　　　　　　　—*Forth* magazine

"Witty, inventive . . . immensely entertaining . . . well-sculpted."　　　　　　　　—*Publishers Weekly*

"Zany."　　　　　　　　—*Booklist*

"Jacob Rubin writes with more vitality, drive, and vision than any young writer I've seen in ten years."　　　　　　—Barry Hannah

"*The Poser* is smart and grand and funny, a wonderful fable. Mr. Rubin is a great hope for comic fiction in the twenty-first century. He's got the spirit and the ear."
　　　　—Sam Lipsyte, *New York Times* bestselling author of *The Ask*

"I yawped—because when you read a book as exquisite as *The Poser*, you yawp. Have you ever met a character like Giovanni Bernini? My heart breaks even now. With astonishing control, Mr. Rubin has created the perfect comic noir tragedy of mimicry and betrayal, of great love and greater loss. Bernini is one of fiction's great ciphers and his parallel universe is such a good imitation of our universe I can no longer distinguish which is which. This is a novel that will be loved and admired for years to come."
　　　　—Reif Larsen, *New York Times* bestselling author of
　　　　The Selected Works of T. S. Spivet and *I Am Radar*

PENGUIN BOOKS

THE POSER

Jacob Rubin's writing has appeared in the anthology *Best New American Voices*, *The New Yorker* online, *New York* magazine, *Slate*, *n+1*, and *The New Republic*. He also writes for television and film. He lives in New York.

THE POSER

A NOVEL

JACOB RUBIN

PENGUIN BOOKS

PENGUIN BOOKS

An imprint of Penguin Random House LLC
375 Hudson Street
New York, New York 10014
penguin.com

First published in the United States of America by Viking,
an imprint of Penguin Random House LLC, 2015
Published in Penguin Books 2016

THE LIBRARY OF CONGRESS HAS CATALOGED THE HARDCOVER EDITION AS FOLLOWS:
Rubin, Jacob.
The poser : a novel / Jacob Rubin.
pages cm
ISBN 978-0-670-01676-1 (hc.)
ISBN 978-0-14-310795-8 (pbk.)
1. Impersonation—Fiction.   2. Singers—Fiction.   3. Self-actualization
(Psychology)—Fiction.   4. Humorous stories.   I. Title.
PS3618.U294P67 2015
813'.6—dc23
2014038538

Printed in the United States of America
1   3   5   7   9   10   8   6   4   2

Set in Bodoni MT Std
Designed by Alissa Rose Theodor

For my mother and father

. . . or if a Sparrow come before my Window I take part in its existence and pick about the gravel.

JOHN KEATS

Imitation is criticism.

WILLIAM BLAKE

THE POSER

"There you are! Christ!" Anthony Vandaline, of all people, came waddling up the stairs. "I'm a pilgrim in the dark. I'm searching and searching. And—ah, finally."

At this late hour, only four men remained at the balcony bar, stoking each other's laughter with shouted stories. One even bent at the waist, gripping the back of a chair. Performing for me. Soon, I knew, would come the sharp compliment or offered beer, and I prepared myself by seeming unaware, a man immersed in his life. I stroked Lucy's hand, doing that thing where I looked from her hands up to her eyes and down again. What she was saying in that low voice, however, the one she risked only when we were alone, I can't rightly say, for I was listening to the men.

Then Vandaline arrived, and they fell silent. Lucy stood to meet him.

"Ugh, you're one of those people who's always *heeere*," she said. "It's like I'm gonna turn around and trip on you."

"Look, my priest is gonna blush at this thing when I print it in full. All my sins. But I was talking to Max, and he said, and I quote, 'the heart of his technique is something called'—yeah, here it is—'the thread.'"

A show tune played through the house speakers.

"Now you answer this," Vandaline said, "and I'm gone. I mean, I walk out the door."

"It's a skill you should practice more," Lucy said.

"Doll, whatever you think of me, I'm after the truth. A servant of the truth. A butler to it, truly," he said. "Now I wasn't wrong about everything, was I? Your man Maximilian printed that profile about Giovanni, so I did what any reporter worth his salt would do, didn't I? I checked the facts, humbly, and published them. Humbly."

"But what happened then?" I asked, half-turning to the men who tittered at the attention, like schoolboys before an upperclassman.

"Did I get overzealous?" Vandaline said. "Guilty as charged. But, boy, oh, boy, did you prove me wrong. Hell, I'm shaken up just standing here. You think I wanna *stand here* after what happened tonight? I'm just a butler with my plate, asking someone to put the truth on it, so I can serve it to the public. Warm and tasty. Now, I'm gonna correct the whole thing in tomorrow's column. My god, am I gonna correct it. This is gonna be the best goddamn advertising you ever got—not that you need it. But, in all seriousness, please, just tell me about the thread."

"If Max lied earlier," I said, "why isn't he lying now?"

"Are you saying he is?" Like a man in a shootout pulling for his gun—with that practiced, defensive quickness—the reporter raised the pen to his pad.

"No," I said.

To my surprise Vandaline didn't harass the pause that followed, waiting for me, I guess, to say more. Bless him. Despite himself, he was a collaborator. When earlier in the night, Max's patter was derailed by the appearance at the foot of the stage of a stubby man declaring that I was a fraud and pretender—well, I immediately recognized Vandaline and was pleased, for I knew he would insist on joining us onstage, where I could do him once and for all.

So it was when he appeared at the balcony bar. In my churning waltz with the public, there was a time to lead and a time to be led, and the upstairs bar of the Communiqué at two a.m. did feel like the venue for a second performance, more intimate than the night's formal entertainment. "The thread," I said. Downstairs they'd started stacking chairs and clearing the stage. Shadowy figures scooped up a table's glasses, four in a hand, and pushed, back first, through the doors. "Well, okay, so most people believe imitation to be an art of exaggeration. There's truth to this, of course. It's important, as a tool, it is. But it comes second." Bernard, I noticed only then, sat at the end of the bar. It might have been a photo of him if not for the smoke rising from his cigarette.

"Now I was fortunate to be born with the elastic limbs, the perfect pitch you and your colleagues have been kind enough to write about. But I would have been lost without this knowledge: The real thing, the heart of it, isn't exaggeration, or even duplication. It's *selection*: knowing which parts of a person to take and which to leave alone." I frowned the way people do to indicate a concept too complex to be articulated. "You see, everyone disguises himself with certain gestures. A man clearing his throat while snapping open a newspaper, the way a woman covers her yawn on the bus—these gestures are a costume. Now some do it better than others. Some have made perfect little suits for themselves: politicians, for instance, movie stars. Those charismatic types who tool around in their bodies like rented sports cars. They're *smooth*, right?"

Vandaline held the notepad at his chest like a cop writing a ticket.

"The miracle of the world, Mr. Vandaline, is that no one's disguise is perfect. There is in every person, no matter how graceful, a seam, a thread curling out of them. It's like a pimple that rouge cannot cover up, a patch of thinning hair. Often, it's the almost-unnoticed thing that's a thread: a bit lip, a slight sigh. But when pulled by the right hands, it will unravel the person entire."

In the silence I knew would follow I found myself thinking of Mama. How she and Mr. Derringer looked that day in the glass of the principal's door: a patch of red (Mama), a blob of black (Derringer). It was a sort of magic, what the closed door did to them, or seemed like it from the outer office where I was made to wait. Across from me, the principal's secretary, Mrs. Chappabelle, mouthed words she clacked on a typewriter, out of view. Every few minutes she'd look up at the desk's basket of candy canes. "You don't want a tasty treat?"

The smile I was holding began to wilt.

"Suit yourself. But if you change your mind, you know *exactly* where they are." She winked and had lowered her gaze to the typewriter, thank God, when I burped up, "Suit yourself."

"What was that?" The phone on her desk rang. "Principal Derringer's Office . . . Oh, hi, Susan. Yes. But. No. He's in a . . . you want me to—perfect. Five o'clock at the—okay, great."

There was a giggling by the door where two girls stood. They grinned like hobos: mouths pocked with missing teeth. "Freak," they whispered. "Monkey." I was standing up when the principal's door yawned open, and out strode Mama. There must have been an event at the library for she wore her fanciest dress: the checkered one with the belted waist and big bow at the collar. It didn't matter what she wore. Mama was the queen of every room.

She thanked Mrs. Chappabelle, took my hand, and walked me out of the office. Outside it was overcast, and the wind sprayed a hint of salt on the school building, Main Street, and the animal-faced cars as if to prevent it all from going bad. When we reached the curb, Mama looked down at me with an exaggerated frown. It did no harm. Beatrice Bernini was a beautiful woman, I'd heard other parents say. "That Derringer's a real crow, isn't he? Some-one ought to tell him life's already started."

With that, she snatched my hand and just short of skipped me across Main Street, past Lipswitch Avenue to the gusty board-walk where she plopped down on a bench and promptly folded her legs. She patted the space next to where she sat, and I joined her. Before us stretched the ocean, its gulls and clouds. "Ah, school's all screwed up. How to laugh. What jokes are. Those should be the first things they teach you. Come." I sat stiff as a post until she'd ducked behind me and lit a cigarette. "Mr. Heedling, huh?"

Heedling. Whatever interests had led him to the profession of teacher, a desire on his part to spend his weeks in the company of thirteen-year-old boys and girls could not have been counted among them. The paraded sense of humor, the jaunty manner some teachers perfect so as to endear themselves to adolescent tastes, Heedling never attempted. He spoke to us like a drunk at a bar: often gruff, rarely dishonest. Word was, he had been dis-charged from the army after falling victim to, or helping perpe-trate, a massacre on a distant, palm-treed island. His method of instruction was one of impassioned repetition. The previous week he had repeated, *Don't you envy Sisyphus?* We were forced to scrib-ble it in our notebooks thirty times.

"What did Helen of Troy look like?" he asked that day.

As he lectured, he stalked and circled our desk-chairs, curling Mary Hammerworth's *Anthology of Greek Myth* around its spine. Since he could fly into a rage if he suspected the slightest bit of daydreaming or note-passing, the class did its best to strike postures of attention. For my classmates, I guess, this involved some theater. Not for me. I loved the Greeks. They weren't like other stories where you, the reader, decide if they are any good. Questioning Atlas's or Icarus's fate was like complaining the ocean rolled the wrong way or the sky carried the weather with too much pomp.

Inspired by those stories, I'd been on good behavior all semester. Each fall was that way, offering a brief window of renewal. In recess I watched the older boys play stickball. The way they strode and wound up to fling the ball, all of it such glamorous evidence of what growing up could do, and every night I went to bed hoping the Big Change would happen, that I would stretch to six feet tall and say goodbye to all that trouble at school.

In fact, things had been looking up. I had even volunteered in class, a once-unthinkable risk made possible by a new strategy. That is, I had begun using the voice of Jimmy Nelson, the bemused and even witty son of Danny Hoagland's neighbor on the popular radio program *The Hoaglands*. It seemed a safe choice. For one, Jimmy Nelson appeared on the show irregularly, and when he did, existed, mainly, to air concern in the face of Rascal Hoagland's latest lawn-ruining mischief. His very *off-to-the-sidedness* appealed to me.

"Tell me now, what did she look like?" Heedling asked.

"My mother," Philip Howes volunteered. Philip sat in the front row and was always offering a first response to Heedling's questions even though our teacher had never approved of his answers and once, in a fit of anger, called him a "true egg sucker."

"You are *wrong*!" Heedling said. He asked Alice Krut, who sat behind Philip: "What did Helen of Troy look like?"

"Rebecca Rell, the cheerleader."

"Absolutely incorrect." He asked Adrienne Chitwood, who sat behind Alice: "What did she look like?"

"A movie star."

"Oh, god." He addressed the classroom. "What did she look like?"

Silence.

"Jesus Christ." He turned to draw on the board. Because Mr. Heedling possessed exquisite peripheral vision, no one misbehaved, even when he faced the blackboard. He often called on Todd Willinger, third seat, row five, while looking at Mallory Mayhall, first seat, row one. Someone once asked him why he did this, and he gave that person detention.

With staccato strokes, he drew a stick-figure face: two tiny circles for eyes, a line for a nose, line for a mouth. Then he drew curly sprouts of hair. "Helen of Troy!" As with many of Heedling's lessons, it was hard to tell what the lesson was, but a fury of passion was behind it, so you knew you were missing something. When he taught us the myth of Orpheus, he kept saying, *Music is when something disappears*, hovering over us as we scribbled the saying ten times into our notebooks. "Helen of Troy!" Heedling said again, looking almost pleased.

"That's just a face," Philip Howes protested.

Heedling stopped and looked at Philip. "Philip," he said, "be very, very careful." He marched behind us, to the other side of the classroom. "*Helen of Troy! The one and only!*"

He was wrong, though. Helen of Troy inhabited our very classroom, three rows to my right through a thicket of profiles. Her name was Margot Stamfield, and she was the chandelier in my brain. Every class I studied her face: the subtle lift of her chin, the hint of a smile. Once when I was heading down the fourth-floor stairs, repeating, "Don't you envy Sisyphus?" (Heedling's phrases were like sucking candy to me), I rounded the landing to find her standing there, in all her Martian beauty, clutching a textbook. "Envy him, goddamnit!" I yelped, and sprinted down the stairs.

"Copy this in your notebooks," Heedling said, stalking the class. A flurry of turned pages. The mouse noise of pencils. "This is a very important face, remember! Essential. Without it, you— what's this, Ms. Stamfield?"

"It's what you wanted," Margot said. Heedling hovered over her desk-chair, I saw when I looked up. "To draw it ten times," she said.

"Is it? Is this what I wanted, really?" With a light-footed movement Heedling all but danced to the front of the class where he drew, with quick, impassioned stabs of chalk, a second Helen of Troy. The chalk dusted his hands, a very specific feeling. This new figure, Margot's presumably, looked admirably close, if not identical, to the first. "The same, *really*?"

"They are, right?" she said.

"Are they, though?" Heedling grinned, approaching her desk again. He could move stealthily, too, with quick, catlike steps I liked to practice.

"I—I think so."

"Perhaps you're *thinking too much*, Ms. Stamfield."

Her lip began to quiver.

"Ms. Stamfield, no need to get *emotional*, I am simply asking—"

"Ms. Stamfield, I am simply asking!" I found I was pacing along the side of the classroom. I grabbed a piece of chalk, to feel it on my hand. "I'm asking," I repeated, "if you can answer me *that*, please? Write the answer ten times, please! I'm asking if you can write the answer and erase it ten times! No, eleven, please, *erase it, yes!"* Mr. Heedling reddened in the corner of my eye, but my classmates laughed uncontrollably, laughed in that bottled way, as if soda were bursting out of their noses, Margot among them, and I turned to them and began laughing, too. Yes, this laugh was so delicious, it burst out of me, more and more of it until their faces blanched, Margot's most of all, as though some mean ghost were parading before them. Yet the laughter kept cascading out my nose, so much of it, like the handkerchief a magician endlessly pulls out of his pocket. Someone grabbed the back of my neck—

"Get out! Get out! . . ." I did it for Mama at the boardwalk. "You little—Brrring . . . Brrr. Why hello, Principal Derringer's office—yes, of course. *Helen of Troy. Of Troy!"*

When I looked back at her, Mama was beyond laughter, already casting her look at me, her Look, I should say, for Mama's eyes were unnaturally big, like sideways teardrops, and could do things no one else's could. It was all the parts of her you couldn't reach, that interior mystery, pushed against their furthest limit, and you gathered how much she hated the rules of bodies, that one person could be only one and that certain spaces would always separate us. Most rooms just weren't big enough for her.

"You found his thread," she said. "And you want to pull it, don't you? Undo his whole costume." She reached out her hands for me, and I sat in her lap. She growled and squeezed me, crushed me for a moment, in the near-violent way mothers do. The sky was getting grayer. Soon winter would come when darkness falls at four o'clock, and the stars make sad dreaming babies of all the world.

"One day everyone will see you the way I do."

She said this often.

"People don't like me."

"Not true."

"I have no friends."

"Friends are overrated. You'll get some soon enough and see what I mean."

"Giovanni," Vandaline said.

"Yes?"

"I said, if everyone has this—this thread as you call it, this *seam* sticking out—well then, I must ask, what's yours?"

The men leaned in. At the far end of the bar, Bernard raised a cigarette to his lips. I didn't dare look at Lucy.

"Why," I said. "I'm the exception."

MAX

ONE

After high school, my mother's friend Julius Weld helped me land a job at the train station in Dun Harbor, a dour nub of coastline twenty minutes south of Sea View. Mainly, I was relieved to finish school, where nearly every week I was banished to Derringer's office. Too much stimulation, Mama said. The girls with their skirts and sculpted hair; the boys oily and mean. "Giovanni!" someone would howl, and I'd come to, like a boy who with every step knocked over an expensive vase.

As I soon discovered, my job as a ticket seller required me to utter the same pronouncements dozens of times a day: "We recommend getting to the track ten minutes before scheduled departure." Or, "Kindly check the board for updates." I kept to the ticket seller's booth. I knew what to say, and if ever the old urge came over me, I dammed it with politeness: the simple rules that, once followed, erected a brick wall between you and the world. *Excuse me, Good day.* "After you," I insisted, holding the door for all strangers, unless, of course, a man my senior insisted otherwise, in which case I dug my chin to my chest, said, "'Preciate it, sir," and strode ahead.

Of course, this meant every businessman and runaway, every stubbly bachelor when buying a ticket unwittingly logged the details of their appearance with me. My politeness, I discovered, made for an acceptable disguise, so when wishing a man a good day, I could secretly relish each detail: the way he checked his watch, say, or slid change off the counter, sharing these bits with Mama at night.

Always she was my strongest encourager. If ever I got into trouble at school, she would tell all offended parties that I was sympathetic to the bone. This, her constant response to the hurricane of hair pulls, harangues, schoolyard exclusions, and teachers' meetings I was always causing the world.

When I was four, for instance, Great Uncle Arthur, Mama's only living relative, visited us from out west. A sigh punctuated each effort of his limbs, and the old man's kiss he gave Mama sounded like tape being ripped from a wall. "Put it there," he said, throwing out his hand. "You heard me, pardner, put it there," I answered. "I heard about this," Arthur said, turning to leave minutes after arriving. Mama jumped in front of him. "You can't, Arthur. He's just—"

Or at Susan Sanders's June party. Lobster, shrimp, and steamers served in their never-ending backyard. The older children cavorting by the tire swing. I remember chasing a freckled girl with straw-colored ringlets around some oaks, believing if I caught her, my whole life would explode, and must've still been exhilarated by that chase when we gathered, fifty of us, around the red picnic table for Susan's annual toast. Many wore white linen suits and pearls. Mama beamed at me from behind a cityscape of champagne bottles. The girl I'd chased was thumbing bits of brownie from between her teeth.

"A toast," Susan said. On cue the adults raised their flutes of champagne, the children their glasses of chocolate milk or ginger ale. "We are just delighted everyone could make it," she said, playing with her earrings. To speak Susan Sanders had to kick the grass or twist her legs around each other. But most of all, she couldn't keep her hands off her earrings, and I often wondered what mute depths she'd sink to if parted from that essential jewelry. "A delight to have you. An absolute delight. With the money, the money, the friends, and the money," I surprised myself by announcing, and soon all I could hear were the birds, and the mouths around the table were getting bigger until Mama draped her arms over my shoulders and said, "He means perfectly well. He's just—"

Or when Mama and I attended Brad Mason's funeral at the Sea View Cemetery, which sits atop one of the few real hills outside of town. Even with its weeds and jagged gravestones the cemetery provided a sort of grandeur because of its view. Seagulls ambled around between flights, like ducks. That day it was overcast and blustery. Me, in a blazer with brass buttons, Mama sniffling out of view. It was the tragedy of that year: Brad Mason, my ten-year-old classmate, smashed by a truck. The women had to keep one hand atop their wide-brimmed hats to prevent the wind from snatching them. The priest's exact words were lost in the wind. You could hear his sincere voice but couldn't make out the words. When he stopped speaking, Brad's mother, behind a speckled veil, buckled to her knees and wept so that two handsome young men in black suits had to hoist her up; and soon they were glaring at me with iron mouths—Mrs. Mason, too, her eyes white as eggs under her veil—because I was buckling my knees and weeping to the sky; *Oh, no,* I think I was saying, *Oh, no,* and poor Mama had to explain—as she had to Uncle Arthur and Susan Sanders, as she had to so many people—that Giovanni, her son, was sympathetic to the bone. She even wrote a note that I was to keep in my pocket and present to people if ever things got out of hand.

By the time I began work at the train station I had gained
control enough of my instincts to spare myself and others these
outbursts, storing them for my performances with Mama. We had
a ritual. After dinner, Mama would sit Indian-style on the couch
while I cracked my neck and stretched as if we weren't alone in
our one-story house but center stage at the Sea View County Theatre. Mama might even shush imaginary attendees and then flick
the lamp on and off, signaling the start of the show. To this day I
wonder how those demonstrations appeared to any passerby
chance may have placed at our picture window: a woman, they
would have seen, upright as a piano teacher, yanking and steering
her boy around with the strings of her words. "Tilt your head."
"*Sloshy* hips." "Raise it, yes! Perfect!"

Sometimes Mama even stopped by the train station to observe
the exact way a favorite of ours doffed his cap or, say, lightly licked
her finger, making a pleased expression of the mouth before turning a magazine's glossy page. This was no mere indulgence. These
field trips felt, if anything, like missions, akin to our jaunts to the
movie theater, a sanctuary of my childhood. There all the dull bits
of life had been excised, the world distilled to *happening*, a dream
in which even homely acts—a body tossing in bed, say—rivaled a
general's howl for sheer immortality. There I could hike knees to
chest and mirror it all. At a deserted matinee, I would sometimes
even gallop through the aisle to hail a cab like the hair-flying pros-
ecutor onscreen, Mama ogling me as much as the picture.

And yet, as I grew older, I preferred to stay in my movie-
theater chair, watching like anyone else. Each moment like learning a new word. The way a man grabbed a woman's shoulders
before kissing her. The flashing eyes of a pursued driver in the
rearview mirror. The correct style in which one combs a bronze
coiffure after removing a hat. Or the way to set that hat down at

the edge of the desk. Or, for that matter, the difference between the way an honest man sets a hat down on a desk and a liar does (the latter removing his hand right after, as if the lid might snap at him, then briefly rubbing his escaped hand with the other before slipping both in their respective pockets, whistling and pacing with shifty eyes).

Yes, I preferred to observe these gestures rather than make them. The same was true at the train station, where my politeness helped make me a viewer. I don't remember when exactly in my four years there my nightly performances stopped—or slowly receded, to be revived only by a rare peacocking figure or bona fide celebrity, as when the movie actress Lydia Peele came up on the south train from Pellview. Mama pushed, but I begged off. To mimic felt like a risk, a frightful departure from a far cozier act, one that began at seven a.m. sharp with the bleeping alarm clock and ended at five when I rode the bus home. Nor did the ticket-seller act have to end then. It carried on past dinner when I read a popular novel in bed and would live on soon enough, I hoped, in a house of my own populated by a ticket seller's wife and ticket seller's children, a family who would kiss and be kissed by me and who would never meet, as long as they lived, the heaps of sleeping strangers inside their man.

One August afternoon I was walking to the bus station when a voice called for me. "Excuse me," it said. "You, there. Excuse!" I turned. There stood a broad and tall man with apple-sized cheeks and a shock of black hair. "You're the boy, correct? The boy with the million faces?" When he smiled, he revealed teeth so white and square they looked fake.

"Correct is right!" I said. "That I am. He is I."

He slapped me. "No games, boy! I'm not some object to piss

on!" A moment later, though, he sucked in a deep breath. He was wearing gray slacks and a satin blue shirt stained with sweat at the crown of his belly. "My apologies for not introducing myself," he said. "Maximilian Horatio, Management and Artist Representation. A great pleasure to meet you."

I weakly accepted his hand.

"I have to say, that was quite a good Maximilian Horatio you did and you've only known me—what—the time it takes for two fits of gas to escape a horse's rear?" He wiped his forehead with the back of his hand. "You're Giovanni Bernini, no? I've heard of your talent, and I think there's money in it. And after money come the other treats—women, fame, girl fun . . . but let's get out of this goddamn sun. Discuss it at my place. Just an hour of your time?"

He kept shifting the jacket he was holding to one hand, then the other, then to the crook of his elbow, so he could point and gesture without interruption. I dug my hands into my pockets. Felt something, a ball of lint, maybe.

"What I thought," he said. "Quotation marks."

I focused on not knitting my brow.

"Now, an imitation like that—you do a dead-on imitation like that with no warning and someone will slap you. Hell, they might wait for you to fall asleep and urinate on you. But do it on a stage, do it for an audience, and they'll piss *themselves*."

We were the only people on the street. Outside of the port, where longshoremen hauled containers on and off ships, Dun Harbor's greatest landmark was the state prison, a dismal knuckle of gray, from which you were wise to keep your distance.

"What's a stage?" he asked me.

"I don't think I know," I said in my ticket seller's voice. I couldn't believe how much effort it took not to do him.

"A set of quotation marks. On a stage, you're not saying anything as *you*. You're saying, '*What if* I said this.' You're saying, '*What if* I were this.' Now, I'm willing to bet you've been living a what-if kind of life all along while everyone around you's been *saying* and *doing*, getting in their cars and drinking cherry soda." He lifted his gaze toward the low, lifeless buildings. "What do you say we get out of this goddamn heat?"

I couldn't say no to him. What I mean is, I was physically incapable. I was like a moon in the orbit of a bullying planet.

"Okay," I said.

He patted my back so hard I rattled. "Excellent! Excellent!"

Together we walked up the sorry boulevard. He talked more and more, his hands dancing to his speech. I pulled out the ball of lint to toss in the gutter, realizing, as soon as I did, what it was.

"What's that there?"

I handed it to him, hoping he'd read it in silence. Instead he cleared his throat. "If Giovanni has given you this note, it is because an incident has occurred. Please understand no harm is meant. He is simply sympathetic to the bone." He frowned, impressed. "A boy who comes with a manual!" Maybe he noticed my expression. "Have you heard the one about the man who wanted to forget his past?"

I shook my head.

"Oh, it's a classic." He smiled like a ringmaster. "An old widower, right? Terrible past. His wife killed, all three of his sons killed, his two daughters, cow, dog, even his lovely, baby pigeon 'Orangutan'—all dead. Someone destroyed his pigeon. It's a whole other thing. Anyway he prays to God, saying, 'How can I get rid of the past? Jesus, please erase my past. I'd rather be ignorant than live with this foul dung on my brain. Please, oh, please.' Because he's afraid, you see. 'With this past, how can I have room for anything new, oh, Jesus.' And so one night the man's praying, and Jesus comes to him and says, 'You want to forget the past?' 'Yes,' the man said. 'Yes, thank you.' 'You want to be freed of it, have it erased?' 'Yes, Jesus,' the guy's saying. 'You really want to?' 'Yes, oh, yes.' And Jesus tells him, Jesus looks at him and Jesus says: *'Forget about it!'*"

He slapped his right thigh and hooted toward the sky.

"Now, *that's* a joke," he said after his laughter softened to a sigh. Then he said, "Oh, right," as if remembering something he'd planned to do for a long time. He held the note with both hands and, with a magician's solemnity, tore it up in the sunlight, like confetti, like a celebration, like he'd made a rabbit disappear.

TWO

"The place is, well, *unclean*," Max warned as we trudged up the five flights in the tenement where he rented a room. The light fixtures droned like insects. "You're my worst disease!" a woman somewhere yelled. When we reached his door, a copper 4 hung sideways, resembling in that position a crude sailboat. He fought with the lock. "C'mon," he muttered. "Mean, goddamn—" Then it yawned open, and the odor hit us.

It smelled like many things, like curdled milk, newsprint, and cabbage, but above all reeked of meat. Either Max had murdered a pig or his native musk hung around so long, had become to the air what wallpaper is to walls. "Home—sweetest—sit, boy, sit." The door opened directly into the kitchen, and he motioned to what must've been the kitchen table, though drowned as it was in magazines, brown banana peels, coat hangers, and, strangest of all, a lady's green pump, its surface could not be seen.

Two green socks, soaked black at the heel, occupied the nearest chair. I gloved my hand with my sleeve, removed them, and sat. Many of the kitchen cabinets swung all the way or partially open, revealing amorphous garbage bags and what looked like deeply used athletic equipment. There was no other room, but a small bathroom, and no bed that I could see, just a mat of towels with a pillow behind the refrigerator. The man lived in the kitchen.

"Beer?" He pushed open the window above the sink.

"No, thank you."

"I was right, huh?"

"I'm sorry?" A delicacy of politeness: *I'm sorry?*

"About the place," he said. "It's a mess?"

I didn't know what to say.

"Damn right!" He grabbed a glass and turned the handles above the sink until the water burped out over his hands. Pipes came alive in the wall, and he poured a lengthy stream of green dish soap over the glass, rotating and scrubbing it under the brownish water. "La dee daa dee daa." It seemed to bring his hands such pleasure I had to sit on mine, or else I would've leapt to his side and scrubbed along with him. This jubilant, bearish man—I'd never met a person so preoccupied with the business of his body. I stared again at the table.

Littered over it was a landscape of crumbs and dishware and almost every forum for the printed word: *The Evening Post*, *The City Times*, splayed hardcovers, yellow notebook paper, not to mention a pale thigh outlined by a garter belt, though the rest of the image—the woman's midriff, bra, and ruby lips, presumably—was obscured by a basket of rotten bananas. An excitable hand decorated every page on the table, circling words, adding phallic exclamation marks, the notes swarming like ants in the margin: "Exactly!" "Memorize." "Money?"

"Some orange juice, young squire," Max said, standing over me. Sweat ticked out of my armpits.

"Thank you." I took the still-filthy glass and rested it on a relatively flat pile of magazines. I then scratched my nose so as to make returning my hand to its initial position less conspicuous.

"Awfully glad you could make it," Max said, walking to the

refrigerator. He swung open its door and grabbed—violently—a beer. "Glad as hell." He tilted the bottle at a decisive angle and then decapitated it against the kitchen counter. After batting away whatever occupied his chair, he collapsed into a reclining position, wiping his brow. "This goddamn heat. There are things going on in my body no man should know."

I shook my head though I meant to nod. This could happen. Sometimes at the station, when tired, I said "Please" instead of "Thank you," winked when intending only to smile. Max hadn't noticed, though. He leaned back in that poor bursting chair. "You're not a talker."

"Oh, sometimes." I smiled my ticket-seller smile.

"Fine with me. Talkers, nontalkers. I don't distinguish. Hell, I don't distinguish at all. People are people. That's what entertainment's about." He swigged his beer. "The best performers— the ones who can perform anywhere and get a self-respecting girl to drop her panties and grin *while she does it*—they don't make distinctions. They say, 'Distinctions—'" He blew his thumb, making a flatulent noise, raised his middle finger, and planted his beer on the table. "Look at Shakespeare. His genius? You want a madman? Okay, I'll show you a madman. You want a king? All right. You want a pauper, pixie? Fuck you.

"But as soon as someone's got that talent—I'm talking about someone who can relate to *anyone*, make *us all*"—he drew a wide rink with his finger—"relate to him. When you got someone like that, what do they do?" He shrugged so much his palms were at his shoulders. "They put him on a pedestal. They say, 'I wonder how he does it. How *does* he do it?'" He shook his head. "Have you ever heard the expression 'People worship the lucky'? It's fucking— it's true, boy." Either the hypocrisy itself, or his facility in exposing it, revolted him. He sighed and raised his arm as if to salute, then slapped his hand hard against his thigh. "I talk," he said. "I talk.

"Well, you know what I mean." He stood and began pacing, fanning the bottom of his sweat-stained shirt. "I was in a café in Sea View when I heard of you. Two men talking like they'd seen a ghost. Real shit-them-ole-panties fear." He clasped his hands in front of his chest, wheeling his thumbs over each other. "Their fear—you need that first. Have you considered it? Performing?"

I made a face that said as much as making no face at all, like nodding while breathing out your nose (to express amused agreement), raising your eyebrows while suppressing a smile (mild scandal), or shaking your head while breathing in through the mouth (sympathy)—all those safe expressions I'd perfected at the station.

"What's celebrity?" he asked. "Being different from everyone. Different, so they want to be like you. Usually, it's beauty. Oldest hustle in the world. People never get bored of a beautiful face. Never bored of fucking beauty. I, for one, am *bored of it*. Me, I like a woman whose beauty is tilted ninety degrees." He mimicked twisting the top off a bottle to express the ninety degrees to which beauty ought to be twisted. "Heavy potential. Because of that added layer. You're not up there saying, 'Like me 'cause I dance, like me 'cause I sing.' You're saying, 'Like me 'cause I'm you.' Quite brilliant. Quite a bit of everything, really."

He muttered this last part, and having completed that sprint of breath, collapsed back into the chair. It groaned. "Hmph." Energies blew in and out of the man. He massaged the meat of his neck, pinched the baggy skin around his throat. "Hmph, hmph, hmph." He was staring out the window, or rather, looking at the air outside the window as if it, too, were a window to be looked through. A quality that attracts dogs and babies to a person belonged to him: a certain largesse, a willingness to share oneself with strangers.

Because of this quality, I found myself asking a question, a thing I hated doing. Questions were holes in my demeanor, windows through which rocks could fly. By then, I used the leavened voice of Richard Nelson, the father of radio-fiction (and previous go-to) Jimmy Nelson. Puberty, years before, demanded the shift. An improvement, really. On the diminishingly popular *The Hoaglands*, Richard stood as the true paradigm of the sensible and wry, qualities, if anything, his son (my first model) had aped. "What are these for?" I asked. "All these newspapers, magazines?"

"Research." He planted his elbow on the arm of the chair, rested his two chins on his palm, and sighed. "Been putting my finger to the wind. That finger. You gotta get it wet.

"Month ago I was down in the City. Wore my ass off attending the latest horseshit day and night. Music, comedy, burlesque. Some were B-plus, I'll give them that, but the majority, boy—it was like watching a child make a brown little surprise in his pants, then walk around the aisles, asking everyone to clap for him. Wouldn't know it by the critics, though. Open up the paper, and the critics *love* Brown Surprise. They want *more* Brown Surprise. After all, what's a critic gonna say? 'These are bullshit times. Take a nap.' No, they say, 'Tour de force. Art's as good as ever!' Nonsense. The time is ripe for something *new*, and when they see it—oh, when they see it . . ." He shot up again, pawing through the newspapers on the table. Whether he was searching for something in particular or the frenzied shuffling was a point in its own right, I couldn't tell. "Well, they'll be making cider in their undies. White cider." He looked at me. "What I mean is, they'll sperm themselves."

I raised my eyebrows while suppressing a smile.

"Well, that's the thinking, anyway." He dug his chin into his palm. "It's not that I doubt it. Doubt and I—no, I don't *doubt* things. I just want *other people* to give us the chance. It's the chance that needs to—ah, God, what can you do?" He squeezed circles into his temples and then covered his face entirely with his hand. Out the window a hammer clinked, a common noise in Dun Harbor. Men in hardhats were always streaming in and out of the train station, the reports of their hammers and drills punctuating the afternoon. The place lived in a constant state of construction without anything, as far as I could see, ever being built.

"What is it you're proposing, Max?" I was surprised to hear myself ask.

His eye studied me from between the knuckles of his middle and index fingers. Then his hand slid down his nose and mouth, unveiling a carnival grin. "How much time do you need?"

"I'm sorry?"

"To go on—I mean, you imitated me in—what—a few seconds. Is that all the time you need?"

"Sometimes less."

"Perfect." He was pacing again.

"Perfect *what*? What are you proposing?"

He grinned. It made him look queasy, as evil men do when smiling in children's movies. "What do you say we go down to the City, show the world your gift?"

"But imitating who?"

"Why," he said. "The audience."

"I can do famous people. I can do the president and Dean Fashion, the singer."

"No! No! No!" He stood again. "Boy, the whole point of this— the *revolution* of it—is in imitating the audience. We do celebrities

and we're another two-bit nightclub act. But we get *volunteers*"—
he grinned again—"and we're *artists*."

"But people hate it when I do that. Hell, you slapped me for
doing it. The only way I've gotten along is by *not* doing it. Don't
you understand that?" I couldn't believe I'd said it. Though this
was months before we downed cheap champagne in the mixed
light of the City's downtown, I imagined that this is what it felt
like to be drunk. Max intoxicated a body.

He was standing again. "Where did you get your name?"

"What?"

"It's like you were born with a stage name. How'd you get it?"

"It's my dad's. My mom liked it so much, she wanted me to
have it. She said it reminded her of a beautiful old country full of
statues."

"And what's Daddy do?"

"He left," I said.

It was the most I'd ever said. What I knew was: he was Jew-
ish, a longshoreman, arrived here from Italy. One night he sauntered up to Mama's beat-up sedan at the Sea View Drive-In to say,
"You are my movie girl?" A month after I was born, he left to buy
a bottle of wine and never came back. It was hard to squeeze out
of her more than that, and I, who couldn't bear to upset Mama
and hated asking questions of any kind, wasn't the one to do it. In
the rare moments she did reminisce, it was like someone else was
making the emotion in her face: she scratched the back of her
neck, speaking in a pressured voice. Most often she said, "Your
father was a *magician*." Just as I was "sympathetic to the bone,"
just as that phrase fenced in all my wandering impulses, so the
Old Man was contained by that word.

For years, of course, I dreamt of his return. I would be sitting
in my desk-chair when a knock would startle the classroom door.

Heedling, grumbling at the interruption, would swing it open and there would stand my father. *So sorry, Giovanni's needed home*, he'd say, flashing me a juicy wink. Or he would stroll right through the heart of the boys' stickball game, bow tie loosened, hands in his tuxedo pants, whistling a jazz number. At the train station he'd find me. *One ticket to wherever.* Sometimes lanky and busy-haired, other times barrel-chested and bald, but always in a tux. At a certain age these fantasies receded, or evolved, to imagine the home he had now, for certainly he had one—in Italy, maybe, or the City—where he stroked his new wife's hair and held in his lap a second, tamer Giovanni.

"Makes sense," Max said. "It's the first fact about most entertainers, y'know. Hell of a painful thing, but it's true."

My hands had gone numb.

When Max asked, "Well?" "Yes," is what I said, feeling like I might burst. "Of course," I added, "you'll have to ask my mother."

That week I burped, sighed, even sneezed like him. At work I slapped men on the back to say hello, doffed an imaginary cap to the hurried women. My coworkers must have thought I was drunk or in love. "Denburg," I lectured one ticket buyer. "'Verdant' doesn't begin to describe the greenery."

For many years I assumed everyone knew something I didn't, a simple lesson had been disseminated, a dictum some angel or authority scribbled on everyone's hand except mine. All my life that certainty clung to my heart, I realized as it left me. The businessmen pacing in tight circles, the women dabbing their necks with kerchiefs—each was a nerve-wracked impressionist.

This view helped especially around women, my experiences of

whom, before then, never progressed beyond the horniness of a wallflower. In high school I was always hiding behind lockers and trees to scrutinize the latest gut-churning pass of Margot Stamfield. And at the station, when certain hip-swayers approached the booth, I ducked, like a man attacked, behind the wall of my manners. But, as Max, I could flirt. "If only you gave me as much attention as that purse, I'd be a happy man," I told a slender blonde who couldn't stop fiddling with her clutch. "Why, thank you, mister," she replied, *blushing! Mister!*

During this period, Mama smiled mistily at my grunts and sighs—content, I think, to see me at it again. At the end of the week, I mentioned Max. "When approaching things that are difficult to say, it's best to come out and say them—no other way, really. Whatever preparations you make, well, they must contend with the fact that at a certain point the thing needs to be said, so it's time—"

Mama leaned over and slapped my back. Burped me.

"Earlier this week, a man, a show-business type, but not your usual show-business type, because there's a bone of honesty in him, several in fact—well, he asked for some of my time. I think he's got some bright ideas. Anyhow, he wants to meet with you to illume, as it were, the brightness of these ideas."

Mama ate in silence. "Must be a charmer, the way you've been stomping around."

"He is," I said. "He is! He's even offered to take us out, treat us!"

She snickered. "What is it he wants?"

"Well, I really ought to let him explain—it's only fair a man gets to present—"

"Stop it!"

"He wants to take me to the City. To perform there."

Mama finished her plate in silence. After a long pause she said, "If he wants to pay, he can pay," and cleared the table.

As the location for this fateful dinner, Mama selected Armison's Famous Lobster and Steak Eatery, a tourist trap notorious through all of Sea View for its overpriced and mediocre lobster. "If this big-shot manager wants to treat," she said, checking her lipstick one last time before we stepped into the balmy night, "he can treat at the Famous Eatery."

The short walk to Armison's, she trotted along so fast in heels, I had to skip just to catch up, me in my penny loafers and navy-blue blazer with its brass buttons. It was a warm, starless night, a yellow moon perched in the sky like an unnoticed owl. Couples held hands and pointed at items in the illuminated storefronts as though watching TV. I wrapped my arm around Mama's shoulder and squeezed. "Here we are, lady, you and me, headed to Armison's!" She smiled the way she'd smiled ever since our conversation about Max—flatly, evasively—patted my hand and removed it from her shoulder.

The host led us through the hushed dining room, a wall-length mirror repeating all the mild sumptuousness: noiseless busboys; white-gloved waiters, each table its own conspiracy of candlelight, protected from silence by the ignored music of the piano player. He led us to a back table near the mirrored wall where Maximilian Horatio—ample hair slicked back on his head—already waited. He escaped from his chair.

"Ms. Bernini, I presume." He took her hand and kissed it. He wore a battered, cream-colored suit.

The host pulled back the chair nearest the wall, and Mama eased into it, the way people do when so dressed. He seated me between Mama and Max. The host then urged us to enjoy the meal and scampered back to the dais. A lone calla lily stood in a vase at the center of the table.

"Giovanni told me he had a mother. He did not warn me of her beauty."

Mama smiled quickly and opened a menu. "It's going to be hard to decide. The food here is just extraordinary."

"If the brandy's any indication, we're in for a *fine* evening of cuisine," said Max, raising his tumbler. He patted my knee under the table.

Mama snickered.

"Something funny?" Max asked.

"You sound like someone I know," she said.

"Someone good, I hope."

"Oh, yes," she said, squeezing my other thigh under the table.

"Resemblance, in my experience, is a finicky thing. If I looked like someone you didn't like, it would be, well, *dooming.* An Indian doctor I met once in the circus, he believed all the faces of the people we befriend in this life—they resemble people we knew in a previous one. Reincarnation, et cetera."

"Good hard science," said Mama without taking her eyes off the menu.

I should've known it would be like this. All week I'd looked forward to the dinner—knew that Mama's wit and eyes would square off against Max's bluster and teeth—but had failed to account for my own position: namely, after a week tramping around as Maximilian Horatio, I had to quit the act. Already I was sitting on my hands.

The waiter, dressed in black, appeared, rubbing his hands together mischievously, as if he had a great secret for us. "A drink, ma'am?"

"A gin martini up, please," said Mama. "Perhaps a wine, too, for the table?"

"In addition to our list, which you'll find at the back of the menu, we have a special sauvignon red—a bit pricey but—"

"We'll take it," Mama said.

"Excellent," the waiter said with a serious, servile pout. "Be back in a second."

"Please," Max said, flashing a seasick grin. "Have whatever you want tonight. My treat."

After the waiter returned with Mama's cocktail and uncorked and served the wine, Mama ordered two appetizers of crab cakes and the day's special, a lobster savannah. Max and I requested the standard lobster plate. Mama encouraged me to order an appetizer, too, since Max was so generously offering, but I demurred. The truth was I didn't think I could trust my hands, eating alone. A line of sweat had broken over my forehead, but I couldn't wipe it, not then.

Mama said, "Giovanni tells me you worked in the circus."

"Circle Top Circus, that's right. Stage manager for four years. Developed some acts of my own, too. Mainly with animals. Animals and I have—it's an almost unnatural kinship. Dogs in particular." Max sipped his brandy. "People like to see animals do extraordinary things—jump through hoops, walk on two legs. You know why?"

"I would love to understand why."

"We think it's because they resemble humans, that they're like us—but no! It reminds us that we—we mighty humans—we're just *like them*. You see a dog dance on two legs, see a parrot talk—and we think, We're animals, just like that, with animal needs: food, water, sex, shelter. It gives an audience relief."

"I see."

"*Perspective*. Like Giovanni's imitations. And, believe you me, Ms. Bernini, there's a market for perspective these days. Which reminds me"—he lifted a finger—"I brought my references since I was sure you'd want to, as they say, *peruse* them." He reached into his breast pocket and produced a swatch of creased, gray documents so thick it was hard to believe it had fit in his suit jacket. He stood and, with both hands, delivered the brick of paper to Mama.

She made a bemused expression and began, as it were, *perusing* them. Max winked at me, and I winked back and then blinked two times to erase the effect, a needless precaution, I was happy to realize, as Max was now eyeing Mama, biting his lip and scratching his forehead with an arched finger.

Either Mama truly had no idea Max was watching her read— sighing and tapping his foot—or she did an excellent job of dissembling, here and there snickering, or nodding while pursing her lips as people do to indicate something has impressed them. When the crab cakes arrived, she set the stack of folded papers next to her silverware and continued to read, as if alone at the table, flipping from page to page as she ate, here and there dabbing the corners of her mouth with the peach napkin. When she had finished eating, she looked at both of us and smiled. "Hmmm-mmm. That was good."

By this point, Max was halfway through his second brandy. He'd pushed his chair back from the table, resting his fist on his hip. A nervous checking of his watch would have completed the pose.

"Would you like to take a look?" Mama asked me after she had restored the pages to their original order.

"Okay," I said in as calm a voice as I could muster, receiving the stack with trembling hands. This was unwise, I knew—freeing

my fingers—but I was curious, not so much to read the papers as
to touch them. The pile, I soon saw, consisted largely of well-folded
letters, but included, too, such diverse media as bar tabs, cocktail
napkins, fortunes from Chinese cookies, and, in one case, a lami-
nated slab of toilet paper on which a man named Russ had attested,
in curling pen strokes, to Max's having "a confused kind of grace."
"You can't do no better than Max," signed Jenny. Most were
unreadable. The only typed reference in the packet was signed by
a Dr. Seamus Finnegan, Director, Circle Top Circus, and read as
follows: "Maximilian Horatio is occasionally punctual." Underneath this note was tucked a peacock feather.

"Lady MacGuffin's head-feather," Max said when he noticed
me twirling it in my lap. "A rare item, indeed."

"I was wondering what that was," said Mama.

"I was glad to see you take your time reading those. Too often
people skip over important documents, contracts and whatnot,
rather than *dig in*, really *sink their teeth in* and read."

"I absolutely agree."

"Too often they just, as they say, *sign on the dotted line*."

"Without reading what they're signing."

"A shame."

"Too common."

There was a long silence.

"What did you think of them if I might ask?"

"Your?" Mama said.

"References." He smiled queasily.

"Oh," said Mama. "Well, I wasn't very impressed, Mr. Horatio."

"Max, please."

"I can't say I was impressed, Mr. Horatio."

"If we can just settle on Max."

"Half of it is illegible. The other half's signed by people with only one name."

"Those so-called one-names are what we call VIP personalities. That Russ, that Russ you see there—that's Russ Banham, owner of the biggest nightclub in Fantasma Falls. Sebastian Foy is *the* most important talent manager in the City. As for the illegibles, well, keep in mind, there's a certain smudge factor here. I'm a traveling man, things get smudged. That's just a reality."

"Lobster savannah," the waiter announced.

"Right here," said Mama, with a smile.

He set down the platter with the butter-soaked cruise ship of lobster and laid down the rest of the dishes: the two pink one-and-a-half-pound lobsters, the pale corn, and small dishes of butter. "Enjoy." The waiter smiled seriously and disappeared.

"Big names or not, Mr. Horatio, they don't mean much scribbled on toilet paper."

"Let's—let's," Max said, pumping his knee. "Let's just pause here to let the food happen?"

"Before such cuisine, how could we not?"

But Max missed this riposte, distracted, as he was, by the seafood's arrival into the realm of his senses. Anyone could see it: how much the impending feast had replaced the tug-of-war with Mama as the true, and only, business of the moment. He sniffed and rubbed his hands and even licked his lips, like a cartoon wolf over a captured infant. Without removing his eyes from the platter, as if the dead, pink creature might still slither away, he cautiously unrolled the Armison's Famous Eatery bib and tucked it into his collar, the news of hunger everywhere in his face. "Let's just let the food happen," he muttered again at the volume of a prayer.

What followed was not so different from one of the documentary films they sometimes screened at the Sea View County Theatre, those movies in which a grassland lion stalks and devours a baby elephant. Armison's provided every patron with a silver-plated nutcracker: Max ignored his, assaulting the animal with his hands. There were three clean *snaps*, then he beheld the lobster's sinewy tail. He eyed it with the respect of a predator and smushed it into the bottom of his butter dish, held it there. Two gulps later, it had disappeared. An emission somewhere between a hum and a groan was the sound of his chewing. The tail gone, Max hunkered down and vacuumed all meat and juice out of the remaining animal, sucking the pink-white fins, cracking the joints, lapping up the green mush of roe. His eyes, during this feast, remained in a state of vivid disuse: glassy, black, unfocused. He belched, sucked air through his nose. Whenever he required water (often, given the intense rate of his ingestion) he sent his free hand on a blind mission for the glass, scuttling over the tablecloth, and finally grabbing it, kept that hand—and the hand gripping a battered lobster claw—at the two sides of his mouth, like microphones at a press conference. His chin glistened with lobster juice.

I had to skip the ceremonious application of the bib. I jumped right into lobster cracking, dunking, chewing. Instead of staring off in a kind of gorged reverie, I had to keep an eye on Max to make sure he didn't notice my humming or hovering over my plate or shoveling chunks of shellfish down my gullet. Twice I nearly choked. The lobster tough, tasteless. Pale bits of corn splintered between my teeth. By the time he sighed, tossed his balled-up napkin onto his plate, and leaned back in his chair, I'd returned my hands to their position under me, though I could feel a beard of mess on my face.

Mama had barely touched her dinner, eyeing Max and me with that mixture of horror, rebuke, and bemusement mothers do so well. "Is everyone okay?"

"Fine," I said.

Max swooned in digestion. "Accch," he said, as if lifting a piano. "Ecccch."

"I take it you liked the food," Mama said.

Max chuckled. "Oh, God, yes," and a quiet settled over the table, as Mama, with an exquisite and almost parodic economy of manners, sliced and nibbled her lobster savannah. I sat with that mess on my face. My stomach whistled. Max, meanwhile, ordered a coffee and, when it arrived, sipped it, groaning in continued ode to the fallen meal.

No one spoke, but things had changed: the weather of the table shifted. A new front coming in. It was Max's appetite, I think, unguarded and unruly, as if some mad puppy had leapt out of his person to frolic on the table, delighting Mama. People who did not comport with the narrow bounds of the world—these were her favorite, and she smiled for the first time all dinner, uncoiling her hands from her lap. I remember being scared of all things, terrified that she might say yes. That she would give me up.

"Where were we?" said Max. "Right, the names. The *names*. VIP personalities, all of them, and if you want, I can get more letters to—"

"It's not the letters, the letters don't matter, Max," she said. "It's my son. You're asking to take him away from me."

"A tall order, I know, but I've got a feeling about it. Giovanni, he's really quite a talent. In fact, I—"

"He's been destined for this since he was a boy." Her voice deepened as if to match the finality of her pronouncement, and a strange, wholly illogical fantasy overtook me: that Mama had been the one to arrange this dinner. That she was trying to pawn me off to this stranger. A fist of gas rose in my throat.

"Well, there you go. Destined!"

"He used to perform for me every day, you know that?"

"You didn't tell me that!" Max knocked my shoulder like a chum. I tried to smile, but my lips weighed too much.

Mama stared off, through a haze of reminiscence, then raised the martini to her lips. "So, what *are* you proposing exactly?"

"First we move to the City. Expenses covered by *moi* truly. I have a room lined up at the Hotel San Pierre, superb quarters. Then I say start at the top. Full Moon Bar, the Green Room. If those don't work, on to the nightclub circuit. The comedy clubs."

"But what's the act?"

"Excuse me?"

"Who will he do?"

"Why," Max said, grinning that same way he had for me. It was like seeing a comedy act for the second time. I burped and tasted lobster. "The audience!"

"Ha!" Mama covered her mouth. "The audience!" In her glinting eyes, I understood, ran the roll call of teachers, class-mates, shopkeepers and parents, my former tormentors, lining up to be copied by Giovanni the Entertainer. "He used to do the silly faces I made when I was feeding him. When he was a little baby in his high chair—everything all right, sweetie?"

"Just the restroom." I managed a cavalier grin. "Excuse me, sir, the restroom?" I asked a jumpy waiter, who directed me to a hallway at the end of the dining room. I jogged the last yard, made it just in time: vomited the lobster in the toilet, and spat and regurgitated, "Why, *the audience! The audience!*" into the shallow acoustics of the bowl.

When I returned to the table, Max had already paid the check.

Mama's wineglass was empty, and her chin was swaying slightly. "Destined for this . . ." she repeated. I smiled in the pursed way I did at the train station, politely asking Mama for gum. Outside we said our goodbyes. Later, at home, I was brushing my teeth when I heard a noise. I hurried into the kitchen where Mama had parked herself at the table, crying. A long time passed with her that way and me standing in the foyer, holding my toothbrush. Eventually she yawned while fingering an eyelash from the corner of her eye. "Come here," she said, I obeyed, and she held me in her lap. After a few minutes, she laughed and said, "You're hurting me. Up."

THREE

Mad cabbies gripping the wheel with stranglers' eyes. Business-men halving the newspaper like a martial origami. Traffic cops blowing whistles amid a second city, of voices in the air, saying, "And I told him, if he needed my compassion, well, I'd have to see some from him first, and that's fair, I think, isn't it?"; saying, "It's not really cool, more hip—or not hip but *now*"; explaining, "If you're gonna get in on this, baby, get the hell in on this now, 'cause we makin' some money tonight," these amid voices more raggedy and berserk, singsongy and desperate, voices calling every ignoring stranger *friend, big man, boss, doll*—these calls of the homeless cluttered among the others', each presenting itself on every block, as in a museum, yes, but a museum of voices. The trucks and cars a city-wide brass band of the vicious and deranged. Men on park benches expressing a deracinated life with a single sigh. Turtle-necked hipsters glaring with unsmiling mouths. And hours into our first foray, I, increasingly dizzy, followed marching Max down to the Fifteenth Avenue subway station where commuters per-formed their own hivelike choreography: toeing the platform's edge, stepping back, checking their watch, jostling a briefcase before the train gusted into the station, upsetting their hair.

The subway car itself was even stranger. Weeks later, I would meet a similar territory in a theater's backstage, that shadow realm where a sheriff unclips his badge and throws on a toga, or elves, between scenes, drowse on pink wooden clouds. Yes, the subway represented a vessel of quick changes and reprieve, a zone where the players of the City dabbed rouge on their cheeks or rested their eyes in a vacant stare, before resuming whoever it was they were aboveground.

Privy to such unveiled expression, I, like a jewel thief allowed into the cutting room, might have rampaged through the car (Max, sensing as much, started to collect me in his arms) were it not for my discovery of a new expression worn by several weary passengers, one they'd clearly donned for outside use but still wore, almost forgettingly, like a scarf. It was new, this face, did not exist in Sea View or Dun Harbor; similar to the thousand-yard stare of a patient too long in a waiting room (that same absentminded physical uprightness, the closed but loosened mouth) but with a dose of alertness injected in the eyes. You might choose to ball and un-ball your hands, or scratch your chin, or keep the body in a slightly tightened state of repose, but what mattered most was the face, on guard but unaggressive.

I began to make this expression myself, and when we emerged at War Hero Square, noticed more pedestrians wearing it, like a uniform. Indeed, in those first few weeks as I adjusted to the tumult of the City, it was this face alone that saved me. Without it all those people would have conducted through me as through a lightning rod—I would have burst into flames. Max would talk and talk, and I hardly listened, taking in the City under the saving veil.

When I did begin to tune in, the news, I gathered, was uniformly bad. It took just one week of calling upon Maximilian's various "friends" in show business to discover none were the slightest bit interested in showcasing my talents. Reactions ranged from apathy to open violence. "You see this bat?" Mo Fisherman, the owner of the Horn Club, asked, brandishing a Kensington slugger.

"Of course I see the bat!" Max said. "What kind of questions are we asking?"

"I'm gonna kiss your skull with this bat." He was advancing toward us when Max grabbed my arm and ran us out the door.

Club owners hurled the names like rocks: Horoscope the Nine-Foot Horror; Darlene the One-Legged Clairvoyant; Rascal Rodriquez, Mexican comedian—Max's run of previous stage acts, failures absent from his pitch in Sea View. They shared a freak-show flavor, unsettling, to say the least, like learning of a lover's exes. It seemed I was but the latest in a doomed and repetitive cycle.

"Mo *fucking* Fisherman," Max said as we walked up Eighth Avenue. "Runs some cabaret, thinks it makes him King Master of Taste."

"He's not the only one," I said.

He stopped dead in his tracks. The people rushed by on both sides of us, like trees through a car window. *"What you say?"* He jammed his finger in my chest, and we rode the subway in silence up to New Parthenon, a Greek diner across the street from our hotel. Max, still grumbling, muttered his order to the waiter, who minutes later delivered a matzo ball soup, two grilled-cheese sandwiches, and a hefty pizza burger, all of which my manager, using what implements he had—namely, hands and mouth—incorporated zealously into his person. When the last bun-tomato-beef matrix had disappeared, he crumpled his napkin into a ball and tossed it onto the plate, sighing like a spent lover.

After two weeks of living with him, I learned that Max's

otherwise buoyant moods could be sunk only by the pulls of hunger. Earlier in the week, I'd seen him shove a Chinese man for walking too slowly in front of him and then whistle in pleasure not twenty minutes later after devouring two veal cutlets and a chocolate sundae.

I understood. A personality such as his required fuel. Just being the recipient of his hypotheses, exclamations, gossip, and complaint exhausted me, though the City, I should say, had largely cured me of him. How could I stay faithful to Max alone, after all, among the hollers of the street? As we went from venue to venue, I watched these folk march out of apartment buildings or pour back into them, where windows higher up, like paintings on a gallery wall, framed certain portraits: a man splashing water over his face with the expression of one coming up for air; a woman removing an earring with two hands. A paltry fantasy, I admit, but this was mine: to occupy an apartment, to be observed by a stranger!

"Be back this afternoon," Max said, tapping me awake. "Office of Permits and Registration. The talent ought to be spared such drudgery."

After two weeks of profitless cold calling came Max's new plan: to perform in Archer Park, a swatch of greenery behind the public library. Buskers and jugglers put on shows there, apparently. "Resorting to street performance is in no way evidence of failure," he insisted, though no one was arguing otherwise. "This arrived, too," he said before closing the door.

When I identified the flat, right-leaning hand on the envelope, any prospect of sleep vanished. I tore it open.

SEPTEMBER 26

My Giovanni,

Oh, my boy, my boy, it's lonely without you. How couldn't it be without my Giovanni? You know how the people are up here, the stupidity they can't help but be and how tiresome it gets (I swear, I think small towns make us all dumb). I walk along the boardwalk and see Dottie Charles with her little pug and Mr. Pitt and think about you waddling around like them—patting your head, straightening your hair—and that's about the only way I can take them seriously. No one should be taken seriously, should they? You know better than me, my loveliest boy. Did it upset you to see Mama cry? I hope not. It shouldn't. My gorgeous little monster, it's only that I miss you. Write me, write me, write me, and know that Mama will be visiting soon.

With all possible love,
Mama

We had talked twice on the lobby phone since Max and I arrived in the City, but those calls were always derailed by some commotion. All in all, the Hotel San Pierre fell well short of Max's description. The staff stank of booze. Empty food carts, shelled with stained plates, drifted squeakingly down the hall. The lobby's row of phone booths, in particular, proved a site of much desperate activity. A man pleading with a creditor with fake good cheer. A woman with wet heavy lips whispering, "Baby, baby, baby, *please* pick up." Most of these people were not occupants of the hotel, I understood, but wanderers, in from the street, and their voices, strained and exposed, threatened to seep into mine, a danger that at least partially accounted for the brief and stilted quality of my phone conversations with Mama.

None of those talks rivaled the life of this letter. It was like receiving a monologue delivered by a superb actress playing the part of my mother. I wanted to try it, too, sounding like someone who turned out to be me. Just then the door burst open and in rushed Maximilian wild-eyed, brandishing a rolled copy of *The Skyline Gazette*. "Clothes. Now," he said. "Luck finally deigned to call."

Down hilly West Highway in and out of traffic we weaved, past the cruise ships docked on the pier like napping dinosaurs, the river beyond the concrete guardrail wind-tossed and moody. "An old friend has opened a nightclub in town! I have a beautiful feeling about it, boy. No more lies."

With eyes as big as moons, with bellowing interest, Maximilian told me the story of Bernard Apache, the man we were headed to see. "We met out west in Fantasma Falls," he began. "An old acquaintance of Dr. Finnegan's, the circus chief. Ran for Congress, I think. Then got into theater stuff. Maybe worked on the movies. Powerful guy. *Connected.* The mob. Dirty cops, all of it. After we left, Dr. Finnegan told me the big rumor, the famous one."

Apache, Finnegan told him, had served in the war as a rear admiral and, as such, oversaw some of the most brutal campaigns in the South Pacific. He summoned a loyalty from his soldiers as great as any they held for a commander. In fact, he was soon to rise to the rank of vice admiral when a correspondence between him and a Japanese lieutenant general, Kendo Ozu, was unearthed from a valise under Apache's cot in which the two, in addition to debating topics as disparate as baseball and *The Iliad*, wagered on the outcomes of war.

Apache, of course, was shackled and thrown into the brig. "They were gonna hang his ass," Max said, but a host of beguiling particulars emerged, complicating what had seemed such bald betrayal. To start, the rear admiral often furnished the Japanese officer with incorrect data on troop strength, giving credence to the theory, harbored by some members of the tribunal, that Apache had been recruited from some other arm of government to perform extraintelligence work as a "mock mole" or "counterspy," winning the trust of the Japanese commander in order to prey on the man's extramilitary sense of honor. How Apache had won, let alone maintained, the credulity of a blind-hearted enemy was a subject of great speculation. Some believed he and Ozu had cemented a real friendship despite whatever games of betrayals had passed between them. Others that Apache had journeyed so far into being a spy he no longer knew what he stood for. Apache answered none of the tribunal's questions.

In the end, the rear admiral's fluency in Japanese, his keeping a handwritten facsimile of the correspondence, meticulously ordered and dated in the valise under his cot, his skill in prosecuting such communiqués from the secure distance of an aircraft carrier, and his extraction of valuable intelligence from the Japanese officer (as well as the secret intervention, it was widely believed, of higher-ups in the government) saved Apache from execution. He was discharged without punishment, though many in the navy still called for his head. To his few staunch champions, however, Apache was a maverick patriot, a genius of war and other things.

"Finnegan said there were rumors," Max told me. "That he was still doing spy work. That the theaters he owned were just a front. But this—" He snapped open the paper with a business-man's panache.

According to the *Gazette*, Apache had purchased the old Tinder Box Theater, a half mile west of Aberdeen Row, the heart of bohemia. "'The relic of the building remains in Western Downtown on Fourteenth Avenue,'" Max read, as our cabdriver nosed toward the Fourteenth Avenue exit ramp, "'an anomaly among the warehouses and meat-packing plants that have since sprung up around it. Renovating the Tinder has remained a cause célèbre among the more quixotic and nostalgic of the city's philanthropists, but was considered foolhardy, if not impossible, given the reestablishment of the Theater District two miles north of what is now an industrial neighborhood. The nightlife and ne'er-do-wells of Aberdeen Row are close enough, this is true, but the theater will need more than a bohemian audience to maintain its costs. And what would draw faithful theatergoers from their velvet-lined boxes in midtown to a rickety cabaret so far west?'

"Apache can do it if anyone can," Max said, as the driver jolted to obey a stop sign and then peeled right onto a potholed street, stopping when we came to a redbrick building. "He once said to me, 'Max, if you're good at killing in wartime, you'll be good at turning profit in peace.' This guy's got something, boy." According to the article, Apache, outside of basic renovations, planned to make no structural changes to the building. But he was giving it a new name. It would now be known as the Communiqué.

Bookending the entrance were two copper-topped bars where men glared at us like deer. Many circular tables, chairs stacked on top of them, filled the space leading to the stage itself, between which hunched sweepers busily worked. On the stage an unoccupied ladder stood under a massive dangling light rig. It smelled like sawdust and beer.

"Is Bernard Apache here?" Maximilian addressed no one so much as the hall itself. The sweepers stopped their work to consider us. The bar hands, a few feet away, continued to peer in our direction as if incapable of speech. Max stepped forward, and I followed, both of us coming out from under the low ceiling, which, we saw now, supported a grand balcony glutted with red-cushioned seats. An illuminated box indicated a second bar above. "Is Bernard Apache here?"

Again, silence.

"Is Bernard Apach—"

"Who wants to know?"

The voice hailed from the far end of the room. Through the forest of upturned chair legs, a plume of smoke rose, like a signal in the woods, and we made our way toward it, around the sweepers. As we approached, we saw four wiry men in suits sitting around a table, playing poker, all of them vigorously chewing gum—producing a street-firecracker chaos of *pops* and *snaps*—except the oldest, a man in his early fifties maybe, who held between his middle and ring fingers a cigarette from which he extracted long, vulnerable sips. His pale blue eyes—amused, I would call them—did not stray from his hand of cards, despite this arrival of strangers, us. His tablemates, meanwhile, greeted Max and me with a uniform glower and even more hostile jawing of gum.

"Who you?" asked the man next to the cigarette smoker. This one, like the other three, wore a pinstripe suit. He had a thin, hideously tanned face, gap teeth and a lightning-shaped vein now flashing in his forehead.

"Mr. Apache, hello," Max said to the older man, but he didn't look up from his cards.

"*Who wants to know?*" the tanned one asked. He ground his gum between the words, creating out of each syllable a discrete phrase.

"But Mr. Apache, hello." Still, Apache, if it was him, didn't respond. He must have gone deaf, been someone else.

"*Who wants to know?*" the other said, rising.

"Maximilian Horatio."

As soon as Max said his name, the older man smiled in a grand lying way, the way politicians smile when presented with a gift on television—the kind of smile that respects size over verisimilitude. The man laid down his cards, stood, and opened his arms. That was the first thing I noticed about Bernard Apache, the man who would ruin my life: He had banished all impulse from his body.

"Maximilian Horatio." He hugged Max, patting his back twice, and then held him at arm's length, taking him in. He was nearly Max's height but lank with broad shoulders and moved, generally, with a lightness, a physical grace evident even in his stillness, like the pose of a magician before a trick. "Long time."

"Too long, Mr. Apache. Too long! I trust you've been well?"

Apache said, "Call me Bernard."

"All right then, Bernard," Max said, anxious to establish levity. "How you been for godsakes?"

Apache ignored this and instead made a show of looking at me. He wore a brown suit, a black bolo tie, and cowboy boots.

"Bernard, meet Giovanni Bernini," Maximilian said.

Apache nodded shortly and turned back to Max. "So. Why are you here?"

"Serendipity, if I ever seen it, Bernard! Here I am trying to decide where to go with this new act—I'm getting offers uptown, downtown, but, y'know how it is, *none of them feel right*—and that's when I happen upon this"—he had produced the *Gazette* from his pocket, snapping it against the palm of his hand—"about your taking over the Tinder, and, well, it's a match made in heaven, you ask me."

Apache casually removed some stray tobacco from his tongue. "Is this person talented with something?"

Max paused for effect. "A master impressionist!"

"Good to see you. Stay well."

"Wait, wait!" He chased Apache with mincing, diplomatic steps.

"I know what you're thinking, impressionist—please, I go out on the street and find twenty just taking a shit. But this kid—"

"Take care of yourself, Max."

"He can do anyone." Max snapped his fingers. "Like that."

Apache had pulled his chair back but hadn't yet sat. "Anyone?"

"At all!" said Max. "We take volunteers from the audience. One at a time, we bring them up and—*boom*—Giovanni imitates them. On the spot."

"Have him do me."

"Then we—I'm sorry?"

"Now, please."

"You? Why, yes, I—I mean, you're sure?"

Apache smiled, though his eyes, throughout the smile, exhibited a hardness, a bedrock of meanness I had not yet seen. "You just asked my least favorite question."

"Sure, sure." Max clapped his hands. "Well, then. Without further ado, I present to you"—he retreated with small steps, like a backup dancer—"Master Impressionist Giovanni Bernini . . ."

I decided to use the moment he heard Max's name and pull

from there. The way he smiled, fakely, and laid down his cards (mine pantomimed) like an actor slowing down routine gestures for maximal effect. "Maximilian!" I hugged Max and patted him, held him at arm's length. I raised an imagined cigarette and sucked it through the wall of my hand, all with his physical looseness. I said, "You just asked my least favorite question," adding, "*You* are my least favorite question," and when I did, a strange light finger pricked right between my shoulder blades, a calm easing down my back, and his thread emerged, yes, there it was—and pulling it, I saw, clearly, that this figure named Bernard was but a handsome shell, a kind of emissary or stand-in for the soul peering in through those eyes, a presence otherwise absent from the room as I was now absent from it. And I was free to look through my eyes without fear of being looked at, for my body, light and airy, was not mine at all.

A knock somewhere. Several. It was Max, I realized, patting me on the back. "Good job!" Each pat seemed to cement me, as if Max were a sculptor rounding out my shoulders.

"Very nice," a voice said. Apache's. He smiled fully, and looking into his eyes, I could still see it: *He was not there.* "Bravo."

"You liked it? You liked it!" Max was still chewing his nails. "Of course you did!"

Bernard pulled on his cig, winced. The promised stage behind him. Perhaps the tingle hadn't worn off yet, for I had a strange premonition. That if I were to stand on that stage, I would become not more visible but less, that I would disappear.

"I've got a slot open on the second at ten," he said. "You'll receive seven percent of admissions. Depending on how that goes, we'll discuss further engagements."

If there were such a thing as a jubilant heart attack, Max suffered one at that moment. "You won't be disappointed, Bernard."

"I suspect not," Apache said and was sliding into his chair when a voice shot down from the balcony.

"What next, Bernard? The monkeys in top hats and the women sawed in half?"

Maximilian and I both looked up to the balcony where a woman leaned so far over the banister it seemed she might fall off. She wore a sleeveless, kelly green dress. "Hello, Maaax."

"Lucy." Max bowed theatrically.

"You don't approve?" Bernard asked.

"Nope," she said.

"Why not?"

"Do I ever?"

"Some of the time, yes, you do."

"Maaaybe." She gave me a look, cocking her head at an angle. In any other circumstance I would've melted under such female attention, but the scrapings of Bernard still covered me—or unfleshed me—so I withstood her gaze, even, I think, returned it. "Well, I'll leave you to the boooores of business." With that, she pushed off the banister. The green of her dress, as if worn by a ghost, floated past a bend in the balcony, and away.

On the street later, Maximilian walked ahead, talking to himself. Me, though, I had a headache. A hangover. That could happen after good ones. "He's the first," I heard Max say as he passed a warehouse with broken windows. "The first one who *liked* it."

FOUR

I discovered it one morning while Max slept. Under the sway of some dream, I woke with a specific desire: to imitate that woman Lucy, the one on the balcony, and so tiptoed into the bathroom where I whispered, "Maaaax," the way she had, and "Noooo," and "Do I ever?" Several times I tried, but each pushed her further away, like a tin my own steps knocked out of reach. I tried the vowel-indulging voice, the headlong posture. But none of the usual feeling, a kind of internal warmth, came to me. "Maaax." My tongue heavy. "Maaaax." I sounded like a sheep.

"What?"

I turned, and there he stood in his sleeveless undershirt.

"Just warming up."

So went the cycle the two weeks leading up to our debut: trying to imitate that woman and failing. When Maximilian showered, I tried her bugling voice. When he used the bathroom at the New Parthenon, I sat in the vinyl booth, bouncing my neck side to side like a swimmer. Wherever and whenever we walked, I tried her gait: that pushing forward, that volunteering of the face before the rest of the body. None of it right. Needless to say, such a blind spot, a limit, had never presented itself before. What's worse, the further I got from her thread, the more individual elements, those units of her person (the tone of her voice, the angle of her head), abandoned me, stranding me with my failed attempts, like a bad mechanic scattered among car parts.

These shortcomings, needless to say, did little to reassure me in the run-up to our debut. In those two weeks I had to mimic homeless men, bus drivers, the ticket taker at the Stone-Wild Museum to reestablish that I still was, despite this recent trouble, Giovanni Bernini, Master Impressionist. This too, though, was about to change.

"Master Impressionist—it's, well, *weak*," Max mused over his pretzel. We had taken to a bench at the edge of Darling Park, two blocks south of the Stone-Wild Museum. "Master Impressionist— it's weak, lame, *flaccid*. . . ."

Max had been moony since our meeting with Bernard. Hypotheticals danced through his mind day and night, hopeful (visions of packed houses, thick wads of money, hearty handshakes) when his stomach complied, doomed (nightmares of faulty lighting, poor sound, no volunteers) when it roared.

No volunteers. Before his snack that afternoon, Max had been worrying about that: "We can always plant someone. Have one of Bernard's goons do it, just to get the ball rolling—but no, Apache wouldn't *approve*. He likes independence—ah! But that's the whole problem, boy, the flaw of the act. It isn't, will never be, *self-sufficient*," he said as we clambered down the museum's steps. The ruminations would've worsened considerably, I knew, if I hadn't steered him to the street vendor where Max promptly devoured two large hot dogs, chili fries, and a tremendous salted pretzel.

We sat under the shade of two oaks. Not ten feet away, a caricaturist with long gray hair and a knock-off earring drew the portrait of a French girl. She sat on the stool, hands in her lap, trying not to giggle while her mother stood sentry behind the artist, eye-ing his paper severely.

"Master Impressionist," Max said. "Horrible."

I might've been pumping my knee, I might've been chewing my nail and not even known it—that's how bad it was. Lucy so crowded my mind I forgot about my heels, myself.

Because of her, the museums had been torture. Max's idea. "For inspiration, boy, and to show you the sights, we'll museum-hop." We'd been at it the past four days: the Natural Life Museum, the Shaustenhausen, the Stone-Wild.

Even had I been spared the specter of Lucy, those visits would have grated. Art, for an impressionist, is a tease. Those objects beckon, call to you, and it's not that you can't mimic them—you can, but even as you are, it doesn't *feel* like it, the thread of the figure always withheld. As we toured the marbled halls of the Stone-Wild, I wondered if this could be the case with Lucy. Per-haps I was getting her after all but couldn't, for whatever reason, recognize that I was. But why would that be? I tried to replicate every object we passed, to verify that I still had my chops, know-ing full well that doubling the lobotomized expression of the Madonna would do nothing for me.

Max tossed the last knot of pretzel to the assembling pigeons. "We'll need to give Bernard notice, though, if we're changing it. For the marquee, of course."

"Who's that Lucy?"

"Of course it could all go to shit quickly if—Lucy?"

"The woman at the Communiqué."

"Ah!" He draped his arm around the back of the bench. "Lucy Starlight. A real character, I'll tell you that. Lounge singer. On the scene for years."

"Character?"

"Let's just say she is—how to put it?—a *friend to man.*"

I tried not to react visibly.

"Not that that's a *bad* thing. No, sir! Some men would toss dirty words at a woman like that—scared men, boys really. There's much saint in a slut, boy. Remember it."

"She with Bernard?"

"Oh, I doubt it. Possible, I suppose, but—" Max stopped and looked at me. He had a queer expression on his face. "Does the genius have a *crush*?"

"Not in the slightest," I said.

Since he winked, nudged my shoulder cartoonishly, and then said "O-kay," I don't think Max believed me, but he didn't press the matter further.

It didn't feel like a crush, I knew that. The world was a smooth case, Lucy a splinter jutting out of it. I'd mentioned her in the letter I wrote Mama. It was the first letter I'd ever composed, and I was shocked by the freedom of it. I could throw the words on the page and not have to stand by them.

SEPTEMBER 29

My Mama,

It was slow going at first, but it seems we've gotten our first bite. Your little ape, Giovanni Bernini, will be making his stage debut on October 2nd at the Communiqué (There's a notice in the Gazette. *Perhaps there's a copy at the library?). The City is a parade of faces, Mama, and I do think I was meant to witness it. A City of threads! I've even met a woman I can't imitate—I say it cavalierly, here, but it's made me*

fairly nervous, as you might imagine. Only you can imagine
it, I know. You'll have to come down here and help straighten
it out. Visit soon, Mama.

With love,
Giovanni

The caricaturist penned a final eyelash, completing the vision. He
had tossed the thing off quickly, competently. The pink bolls in
her cheeks, the fine curling eyelashes: If the girl had been born a
cartoon, it would be what now appeared on his easel. Seeing the
final result, the mother loosened her mouth. A grin startled her
cheeks. This street man, entrusted with her daughter's face,
hadn't attempted a crime, and she could now relax. He squinted
at the drawing, plucked it from its wooden hold, and handed it to
the girl. She readied herself for the unveiling, held it wide in her
hands. She stared and stared at it. Her smile did not get bigger or
smaller. Only children can be let down that way, invisibly, before
time has taught them a measure of expectation. Rejuvenated, the
mother tiptoed around the cobble and rubbed her daughter's
shoulders, confirming the experience had been a success.

"World's Greatest!" Maximilian exclaimed out of nowhere.
"Giovanni Bernini, the *World's Greatest* Impressionist!"

FIVE

From the network of rafters above to the stage below, the comedian's shadow stretched like a jinni out of its bottle. "Y'know, my wife and I. We've been married for ten years—I think it's ten, right, Doris?" The comedian in his rumpled velvet suit turned to the wing where Max and I stood. "Doris, is it ten or twelve? Doris! Oh, Jesus. Asking how long you've been married—that's like diggin' up a grave and askin' the corpse how long he's been buried." The crowd groaned, a notice of pain somewhere between plea-for-help and war cry.

Pacing in the shadowed wings, Max and I could judge the audience's size only by these spurts of noise. Glasses clinked. Chairs scraped against the floor. Voices rose—"Be funny!" "Get off!"—like sea-thrown bodies, surfacing for a moment before sinking again into the black depths.

"Don Q., more like Don *eewww*," Max said, pacing. All day he had been anxious. That afternoon when one of the microphones kept emitting feedback, Max, in a huff, referred to one of the stagehands as a "pig's heart."

"My wife, she's quite a doll." Don Q. scratched the side of his head. "I mean, literally, she's a doll. I bought her at the toy shop on Sixty-third Street and I tell ya, I got no complaints."

His shadow extended its arm like a dancer at the end of a routine.

"My wife—when we get home, we're in bed, and she says to me, 'C'mon, baby. It's been so long since we made love.'" His shadow, the second comedian, gave the line a real what-the-hell-can-I-do oomph, and the most absurd picture came to me: of the lanky shadow in bed next to a bewildered woman tugging the sheets up to her neck. "'C'mon, let's make it a special night, honey,' she's saying to me. 'When we were young, we did it all the time. C'mon, make love to me,' she says. So I tell her, 'Baby, I already *did*. You didn't notice?'"

He was an excellent comedian, the shadow. He made the circumstances so unamusing that one had to laugh.

"You find this trash *funny*?" Max asked.

Just then we heard Don Q. say, "Thanks, baby. Thank you!" A thin bouquet of applause was tossed at the stage. He exited through the far wing, the shadow behind him distending, then collapsing, like an umbrella.

The spotlight beamed upon the microphone, not ten feet from us. It seemed music should be playing. Music should be playing. There was a palpable vacuum of entertainment, the kind of parlous lull that required music, that could only be cured with music, yet no music played. The crowd, already testy, grabbed on to the kindling of silence until a conflagration of talk, shouting even, flared up in the hall.

"Where is he?" Max ragefully pulled the ears of his bow tie. We wore tuxes (cummerbunds, bow ties, wingtips), rented from a tailor Bernard knew in the Garment District. "Where the goddamn is he?" We were under strict orders not to move until the stage manager found us. This had been the principal lesson of the sound check.

Footsteps seemed to imply milling.

With a swift waddling motion, like a man with pants around his ankles, Max hurried to peek around the proscenium. He rushed back. "People are leaving, goddamnit." The illuminated microphone was not ten feet from us. "In five minutes we go onstage no matter what." Then he said, "Right now. Ready?" and, with no warning, nudged me onto the stage.

The instant I stepped out, a spotlight found me, like a prison's searchlight locating an escaped inmate—too bright for me to see the audience. Max soon joined me onstage and, in his own spotlight, took long, butlerish steps to the microphone, a few paces to my right. I clasped my hands behind my back and stared at the circle of illuminated wood at my feet. This was the plan. Before an imitation, I was to appear like a wind-up toy not yet wound: arms clasped behind my back, head bowed. When a volunteer came to the stage, I was to spring to life.

"Ladies and Gentlemen . . . Ecchem . . ." The sound of Max clearing his throat was grandly amplified. "Hello-OOOO—ANAEEEENNANENANA!"

The feedback shrieked, leaving in its wake a series of gasps.

"My . . . my . . ." Max's voice sounded meek, of all things, now that it commanded the hall. "My apologies. Perhaps I should have asked the microphone for a date before approaching it so rudely?" From the crease in his voice, I could tell he was smiling, but the crowd had disintegrated from a unified audience to factions of conversation.

"It is my great pleasure," Max tried again, sucking in a deep breath, "to present to you Giovanni Bernini, the World's Greatest Impression—AEENENEEEENENNE." Groans and gasps and what you had to assume were cross expressions emanated from the dark. The heat of the spotlight was unbearable. My collar clamped around my throat, and I was feeling very embarrassed to occupy a stage in such a costume with so many strangers expecting me to do something. It seemed absurd that I, of all people, should stand in front of others as an example of what a person is.

"This goddamn . . ." His mutterings amplified, Max grappled with the stand, trying to rest the microphone in its perch without causing further disturbance. Once he had, he lifted up the stand and walked it to the edge of the stage. Sweat coating the sides of his face, he returned to center stage, smacking his hands. "My plain voice will do!" he declared from his spotlight, his baritone carrying without problem across the hall. I lowered my head again. Out of the dark came purposeful coughs. They disliked us now.

"Ladies and Gentlemen, without further ado, I present . . . GIOVANNI BERNINI, THE WORLD'S GREATEST IMPRESSIONIST!" Without looking up, I knew Maximilian was sweeping his arm toward me, folding his legs in an exaggerated curtsy. I was doing the same. This was supposed to be comical—the oddly matched pair bowing in unison—but there quivered only that tightrope of silence. I thought I heard a boo.

"I know *I've* always distrusted performers who require volunteers. If I were down there among you, I would most certainly *not* volunteer myself. But! I *would* hope someone else had the guts, the temerity, the courage to step across this stage, to join us in this bath of light, so I, safe in the darkness, could see what all this nonsense was about!"

A raggedy gust of coughs. Snickers.

"One brave soul," Maximilian said again. His tone remained jocular. It was as if, since stepping onstage, we'd somehow exchanged moods. "Who will be brave enough to grace this stage, to make this night a memorable one for all of us?"

"Okaaay, I'll do it," a voice shot out from the dark.

"Excellent!" Maximilian was saying. "No one will be disappoint—" He managed to feign composure, to not suffer some baroque seizure, as I was sure I would, when recognizing the bewitching figure cutting a path through the tables. Who knows how white my face became, how taut my mouth, when I made out that shape in that kelly green dress excusing herself from between the backs of chairs.

As soon as Lucy Starlight mounted the stage, a spotlight cocooned her, too. I was supposed to be firmly in my *wound* position, but I watched—gawked, more like—as this was my first real chance to study her. She ranged over to Max, the rim of their spotlights touching, feet away from me. Her shiny calves, her wriggling hips, the whole female affront she aspired to—where was it? Her thread?

"What's your name, sweetheart?" Max asked as she sidled next to him.

"Lucy."

"Lucy what, dear?"

"Starlight."

"And what do you do, Lucy Starlight?"

"I'm a singer," she said in a mock baritone.

"And what do you sing about?"

"Horrible tales of heartbreak and love," she said in that same deep voice, drawing some laughs. I wondered if it was supposed to be an imitation of Max.

"Now, Ms. Starlight, have you ever been impersonated before?" In the absence of microphones they were both consciously projecting. It gave their dialogue a scripted, ironic tinge. Nothing I could use.

She shook her head and hid her cheek behind her shoulder, like a shy child.

"Are you ready then, Ms. Starlight, for the amazing transformation, the incomparable experience, the thrilling adventure, the delicious delirium of being mimicked by the *World's Greatest Impressionist*?" Max asked, swinging his left arm toward the crowd as if opening a cape.

She nodded hard.

"Giovanni, take it away!" His spotlight went out. It was just Lucy and me, floating. The light encased her like glass, the motes dancing above her like snowflakes. Given her posture, it seemed that her hands should have rested on her hips, but she instead held them limp and expectant at her sides as if, despite the jeering tilt of her head, she awaited a kiss.

The rim of my spotlight inched toward her, ahead of me.

Any connoisseurs in the audience would have gnashed their teeth at what followed, would've mistaken me for a noisy, foot-stomping poseur for at that moment, before a large audience, Giovanni the Fraud commenced a rank parody of his art. He copied as best he could her vowel-happy voice, her tilted head. He stumbled around in that rangy gait, despite not having her thread, the seam that when pulled would unravel her whole. I was no better, really, than a younger sibling who echoes what his older brother has said immediately after he's said it, to grab on to his coattails, as it were, and leach some of his person. I faced the audience and said, "Horrible tales of heartbreak and love." I said, "Oh, I'm a singer, I sing, and please, I sing." I leaned my head forward, lunged in a circle. That's when they started booing.

They threw boos at me like bottles. Those boos whizzed by my ears. Boos smashed against the stage, echoed through the rafters, and I, believe it or not, was thankful, for it's what I expected all along. To be thrown on my ear, railroaded back to Sea View, for Giovanni the Monster to be tarred and feathered and cackled out of town. Those boos purified me. I closed my eyes and stood still, washed as in a cleansing rain. And just then, with my eyes closed, my arms outstretched, I realized they weren't booing at all—they were chortling, hooting, *applauding*. What I heard was the sound of mob laughter. I was terrified.

"Ladies and Gentlemen, I present to you, Giovanni Bernini!" Max shouted, and the hall filled with applause. "Giovanni Bernini!" It was a misunderstanding. I was going to be caught, I was sure. They would pelt me with ashtrays and glasses when they realized I'd tricked them, that I hadn't really done it. *"The World's Greatest Impressionist!"*

With protesting hands and a modest smile, I accepted the applause, though my heart was pounding. I stole a glance at Lucy, who, confined to her spotlight, leered at me like an angry sibling. Her look indicated that we shared a secret, but whether that secret was my failure or success I couldn't know.

Max said, "A round of applause for Lucy Starlight," and Lucy batted her eyes and curtsied with that theatrical irony, though something about the act, you could tell, had rattled or satisfied her. Before that first wave of clapping subsided, she had already disappeared down the stairs, through the maze of tables—ignoring hands offered to congratulate her—her green dress eaten up by the dark. I nearly sprinted after her, began to, actually, and then remembered I was onstage and, wind-up toy that I was, wound down.

"Giovanni Bernini, the World's Greatest Impressionist!" Max declared, the vindication like wine in his voice. At this there was

no applause, just the quiet of anticipation. He was right. Everyone wanted a nibble of magic, the duet of spotlights.

"Who would like to be next?" he asked now. "Who next will
be impersonated by the incomparable, the inexplicable, the inde-
fatigable Giovanni Bernini?" Immediately, fifty hands went up.

"You demented genius!" said a jubilant Maximilian after we'd
exited through the wing to a shadowed nook backstage. "This is
just the fetus of the whole thing, boy—just the goddamn slimy-
headed fetus!" He hugged me. "I know you sensed it, my boy. I
know you did 'cause I did!"

A hundred hands must've cluttered the dark that night, but
we had time only for ten. All of their threads, thank God, curled
out of their person. I gave a tug, and that was that. A paunchy
lawyer. Two transparent teens.

Our last volunteer that night was a schoolteacher. She liked to
nod four times after saying something true. Max asked her: "You
teach which grades?" And she said, "Second and first graders.
That's right," and nodded four times. After the imitation, I'd
returned to my default position, staring at my feet when she all
but tackled me. She pecked me on the cheek and then rushed back
to her spot beside Max, eyeing me like a bashful fawn. The crowd
ooohed with delight, and, without thinking about it, I scampered
over to her, pecked her on the cheek, and hurried back to my
mark—the spotlight running with me—batting my eyelashes.
The crowd ate it up. I bowed, they *hurrahed* more. Giovanni the
Thief bowing! I was delighted, it's true, and yet I could not shake
the feeling that I was tricking these people, or they were tricking
me, that together we were collaborating in some vital deception.

Despite these strange notions, I said, "Mmm-course" to Max,

because I had been confined to that spotlight all night, and it was such an odd, pleasing feeling to be hugged.

"Just the beginning!" he said, walking to the corner where he crouched down, and from behind a wooden scenery of pink clouds, dragged what appeared to be a bucket. It contained, I saw as it came closer, two bottles of champagne. He removed one. "I got these in case tonight went as swimmy as it did," he said and then turned to face the wall as if for the privacy of a urination. There was a *pop* and he tilted his head and the bell of the bottle rose into view over his considerable hair-scape. He turned, wiping his mouth with the back of his hand. "Ah!" he added viciously, then handed me the bottle.

Not wanting to disappoint him, I poured too much down my throat, bent over, and managed to swallow before hacking hard. Max slapped my back. "That's it, boy. Drink."

Before long we were on the second bottle. I was telling Max things. My predicament with Lucy, for one. "You can just imagine how I felt with her coming to the stage." I was making severe shapes with my hands. Only later did I realize I was imitating him.

"You *were* her." He stood with one foot against the wall, a sleepy smile on his face.

"No, my great friend, not in the slightest!" Like that, I began a drunken excursus on the thread. It was the first time I'd discussed the concept with anybody but Mama, and the words, existing aloud, sounded both miraculous and thin.

"You got it, man," Max said, the two of us carrying on interlocking monologues. "That shining star in the belly. It's not something you get if you're lucky or you try real hard, you know that? You're born with that seed inside you—you either are or you *ain't*—and if you've got it and the world *waters* that seed, then you become *fame-us*." He pronounced the word like a spell, and a shiver went through me. "I'm gonna find Apache," he said, pushing himself off the wall. "See what kind of green he's got."

We pawed our way around dark corridors to a side door and parted there, agreeing to meet backstage later. Given the fifty or so ounces of champagne sloshing around our guts, it's unsurprising, perhaps, that ours was a dramatic goodbye, rife with sustained hugs and hardy pats of the back. We were like two diplomats hamming it up before an international press corps.

When I rejoined the world of the hall, big band swing was blaring out of the house speakers. The balcony bar was alive with heady, flushed people, all eager to establish an intimacy. They patted my shoulders; one pinched my cheek. I was like a lucky stone that had to be rubbed, and yet it was as if the spotlight still separated me, so that no matter how much they jostled and mussed me, I could not be touched. When they offered me a drink, I said, "Oh, thank you, but I can have no more." When they inquired about the act—how long I'd been at it—I said, "All my life." Nothing I said was impolite, which made them all the more curious, I think, to see the buried genius inside me emerge and yawp. I was drunk, that was clear, and at times grabbed the banister and leaned over it to peer down at the carnival of heads below. I tripped around for some time before making my way back to the stage door. With some work, I opened it, the heavy thing closing behind me with a shotgun's report. "Max!" I tried. My hand thinned to a sliver of white.

I hugged the wall, followed it, drifting deeper into the interior of the stage. I stopped only when the glass shattered. A ringing pain in my knee and hand. "Fuck!" I screamed. Yellow light unpeeled the shadow on the far wall. A toppled glass table sat before me.

In the opened door appeared a silhouette. "Who's there?"

"Who's there, too?" I asked.

"Giovaaanni?"

"Oh, God." It was her.

"What are you doooing here?"

"I could ask you the same." I stood. "There are a number of things we ought to discuss posthaste. Like, what the hell you trying to do to me, huh? That's first off." Whose voice was this?

"God, you're weird." She was backlit, shadowed in the doorway. All the clues and tics, the theater I depended on—those weaknesses in her face were hidden from me.

"Always in the shadows, isn't that convenient."

"Are you druuuunk?"

I cleared my throat. "I'm sorry?"

"Drunk," she said. "For the first time?"

"Fine, change the subject."

"I didn't know we had one to change."

"Who gets to tell when you're pretending?"

"I could ask you the same," she said—a quick rejoinder—but my question had reached her. She stepped back from the door. I walked in. It was a greenroom of sorts, outfitted with a vanity mirror next to which were piled wigs and brushes. There was a cot in the corner, and a wardrobe packed with dresses.

She stood closer to me than most people would. "Look at you," she said, smiling. "You play it sooo innocent. Fumbling around like a little boy, then you get onstage and trick everyone." She bit her lip and batted her eyelashes. A gesture of flirtation or sardonic commentary on such a gesture?

"Why'd you come onstage?"

"Seemed like you could use the help. Besides, I wanted to see if you could doooo it."

"Could I?"

She frowned, as though distracted, and took my hand from where it rested at my side, raising it above the waterline of shadow. "You're bleeding."

It was true. A mess of glass in my palm.

"A boo-boo," she said, and with her other hand gently plucked the glass from my palm. "You have to be really caaareful." She blew on it, and the cold rippled up my hand and arm. "If this gets infected, it could travel down the arm—"

"It's all right, really—"

"It's called celluuulitis."

"Biology's really not my—"

"Untreated it can be quite severe and spread to—"

"I think it'll be all right. Really, I—"

"God, you must be some klutz if—"

"It's my hand not yours!" I hadn't meant to sound so shrill.

She seemed to scowl. She returned her hands to her hips, tapping her foot.

"I, I'm sorry," I said. "I, I didn't mean . . ."

The twinkling in her eye seemed to condense and sharpen, and I was sure she would either slap me or yell for help when she dropped to her knees, unbuckled my belt and unbuttoned my jeans, tugged them to my knees—underwear, too—and put her mouth around me.

I yelped. I tried to grip the wall behind me, but there was no wall to grip. The back of her head bobbed and bore, flashing in and out of the light, hidden by her hair as if under a photographer's hood. "Yes! Yes! Sure thing! That's the ticket!" I said it in Max's voice because I knew I ought to say something, but all I could see was her black hair, that hood, under which she was taking photos of me. "Please stop." I was yelping. "Stop it, please!"

At these words, her face appeared out of her hair. She looked up at me with pleading eyes, an expression of the wronged or hunted. Later I'd remember it: that vibrating moment when I grabbed her hair. Her eyes pleaded with me in that cold room. In my hands, she unraveled. We were stuck in the rooms of our bodies, but our eyes were keyholes, and as through keyholes, with that freedom, we caught each other.

When it was over, I understood I was naked. I yanked up my underwear and pants. She grinned. "I knew it," she said, "I knew it," and sped off, headfirst, around the corridor.

SIX

Days later Max confronted me at the Old World, a French restaurant on the edge of Lilac Park. "You tell me right now what's going on," he said upon my return from the bathroom. "Either a worm's jumped into your dick or up your ass, 'cause every five minutes it's a bathroom adventure."

Claiming an upset stomach, I had disappeared into the bathroom minutes earlier. There I frowned in the mirror, as she had. I tried her pleading eyes. But my thin, wanting face was all that peered back. It was getting further away from me.

"Out with it." He said this while (1) chewing with an open mouth, (2) wiping the corner of that mouth with his napkin, and (3) imbuing one of his eyebrows with a giant, bawdy curiosity.

I took a deep breath. "Lucy—"

"I knew it!"

My mouth grew heavy at its hinges.

"All. Tell. Now."

"She—we had a-a-an encounter."

His mouth hung open. "On my mother's expensive grave, Giovanni, do you mean *sex*?" The last word hissed out of him with a sibilance that snaked up my spine, up the waitresses' loose black aprons and around the jabbering eaters, as if a director somewhere had yelled "Action!" and all things obeyed. "Tell me a fucking tale."

I did, wincing when certain words and certain things for which there are no words (the hurt in Lucy's eyes, the rumbling in my head) required description. The entire time he listened visibly, and if it had been any face other than Max's at the end of the table, my tongue would have wilted. When I stumbled or blushed, he filled in for me, planting hard terms in the holes of my speech. He yanked the story out of me and tackled it to the ground.

It was my first time kissing and telling, and I learned what every man learns the first time he tells: that the narrating of an experience like that is no repetition, no rehashing of that wet, combustive moment but that moment's midwife, what pushes it out into the noisy world, births it, and in that way forever separates you and the unspeakable seed of what was or might've been. As Max pulled the wheres and whats out of me, like a detective, I waved goodbye to the impossible reality of Lucy.

"In-motherfucking-deed," Max said when the tale had been patted down to his satisfaction. He leaned back in his chair, shaped an ostentatious O with his mouth, and breathed heavily. If there had been smoke in his lungs, rings would have drifted between us. "And so what—you're in the bathroom tugging it, I bet? Tugging it like a fiend, eh?"

To my relief, he didn't seem to recall my drunken confession backstage, my admission the night of our premiere that I couldn't do her. I nodded, not wanting to say more.

"It's tough, boy. You get that taste and you want it again. There's a lot of talk of penis envy. Lord knows I've contributed to it, but there's the opposite, too. We envy what they have. That slit. Yes, boy, yes, there's far too little mention of *absence*-envy." He continued to ruminate at a high volume. Already I regretted saying anything. It was always that way, as if the punishment for sharing were being heard.

We paid the check and walked west toward the train station just as the sun was going down, in the human silence sunsets enforce. As I learned, it was best to be aboveground for sunsets. Otherwise, you entered the subway in the day and emerged from it at night, feeling stranded. We were turning onto Eighth Ave when Max started. "My God."

It had been painted on the side of the Eighth Avenue Church: a face, or the blueprint for one. An oval with two circles for eyes, a triangle for a nose, circle for a mouth. Underneath was written G. BERNINI. Like an animal it appeared both enlightened and permanently bewildered, the eyes and mouth the same size. I wanted Mama to come down there and peel it off the wall. But it was writing, and writing cannot be peeled.

"Any publicity is good publicity. That's what I say," Max tried.

I must've looked how I was feeling, since Max put his arm over my shoulder. "It's the beauty of the act," he said as we walked up Eighth Avenue. "Everyone wants to be you, because you're being them."

That Saturday, ten new strangers. A haberdasher who cupped his left elbow in his right hand, shyly. Giggling sisters. A cop.

Who knew the City's jaded public hungered for an art as basic as imitation? In our first ten performances we would meet with sold-out crowds, a sea of heads who each Saturday carted a tense breed of silence into the Communiqué and left it with crackling pleasure, like teens bounding out of a dance hall. Those who wished to be imitated would soon call in advance or arrive at the ticket window days before the performance to receive their "stage number," an option so many chose that our list of volunteers soon stretched comfortably into April. Bernard, eager to extend this success and masterful at garnering attention, would purchase a weekly ad in both the *Gazette* and *Daily Scribe*, even billboard space over the shipping docks, featuring in bold red letters THE EVERYMAN and under it, quotes from critics who'd discovered me as an object of hyperbole.

In time, Max would inject new quirks into the act. In one of our more popular twists we'd call family groups to the stage—a husband and wife, say, or mother and daughter. Stage right we would stand a wardrobe screen behind which Max would lead me and one member of the pair. So hidden, we—the towheaded child and I—would take turns saying, "But I hate peanut butter!" and that separated mother, or wife, stranded stage left, would then venture a sometimes exultant, sometimes quavering, guess as to which of those voices belonged to her intimate and which to the famous impostor, Giovanni Bernini. The entertainment, of course, lay in how often they were wrong. A mother mistook me for her son. A man *knew* my voice was his wife's, at which point I would appear from behind the screen saying, "It's *me*, honey!" provoking the sincerest hurrahs from the audience.

In fact, from the crowd's reaction one would have thought I'd *created* a child from behind that screen. Not to speak of the volunteers themselves who, seeing me emerge, who a moment ago *knew* that I was their wife or daughter—these volunteers, upon recognizing their error, would hug me or even jump up and down, ecstatic, really, as if I had introduced them to their own flesh, as if inside the most familiar people (their wives and husbands) and inside themselves, too, lived a stranger they might never know, or the *space* for such a stranger, a prospect that thrilled them.

Afterward these volunteers would often track me down at the balcony bar. I would say to them, "Thanking me is like thanking a mirror," which they took as an example of wit, and I suppose it was, though I didn't intend it to be. More and more I would be deemed witty or ironical when I was trying only to defend myself, and yet I'd be lying if I claimed there wasn't some hope, underneath all that success, that Mama was right after all, that I really was sympathetic to the bone.

"One more time for Giovanni Bernini!" Max said at the end of that second performance, and the applause crashed down.

Again my conniving manager had snuck champagne backstage. Again we guzzled it and fell into a nostalgic, dreamy dialogue, and again I wandered out in the crowd, and again, through that carwash of hands, found Lucy, this time moping on the balcony's red steps.

"There you are," I said, fortified by booze.

Lucy looked up lazily. "Drunk again."

"Little sauced at the edges," I said, like a noir detective. Drinking seemed to scramble my channels.

"You hold it well."

"Shoulda known you'd be cold with me."

"Yeah, you should have," she said and like that, warmed to me. You could almost hear it happening.

"You like the show?"

"Toast of the town. Amazing, of coooourse," she said. "But sad."

"Sad? Why's that?"

"Whenever something's funny, when a joke works, it's sad."

Other people would have probed. They would've said: "Because you feel like someone's being made fun of?" Or, "Do you like being sad?" But I hated asking questions.

"How 'bout we go."

I wouldn't remember the walk beyond the warmth in the night air and the big bright moon. I wouldn't remember entering the brownstone on Chaplin Street, or the three-flight walk to her cramped apartment, or the act itself beyond the pockets of new warmth. I woke at dawn, kind of jet-lagged to be on Earth, our unhumiliated asses in the air.

"To the roof," I said, still drunk. We climbed the stairs. A few times she slapped my behind and I shushed her, and then slapped hers, too, and dashed up the stairs. She wore my tux shirt over her panties. I, in my jacket and pants, lunged against the rusty door, and we emerged into that brief calm after dawn, when you can't tell if the day is beginning or fading, but you know it can't last. The bridges spanning the river looked as if they'd been built strictly for us, for our tiny lives, and I yawped because when it's dawn-time, when you've tossed your virginity out the window and watched it spiral down to nothing, you yawp.

We kissed, and I watched her eyes open after the kiss, thinking it might help me. It didn't. She shivered in my arms. It *was* cold. Winter coming.

"Look," she said.

By the far ledge a squadron of pigeons, fat and thrumming, had landed. You saw pigeons all the time in the City, but they were always roosting on skyscraper ledges or dodging commuter shoes, and yet, even in this sanctuary, they seemed uneasy. Lucy rested her head against my chest, shivered.

"Here." I slid my jacket off my arms and rested it over her shoulders.

"Look how *skinny* you are!" she said once I had.

I looked down at my silver-dollar nipples, the pathetic clutch of hair on my chest.

"You're like barely *here*," she said again.

"Skinny, yes. But you need to show these birds you're naked if you want any shot with 'em. Pigeons. Dirty creatures, boy. But disciplined. You can train them—oh, shit, yes, you can. Just need to know how they talk." She cackled. "Tough to learn. Ugly as hell, but you need to know it. Would you care to hear it, madam?" I said. "Would you care to hear the language of the birds?" I nearly cried with relief, to know that I could always be Max.

SEVEN

It snowed for days on end. One week, forty inches. The air gnawed at your skin. Frost clouded the windowpanes. Mounds of snow, shoveled to the curb, were like castle walls, so high only the balled tops of wool hats, the crowns of fedoras, floated along. Streetwalkers retreated into bundled privacies: upturned collars, hunched shoulders. Night was a brighter, quieter event. In diners people thawed rather than conversed. You'd see couples staring at each other like they'd never met before.

Max and I convened for lunch every Tuesday at New Parthenon on 105th Street, ostensibly to plan for whatever performance was upcoming but really to bathe in each other's company. (Among the tidal surge of new experience, Max's companionship relaxed me. Watching him roll his thumbs over each other or pull the waist of his pants up after a meal was like listening to a favorite song over and over.) After all, the heat from the scandal had finally cooled, and there was little business to discuss.

The drama began with an Artist's Biography of Max's creation that was soon picked up by local papers. The bio read as follows:

The exact origins of the man called Giovanni Bernini, commonly celebrated as the World's Greatest Impressionist, are unknown and, among those who study his origins (scholars, lawyers, etc.) in great dispute. We will present only the most agreed-upon account of his earliest years since there are hundreds of versions, few of which are suitable for printing. The most common, however, has it that twenty-three years ago an infant was discovered by immigrant officials near Cape Host, sleeping in a canvas shopping bag in the hold of a flat-bottomed boat arrived from Italy.

Despite knowing the origins of the ship, the baffled officials had no way of determining where the baby himself came from as he was without identifying papers and could utter even the simplest "gagas" and "googoos" with distinctly French, German, Scandinavian, Iranian, and Chinese accents. One official, taken with the foundling, brought him home to his childless wife and raised him as his own. As the years passed, this innocent man came to learn how strange and mysterious the boy was. For one, he could imitate perfectly any sound: the mad barking of stray pit bulls, the foghorn blasts of twenty-ton steamers, the faint mewling of their neighbors' lovemaking. Even stranger, the boy often slept standing up and could stick his hand in the fireplace without so much as a scratch. Deer sometimes lined up outside the house, and the boy would ride them through the woods. By the age of five, the child would not stop impersonating the voices of his adopted mother and father. Believing this creature cursed, the man woke up early one winter morning and drove thirty miles south to the nearest train depot where he stowed the boy on a westward freight, leaving him with only a bowie knife, a box of crackers, a crate of seltzer, and a Slinky (for entertainment).

On these freights the boy received his education, and an ugly, pitiable education it was. He was attacked repeatedly by tramps, wolves, wild dogs, horses, and that sick breed of wealthy individual—there are many in this country—who loiter by the freight tracks in order to thrash the homeless with golf clubs. He nearly died of hunger twice, thirst once, and food poisoning too many times to count. He fed himself on hay, coal, straw, and (God forgive him) dog. He taught himself to read with the help of stray scraps of newspaper, road signs, and the spare book thrown at him for sport by malevolent teens. Eventually, he joined up with a makeshift traveling circus in which his most popular act was to imitate the noises of planes flying overhead.

The boy would no doubt have fallen, as they say, into the dustbin of history if famed circus organizer and humanitarian Maximilian Horatio had not, by chance, attended one of these performances at which he instantly recognized the boy's talent. Through the layers of dirt, rags, and grim, grim odor, Horatio saw a star. Of course, it took a lot of work, a lot of sacrifice, but soon he burnished to a fine finish the raw talent inside the degraded soul. In the end, Horatio dubbed him Giovanni Bernini to honor the spirit of the Italian vessel that bore him. While Horatio has a well-known heart condition, he agreed to travel east with Mr. Bernini in order to share his exceptional talent with the world. (The Communiqué; Saturday night; ten o'clock; $6/one drink minimum.)

It didn't take long for one Anthony Vandaline, a dogged columnist with the *City Press*, to grab hold of the story and, after some modest investigation, debunk it:

Like many folks around town, I've been impressed by "Giovanni Bernini" and his impersonation act. The kid's talented, borderline uncanny, no doubt about it. But like a lot of folks I'm sure, I found his "Artist Bio" a little, well, outlandish. So yours truly did a little research, and it turns out the entire thing—all of it—is complete baloney. "Giovanni Bernini's" real name? Giovanni Bernini. Found in a boat? "Educated" on the freights? Fat chance. The kid was raised in Sea View, five hours north of the City, by his librarian mom, Beatrice Bernini.

This lie, once exposed, paved the way for greater accusations. Soon "anonymous volunteers" came forward, claiming we had rehearsed

the impersonations for weeks in advance, making use of complicated microphones to throw their voices. It did not help when word
got out in the *Monocle* and *Daily Diary* that the act's first volunteer, a Lucy Starlight, had been sighted repeatedly smooching
Bernini at the bars of the Communiqué. Vandaline himself waged
a vicious print campaign against us, much, I should say, to Bernard's and Max's delight, since the spate of articles only amplified
the interest in those Saturday performances by doubling the
drama: my imitating the volunteers on the one hand, and the audience's scanning the stage for invisible strings, microphones, etc.,
on the other. None of this bothered me: not Max's fake biography,
nor the public's suspicions. I liked it, in fact. I was no longer a
genius but a charlatan, a role I knew how to play.

This siege on my reputation culminated in Vandaline's unexpected appearance that night at the Communiqué when early in
our performance he rose near the foot of the stage, demanding
that I imitate him. Max milked the moment for all it was worth
("Have *ye* no shame, sir?!"), ushering the pompous reporter center
stage, where I mimicked him with no difficulty and much pleasure. The crowd applauded, and Vandaline went on to publish his
lengthy mea culpa, which, to my great relief, was too glutted with
self-aggrandizing caveats ("Did I push it all too far? Okay, but so
did Bonaparte") to leave any room for mention of the thread.

A week later, though, I learned from Max that Bernard had
secretly arranged the whole thing, persuading Vandaline to go
along with the stunt, knowing full well the spectacle it would create. "Y'know how he is," Max said. "Mysterious as an end and as
a means."

It was true. When he wasn't attending to business in his office
upstairs, Bernard kept to the back room, playing five-card stud
with an unchangeable crew. There were those toughs we met the

first day as well as two constant associates: Frankie Diamond and Lou Dust. According to rumor, they were uncle and nephew, strangely close in age. Others said they had nearly killed each other in a bar fight years before and, each stabbed by the other, recovered in adjacent hospital beds, after which they had been inseparable. An odd pair—Frankie tall, with largely veined hands, Lou bell-shaped. They served Bernard in ways both formal and informal, and as they counted their chips or studied a hand, sniped at each other in the style of soldiers or teammates, a banter dense with references to old slights and mutual enemies. Mostly they spoke of Fantasma Falls, out west.

Around these associates, or the bar hands, or sound guys, Bernard kept silent. This was an expression of power, I understood, one that implicitly equated talk with weakness, and when he did talk himself, his tone was either cutting or grandly deferential, as if he were making a show of lowering himself.

With me, he was the latter. Sometimes he would give important visitors a private tour, of which I seemed to be the central attraction. One week it was a bone-white dowager noting each detail with delighted shock: "Oh, and people drink here, how vibrant!" Or an important painter, a guy in a long flannel shirt compulsively rubbing his nose with the back of his hand. "Come meet our star," Bernard would say another time, introducing me to a tall, eagle-faced man with discerning eyes. A senator, apparently.

"The imitator, got it," the man said.

"Oh, he's a load more than that, Charlie," Bernard said. "Give him five years, and he'll have your job." He told me I would one day run the country. "Once you've mastered entertainment," Bernard would say, clapping me on the back, "any field is open to you in this country."

Always, he was trying to get me to play poker. The one time I did join, Bernard stood so quickly his chair slid against the floor. "Here's the kid keeping this whole place in business." He waved me to a seat next to his, and as the game got under way, draped his arm over the back of my chair. Smoke clotted the room. A long-necked pianist in the corner played an angular melody. Bernard whispered in my ear how Lou never bluffed or to watch out for Clem. Hand after hand, that same feeling descended, as it had the first time I imitated him. Teeth exposed in laughter. Arms hugging the puddle of chips at the center of the table. And it took all the energy I had to peel myself out of the chair. Lou and Frankie stood, as if seeing off a dignitary, and in the parting of their suit jackets, metal briefly gleamed and then disappeared. "Come again," Bernard said. "Anytime."

That night, on my way home, a skinny man with a misaligned collar asked me how to get to Aberdeen Street. "Oh, it's very easy," I assured him and calmly and very clearly sent him in the opposite direction. I waved off his thanks with a big, fake smile. Then I hopped up the steps of the corner store and bought some cigarettes. I smoked one but coughed so much I threw the pack out and woke up that next morning with a torrential headache. After that, I did my best to avoid that back room.

But Bernard knew what he was doing. The Vandaline affair increased my fame. Like some urban eczema, those faces appeared more and more on the skin of the City: on the side of a delivery van, in chalk on the sidewalk, in spray paint on a fifty-foot rail bridge. People recognized me on the street, asked for my autograph, buttonholed me by the entrance to the train: *How do you do it? How can I learn? Teach me.* For a time the scandals hardened these public interrogations: "I knew it! Is it true?" "They say you a fraud, man," a baggy-eyed man told me under the awning of the Hotel San Pierre. "Of course I am," I answered.

That's how I talked now. As I understood it, the public ached to know me and yet refused to believe they did. To understand me would disappoint them as much as not knowing me at all, a paradox that expressed itself most often through touch. Passengers on the subway, waiters at the diner were always patting my back, for instance. Yet, after this presumptuous leap, each would back off, nearly recoil, as if to reestablish the moat that ought, by all rights, to separate a talent from his devotees. What they desired, in other words, was to be confounded, but confounded *warmly*, a want I was happy to meet.

But all of that broke down in Lucy's apartment.

Given the cold, we spent most days tucked into her L-shaped studio apartment, in a new proximity I found both thrilling and frightful. With Max and Mama, the more I hung around them, the more their gestures seeped into my very person, but with each hour Lucy only wrapped herself in a denser mystery, a thousand details still burying her thread: the way she puckered her lips to blow a hair fallen over her face, the angle at which she rested her head when twirling spaghetti with a fork.

It had to do with her body, soft and round and the first I'd ever known. I don't just mean the first I'd ever laid against, shared a bed with, or made love to (a phrase Lucy despised—"We don't make love, Giovanni, we *fuck!*"), no, she was the first person, in my life, to exist apart, as a whole. Perhaps I did not always allow for the fullness of people. In the case of Max, for instance, perhaps I was too busy charting the movements of his hands, too busy concocting my "Max" rebus to encounter the reality of his presence. And perhaps (I thought, watching Lucy constructing a lipstick-applying moue in the mirror) the same held for my current volunteers, each of whom I reduced in the moment I met them to a gestural acronym. Perhaps (I thought, watching Lucy, post-shower, brush her hair with strong untangling strokes) all my previous work *had* been a deception, as I'd felt instinctively our first night at the Communiqué.

Nearly unraveled by these notions, I sometimes acted in strange ways. One afternoon I took out her tape measure and measured the length of her thighs, the distance from pelvis to breast, knee to ankle, the length of her longest strand of hair pulled down to her chest. She lay there while I did it, without peep or complaint, shifting only to giggle when the metal tape tickled the nape of her neck. "Giovanni, where did you get so straaange?" she said, leaning up to kiss me.

Generally, though, I was terrified she would grow bored of me, would exile me from her apartment, or body, and so imitated whomever I could to keep her amused. Strangers on the subway, waiters, friends. Half the time, I was Max, the soundman Alexi, anyone. Each cackle (she had a raucous laugh—cocked her head back and shouted it loud enough to quiet most rooms) I coaxed from her soft and vulgar throat guaranteed me a few more hours of closeness.

My performances at the Communiqué seemed especially to excite her. "It's almost *creepy*," she'd say after, running her hand up the thigh of my tuxedo. Often she'd sit me down in a chair at the center of the Communiqué and hop on my lap, kiss and tangle with me, even with all those people watching. And yet, in those days I was still very polite and would often say, "Jeez, thank you," when a waiter brought us soup or "Excuse me," when shuffling past strangers in the subway. "Where the fuck did they make you?" she often asked.

She would not give me her real name. "It's not the one I chose" is all she said. Her sole memory of her father, a goateed professor who left when she was three, was of him, in a silk waistcoat, holding her above the crib in a room of laughing construction workers. She produced a photo of her mother, looking like Lucy in disguise, with fake eyelashes and a fur stole. A minor stage actress in her time, she catered to men her whole life, as Lucy described it, and now lived without memories in a nursing home in China-town.

Lucy described her own men to me, with a detached, if vivid, interest. Among this crowded list she included Bernard casually, as if I already knew. "We went around for a bit," she said. "He's a good man to see when you're feeling low because he makes you just a little looower." Only when she was spontaneously cold, as she could be, or strangely remote, as happened, did the specter of these men, Bernard among them, haunt me. After all, I knew what they wanted. We, all of us, were like tired desert animals lining up to sip from the same oasis. Mostly, I enjoyed hearing her talk this way because there was a softened, hesitant, dreamy quality to her voice that I thought might lead me to her thread.

To Mama alone did I recount my secret repeated attempts to imitate Lucy, scribbling it to her in my letters like some deranged taxonomist. "So I've tried the way she walks (headfirst, rangy) in combination with the way she talks (loooong vowels), the way she talks in combination with how she tilts her head (a kind of smirking tilt). I've tried the way she pares her toenails, dries her hair, ties her shoes, opens envelopes, but Mama, none of it works!" It was Mama who first suggested I watch how she slept, not knowing the great frustration this would cause me. "That's a start at least," she wrote. "No one's pretending while they sleep."

In fact many nights I couldn't sleep anyway, hearing Lucy breathe, trying to match the rhythm of it. In slumber, though, the mystery swallowed her whole, contrary to Mama's theory. Lucy, a self-contained mound. I couldn't stand it, and once while she lay on her side, I reached under the covers and ventured a finger inside her—dry at first, but then wet. She stirred but didn't wake, produced a "Hmmpph" sound, as if considering a pleasant puzzle.

Yes, what I kept from Mama was how close fucking brought me to Lucy's thread. This goes a long way in explaining why I could barely keep my hands off her, even in public, why our sex mattered so much, and how unsettling it was when she withheld it.

We'd lie in bed, the radiator baking our cheeks. I'd run my finger up her thigh and lightly kiss her neck. "No, not tonight." I'd try again. "I'm tiiired," she'd say or, "A gal needs her beauty sleep, Giovanni, those performances can be *ex-hawww-sting*," and I'd toil over the covers, corked and jittery, while she heaved in sleep next to me.

But this one time I needed her: that moist buried star inside her, I needed it. When we made love ("fucked!" corrected Lucy), her eyes, her smell—she began to unravel. I saw her shape emerge, as if out of a deep mist. Her thread almost—*almost*—appeared. I nuzzled her neck.

"C'm*oooon*," she said.

"*You can't do this.*" Tears were piercing my eyes.

"Do what?"

"You can't give it to me sometimes, then keep it away!"

"What? My pussy?"

"Yes," I said, though it wasn't what I meant.

"*Okaay.*" The smirk was nearly audible. "Come and get it."

Afterward, she'd kiss my chest and go to the bathroom, and I'd lie in bed, waiting to hear the water start. Once it had, I'd tip-toe to the mirror and attempt that shocked, hunted look, but it wasn't, *was never* right, and as soon as the shower had cut off, I'd retreat, heart pounding, to bed. Before that, though, for a delving moment, I'd lie there, considering the windows walled in frost. A stranger might be looking up at them right then, I'd think, wondering who was up there. And it made me nearly tearful, yes strangely joyful to think, I am.

Lucy performed Sunday afternoons at the Communiqué with an effete piano player named Geoff who snapped his head at the striking of certain high notes. Lucy herself sang huskily into the microphone and swayed in place like a mechanical doll. No banter, no seductive preambles introduced their songs. Geoff injected what life he could into each piece, but Lucy seemed bothered up there.

"That was sh*iiii*t," she'd say afterward, Geoff trailing contritely behind her. Each Sunday I wreathed compliments around her neck, and each Sunday she shrugged them off.

"It was great," I'd insist. "Best yet."

"Lie-er!"

It was true. All of Lucy's ballsiness abandoned her onstage. Through most songs, she seemed hesitant to leave the microphone stand. The few times she did venture to the hemline of the stage or kicked out her leg or shimmied to her knees, it was always with a curbed physicality, an awkward smile, like that of someone apologizing for a misstep.

Yet I looked forward to these sets as they were a rare opportunity to watch her without being seen, and often in the dark, I would sway and tap my foot as Lucy did in that tollbooth of light. But it didn't help. Her voice was too husky, her hips too bridled.

"I do wish she were better," a voice said one afternoon. I turned, and there was Bernard, raising a cigarette to his mouth.

"She's improving."

"You're too kind," he said. "Or think you ought to be. The stage always calls her bluff."

Years later a man at a party out west would tell me that he once snorted a drug so good he refused then and there to ever do it again. That's how I felt with Bernard. I could feel it happening again.

"I assume Lucy told you about me and her," he said.

"She did."

"That doesn't bother you, I hope."

"It doesn't."

"Her goal is to undress the world. That's what draws her to people like us, who can't be undressed so easily."

Together we watched the object of our talk, in her sleeveless green dress, swaying indecisively.

I said, "And the girl likes a good dicking, too."

He said nothing, smoked. Like that, I hated myself.

Their song ended. Lucy and Geoff struck up a new, stilted number.

"I was surprised how much trouble you had doing her," he said. "Onstage, I mean." With that, he patted me on the shoulder and walked away.

EIGHT

From the beginning we had planned on Mama's coming to the City—first in the fall, then Christmas, then late January—but bad luck kept delaying her visit. Days before she was to take the train in October, Sandra DeMille, her beloved coworker at the library, suffered a stroke while shelving a textbook on naval history, cracked her skull on the fall from the ladder, and fell into a coma. The resident brain doctor at LaClaire County Hospital implored Mama to contact a member of Ms. DeMille's family, as the human voice, he said, reading or simply chatting, represented the patient's last tie to the living world. Since Sandra had no family to speak of (her husband had died of a cardiac thrombosis years before), Mama canceled her trip and spent the next five weeks running shifts, along with Mimi Washington and Doris Huitt, sitting by tube-fed Sandra in the hospital, reciting passages from *Journey to the North Pole* and *Everest, At Last!*, tales of exploration always having been her favorite.

The week before Christmas, with Mama planning her second trip—having recovered from the initial devastation of Sandra's fall and having arranged for Wendy Delacroix to take her afternoon shift by the patient's bedside—Sandra died. "Our time here is very short," Mama wrote in her letters. "I must see you." Because there was no one else, it fell on Mama's shoulders to organize the funeral and oversee the devolution of Sandra's considerable estate (her deceased husband the scion of one of Sea View's oldest shipping families) in the absence of a written will.

Herman Mayfield, local lawyer, aided in the stickier legalities. As it had been established town gossip for years that Mayfield adored, and perhaps in his timorous way, loved Sandra, no one questioned his motives in the matter, and it was with the unspoken, but essential, blessing of all of Sea View that Mama and Mayfield donated the lion's share of Sandra's estate to the small, cherished library where Sandra had devoted so much of her time, both personal and professional. The remainder was bequeathed to the county's public school system in keeping with the beliefs and philanthropic history of the DeMille family. There appeared a sweet obituary in the Sea View *News*, which Mama clipped and mailed to me. "There was too much ice on the road for many people to come," Mama wrote of the funeral. "But there was a memorial at the library where all kinds of folks came to pay their respects. Mr. Halberstam and others gave very eloquent speeches. Who knew? You can live next to a person all your life and not know the feelings inside them."

Those weighty matters settled, Mama rescheduled her twice-delayed trip for late January when bad luck, this time in the form of one Jesse Unheim, a rakish and far-flung nephew of Sandra's, sauntered into town. Unheim was a known entity in Sea View, having gone to Sea View Middle School, where, two years my senior, he readily established himself as the town's miscreant. In fact, I knew Unheim personally, as he and I were often sentenced to afternoon detention at the same time—me for having once again duplicated a classmate, him for a whole menu of sin. Most famously, he drowned Arnold Polski's gerbil for sport. Another time, he prank-called the office, pretending to be the husband of his homeroom teacher, a man everyone knew to have run off weeks before with a checkout girl at Sawyer's Market. Inspired only by a dislike for Ms. Edinger, Jesse left a choked-up message, saying he had made a terrible mistake for leaving a woman like that, and would she find it in her heart to take him back?

After he was expelled from Sea View Middle School, Jesse's father moved the family to Dun Harbor, where by all accounts Jesse worsened. There was a petty theft, car theft. He went to prison. Once out, he moved west. Many presumed him dead, including the late Sandra DeMille, who referred to her nephew, the few times she could bring herself to (being a woman of famous discretion), as "the poor boy."

And so, one frigid Wednesday, this very same Jesse Unheim knocked on Mama's door, dressed in a canary-yellow suit despite the icy weather, accompanied by a short, energetic lawyer he introduced as Morgan Le Fleuer. Ashplant in hand, Unheim demanded his aunt's estate be returned to him, her only surviving relative.

"Some of you may have thought I'd never come back," he informed Mama. "I'm sure you wished I wouldn't! Anytime a person gets out in the world and escapes this rat-trap, they must be dead, huh?" Unheim claimed he had found work as an actor in Fantasma Falls, and, though he had sworn long ago "never to return to this site of youthful struggle and underappreciation," he had collected his lawyer (this is when he introduced Le Fleuer) and flown back to Sea View as soon as he received word of his aunt's untimely collapse and death. He then informed Mama that he was suing her and Herman Mayfield for fraud and for a "baseless and altogether illegal misappropriation of family funds," a phrase ominously exact in its wording.

Common sense, however, dictated that Judge Sutpen, who

knew Mama's and Herman's motives could not have been purer, would toss the case in a heap of rage, but Sutpen soon fell ill (bone cancer, bad chance) and was replaced by a new circuit judge from the landlocked county of Dyersburg, a tough, ruddy ox named Judge Thomas Tunder, who carried no loyalties to the community and exercised a clinical, dogmatic approach in all matters of jurisprudence. What's worse, Le Fleuer proved oddly well versed in the byzantine narrows of inheritance law, convincing Judge Tunder early on that a fair trial could not be conducted with a jury culled from the townsfolk of Sea View, since the community more or less abetted the decision made by the defendants. Mayfield objected and was overruled. The judge knocked his gavel, and soon Mama and Mayfield faced a gallery of twelve strangers from the town of Desperate Pines, fifteen miles away.

The trial lasted two months. A day didn't go by that Mama didn't write me to reprise the latest indignity she and Mayfield were forced to suffer. Included in her letters were newspaper clippings (the trial metastasizing into a major county scandal) that contained in their own right a skilled court artist's inked sketches of the trial, so I came to possess a piecemeal cartoon of all that strange drama: I saw cartoon-Mama sitting at the defendant's table, a righteous skein in her eyes. I saw Jesse Unheim, that haughty dandy, smirk etched into his face, hair parted down the middle, thin legs tapering into squiggles. (I remembered him as chubby with intelligent, scheming eyes, but he had lost weight and grown handsome.) Mama had said about Unheim, "He's the kind of man who struts around in borrowed clothes," and I knew what she meant from the pictures. His whole dandy act, even in cartoon form, was fraught with unease.

Mayfield, who in the drawings was always chewing his nail or tapping his fingers on the defendant's table, Mayfield, whose very neck was a rectangle of queasy pen strokes, called as witnesses the entire cartoon population of Sea View to exhibit (a) how much the devolution of DeMille's estate resonated with the conscience of the community and (b) how little love the late woman had harbored for her nephew. Many witnesses recalled her referring to Unheim as "a scoundrel," "my good-for-nothing nephew," and (to gasps in the courthouse) "a cocksucker."

Even sure-footed Le Fleuer (who in those drawings appeared as a kind of French horn of a man) buckled a bit under this avalanche of testimony and, in what many local reports took as a sign of his increasing desperation, produced a letter supposedly written by Sandra DeMille to her young nephew in which she wondered, "Where is this young Jesse? I know you've made mistakes in the past, but I don't think it's right for those mistakes, especially for a young man's mistakes, to define who he is. Home can be a cruel place. You are, Jesse, and have always been a part of the family." Le Fleuer carted in his own handwriting expert (an undertaker by the look of the court sketches) who verified the "authenticity" of the letter.

Things were looking up for Mama and Henry Mayfield when, during a nasty spell of rain in mid-March, Jesse Unheim and Morgan Le Fleuer disappeared. *Poof.* Not at the Home Away from Home Inn. Not at McSteven's, Connell's, or any of the county bars. A garbage man, interviewed by the Sea View *News*, reported seeing four men in overcoats shove Unheim and Le Fleuer into a gray van around four-thirty a.m. one Tuesday. In their absence, Judge Tunder was forced to drop the case, and in the following weeks, word fumbled down the ladder of gossip that Unheim had owed money to the mob out west. By dangling the carrot of his aunt's estate, he had persuaded his creditors to lend him their lawyer—hence the bizarre competence of Morgan Le Fleuer. But the mob grew impatient with Unheim, lost faith in his chances of winning in court, and removed him. Or so the story went. As before, he was now presumed dead. He had come—hijacked Mama's life—and disappeared, this pathetic Unheim, who failed even at villainy.

Throughout this ordeal, that trial sketch of Unheim seeped into my imagination. I dreamt I caught that sketch of him in bed with Lucy, enmeshing its squiggly legs with hers. Dreamt I was lost in the bowels of the Communiqué, racing to find the stage, and when I reached the wing and stepped out, there stood that sketch of Unheim in my spotlight, Max next to him, the stage transformed into a courtroom.

Why, in all those months, didn't I take the five-hour train ride to Sea View and sit by my poor mother's side? Why did I content myself with writing her, with a leisurely reading of her struggles? There were reasons, though they all seem pale and tired now, like suspects under an interrogator's lamp.

For one, I'd offered to come. In letter after letter, I'd *insisted* on coming—even booked a train ticket—but Mama refused: "I miss you more than you know," she wrote, "but please don't involve yourself in this mess. This Jesse is a joke, your Mama will be fine. Besides, what would your volunteers do if I stole you away from them?" And I, as always, obeyed, too naïve to know a woman's insistence in such cases is asserted solely to be overruled.

Even so, I might not have risked leaving for fear of deserting Lucy. In my absence, I was sure, she'd forget who I was or vanish altogether. Like Unheim. Thrown in a van, whisked away. If Lucy was five minutes late for dinner, if I couldn't find her after a performance, I experienced a light, if well-hidden, panic. She was one of those people who seemed ripe, *primed* for disappearance.

Plus, I had developed an allergy to Sea View. Or the fear of one. So many smiling angels had descended upon me since I'd escaped—Lucy, the Communiqué, these new handsome manners—all of which would float away from me, I was sure, if I so much as entered Sea View.

Besides, Mama and I had recovered such naked words in our letters it seemed a shame to test them with faces. A few times she and I spoke on the lobby phone, but it was never the same: We were tentative and alien. We hung up, ran to our pens. Our retreating hearts needed those letters, the distance and redemptive *fiction* of letters. That's what Jesse Unheim was now: insidious and pathetic, but *fictional*. He, and the home from which he and I had both fled, transformed into a cartoon. Ah, that Sea View could have remained so, that Mama and I could have lived as pen pals!

She visited on April 15, two weeks before Max and I were set to leave on a ten-city national tour arranged by Bernard and financed by the famous eccentric and patron of the arts, Marguerite Harris, granddaughter of the late oil baron D. W. T. Harris. Bernard had invited her to a March performance, and Harris, who above all sought out that which was "fresh," declared me just that. A week later, Max and I met Ms. Harris and Bernard at the Harlequin Club on Forty-third Street. Within fifteen minutes Bernard and Max were phoning her lawyer. It amazed me how quickly the business was settled. Fates sealed with a handshake. As if to confirm a process already under way rather than inaugurate a new one. How long did it take Achilles to return Hector's body to Priam? For the Trojans to accept the horse?

There was *one* hitch, however: Giovanni, who delighted Ms. Harris's appetite for wit—*He's something, isn't he? Oh, what a strange boy!*—insisted that an obscure singer, Lucy Starlight, open for him on these twenty tour dates. Lucy who? Ms. Harris asked. Bernard laid his hand on her elbow, whispering in her ear. "Why then it's settled," she said. "A boy needs his toy."

The day Mama was to arrive, I took a cab to Central Station and waited under its canopy. I wore an old pair of jeans and a suede jacket, an outfit I had owned for years, so as not to betray Mama with some new look. And yet, while waiting, I adopted a posture of cavalier world-weariness: shoulder against a lamppost, legs crossed, hands buried in my jacket pockets, a kind of cowboy's pose I never would have assumed in Sea View.

In front of me, as I waited, unfolded a tableau of arrival and departure common to any airport, bus terminal, or train station, any depot where travelers stricken with luggage ship off or dizzily return. Families hailed taxis and picked at the luggage-loaded arriver until he carried no bags. Many kissed and patted and hugged, and it was always so clear, just from the tension and grip, whether the hug meant hello or goodbye. A stranger in that scene looked amazingly like my mother, craning her neck in the timid way one searches for someone in public. "Mama!"

She smiled. I couldn't believe it. It had been just seven months, but Mama was years older. That can happen: in a month, a week, going to the kitchen for a glass of wine, a person can age fifteen years. Maybe the trial had done it. Her hair, shoulder length, was stippled with gray. Her cheeks puffed and pouchy. Yet her eyes were the same. We hugged.

Amazing how easily you forget the only things that matter, I thought, as we motored uptown to the Restless Sailor Inn. Right there, in the vinyl backseat, Mama. "The train ride was just fine! Just fine! Oh, you don't know how good it is to see you." She rested her head on my shoulder. I put my arm around her, an action I'd performed for the first time with Lucy. "This trial, Giovanni, beat the life out of me. Jesse Unheim, that little prick—excuse me, Giovanni, you know I don't like to curse."

"I had dreams about him. He—"

"Why didn't you come? Just a couple days you could've come. You know how *lonely* I was?"

"Mama, I—"

She slapped my thigh with zest. "I know, I know. You have your precious Lucy here." She wagged her finger. "And we'll get to the bottom of *that*."

I knew she would calm down once we had her settled in her room, which in no time we had. She took it all in—the brocaded wallpaper, the plastic flowers, the heavy maroon comforter—with the same head-swirling attention she gave the busy city streets walking to Leaning Tower, the Italian restaurant where Max awaited us. All the while, she stayed close, laying her head on my shoulder, frisking me with those eyes.

Dinner was a play of two voices: Mama's and Max's, the latter reporting all the perks of city-wide success Giovanni had been too modest to include in his letters—how, for instance, a TV star and a famous lawyer had recently volunteered—the former exclaiming, "Oh my!" and "Of course!" and rubbing my back. Talk plowed over the expected fields of conversation: revenue (increasing by the week), the upcoming tour, the cities we'd visit, the generous patronage of Marguerite Harris, who, as it turned out, was hosting a major fête at her town house that following Saturday, Mama's last night in town.

Over the course of dinner Mama drank three martinis, performing the usual program of memories (my unappreciated genius growing up in Sea View, my old performances for her). Then she started in on me. "I'm angry with you," she said. "I was all alone up there. Have you *forgotten* your mama already?" It went on for a while, with Max smiling queasily and Mama wagging her finger at all the sins in the air.

She drank so much, I had to help her into the cab and guide her by the elbow through the hotel lobby, up the old whirring elevator, and, after a brief burlesque of keys, into the room. I helped her onto the tightly made bed. She motioned with her hand for me to lean in, and when I did, kissed me on the lips. "Ah, here we are, still in life."

"Yes, Mama."

"We're gonna find this Lucy's thread . . ."

"Yes, Mama."

"I guarantee it!"

"Rest, Mama."

"I tell you, you know . . . your father used . . . when he was . . ."

"Mama?"

But she was snoring.

"Oh, Giovanni, let me."

Lucy and I sat on one side of the table, Mama the other, the three of us at a tea shop downtown. On the train ride there, two kids with baseball mitts had tugged on my sleeve with an autograph request. I obliged, signing their mitts with my standard, "*You're* the star." Mama had watched it all, looking offended by joy.

"Isn't he just delightful?"

"Mama, please."

"He's a strange one," Lucy said. "That's for sure."

"Strange. Is that a good thing to be these days?"

"Of c-ore-se," Lucy said in an ironic voice.

"'Of course,'" Mama said. "I liked the way you said that." I felt something under the table: Mama kicking me. "And you're going on tour together. Exciting."

"Yeah, well, I was the tax. They wanted Giovanni, they had to pay for me."

"Oh, I don't believe that."

"Believe it," Lucy said.

"No, it's," I said, "it's not true." A sore spot. When I first came back from that meeting with Marguerite—tipsy after some mandatory drinks with Max—and delivered the news to Lucy, she refused to go. We argued. *I'm not your sidekick* is one of the things she said. I had to beg, make a whole jokey campaign of wanting her.

"What do you sing?" Mama asked her.

"Oh, I don't know if it really fits into a type."

"How would *you* describe it?"

"I don't knoooow."

"If forced, how would you?"

"*If forced?*" Lucy made a pained expression. I felt Mama again under the table. "Lounge songs, I guess."

"What about?"

"Giovanni! I didn't know I'd be interrogaaaated!" Lucy laughed. "What are they about? I don't know." She asked me, "What are they about, Giovaaaanni?"

"Well, Mama, they're . . . really, they're excellent. . . ."

Over the course of our brief sit-down, we each had two teas. Many times I'd imagined Mama and Lucy meeting, and every time they talked their way into each other's hearts, and we realized we were family. Only now that we were seated together in a kind of stunned trio did I realize how stupid that was. As Mama and Lucy tiptoed verbally on a heightened, high-wire form of small talk (discussing, eventually, Jesse Unheim as well as the scene at the Communiqué), the afternoon recalled more and more that first, nauseating dinner with Max when there was no room, really, for me to be anyone. Yes, between Mama and Lucy, I shuttled in tone between two Giovannis—the bold, strange lover and that thread-hunting boy—and not knowing what to say or how to say it, kept ordering new hot teas and downing them too quickly, kept going to the bathroom to escape, feeling like I might at any moment shout out something wrong.

At one point Lucy herself went, and Mama leaned across the table. "It's in her head—the tilt of her head, Giovanni. I'm sure of it."

That Saturday night Giovanni Bernini, the World's Greatest Impressionist, devoured ten downy strangers before a packed house at the Communiqué. All show I could feel her: through the mist of smoke, the shrieks of laughter. Like a soft breeze or ray of light, sometimes harkening from the hinterland of back tables, sometimes from the wings of the balcony, I could sense that abiding presence, the bottomlessness of a mother, and many, both in print and out, would stretch the furthest reaches of superlative to describe the power of that night's performance. The most transporting, they said. A work of art.

Before the performance I had arranged to meet Mama and Lucy by the balcony bar and there they stood, as planned. There *she* stood, like some prophetess: Mama, in her old dress, the one she wore to Derringer's office, with the belted waist and giant bow. "Mama—" I was saying, when Lucy pounced, peppering my cheeks with kisses. "My *freeeak*." It was as if she wanted to tattoo me with her kisses, so that any onlooker, in order to see me—and there were many idling by the bar trying to do just that—would have to penetrate the very public veil of her affection. I managed to hold her at arm's distance. "Max says the car's downstairs," I said. "We ought to go."

Soon Mama, Max, Lucy, and I were crammed into the hired car, motoring to Marguerite Harris's town house, ten blocks away. Lucy sat between Mama and me, the whole time petting my thigh, this with Mama sitting right next to her, transforming the streets out the window, with her very gaze, into a kind of poster for longing.

Max swiveled around noisily in his seat. "Proud of your man over there?"

Mama smiled absently.

"Proud as a *peacooock*," Lucy said, inching her hand up my thigh. I smiled, removed it.

The driver stopped at Mandel Street in front of Marguerite Harris's four-story town house bookended by pear trees in full bloom. Figures could be seen milling on the roof like the building's hair, their voices echoing down to us, glib and jocular. That throb and chatter emanated, too, from the building, a sound that stings any passerby with a prick of loneliness and any invitee with dread.

Max, at the head of our group, employed the heart-shaped (not the heart traded on Valentine's Day, but an actual organ-shaped device) brass knocker to the impressive door. Lucy, in the shadows, pecked at me. "Not right now," I whispered, and smiled, which she took as countermand to all I asked. Max knocked again. "Hello!" he greeted the loud impassive house. "You'd think there'd be a buzzer," he muttered, and just as he was arching his head to call up to one of the figures on the roof, the door swung open, and there stood before us a seventy-year-old man in a chiffon wedding dress.

"So difficult to hear this bloody knocker," he said. "Why the Whore doesn't install a proper buzzer, I'll never know."

Marguerite Harris, it should be said, was known among her friends as the Virgin Whore because even at the age of fifty-five (or thereabouts, no one knew her exact age) she had not yet parted with her virginity. Her lack of desire for sex did not originate in any deep-seated belief, religious or philosophical. Aesthetically and from the absolute depths of her, she found the act uninteresting, failing to be "fresh," the sole criterion for her attention. Years before, she had hosted an infamous orgy to see what "this sex thing was all about." As rumor had it, Marguerite invited to her town house some friendly, hirsute professionals along with famous artists, renting, for the experimental purposes of the evening, a haul of trapeze equipment from the Big Tent Circus as well as several live farm animals. A wardrobe was wheeled in filled with such diverse costumes as nuns' habits, adult diapers, judge's robes, lederhosen, overalls, and several fake long gray beards (fitted for both the male and female face); having covered her chaise longue and ivory bookcases with plastic tarps, and catered the event with genitalia-shaped cuisine from all over the world, Marguerite then sat with her secretary on adjacent wooden chairs as the seventy or so guests delved into busy, crowded intercourse. By most accounts, the heiress lasted twenty minutes, the whole time yawning and sighing, and soon repaired to the downstairs study in order to appreciate an eighteenth-century washbasin.

There passed between us a silence to confirm our greeter had been wearing a bridal gown. Max motioned for Mama to pass and then followed her through the open door. Lucy pulled me aside. "Let's find a bathroom and *fuck*."

"Lucy, I don't think it's—"

She grabbed my arm.

With alacrity, with a smirking sense of conspiracy, she separated us from Mama and Max. Down a hallway lined with cater-
ers; through a sitting room where a string quartet played, the
musicians—we saw as we passed through—wearing wolf masks;
up the staircase, along which a series of black-and-white photographs showed in a flip-book sequence a black woman pushing out
the corona of her newborn, who, at the top of the stairs, proved to
be Caucasian; past a pear-shaped man in a silk waistcoat bounding after an escaped gerbil; past a woman with a hat made of plastic fruit kissing a woman with the same succulent hat. Around
another hall Lucy led me to an unoccupied bathroom where we—
as she ordered—fucked.

After, she sabotaged the reconstruction of my tux. "Kiss me,"
she said. "Kiiiiss me."

"I need to find my mother."

"Giovanni loooves his mama."

"But she's leaving tomorrow," I said, making my way to the
door.

It didn't take me long to find Mama and Max, standing in
conversation with Bernard below the famous portrait of Marguerite's grandfather, the oilman D. W. T. Harris, the one on posters
and the covers of hardback books: Harris in top hat and tie, about
to scowl. His eyes are gray and humorless, his face as delicate as a
horse jockey's. In the painting he has perfected the imperious
glare of one who's amassed huge sums of money precisely to com-
mission such portraits and have them hang over the living.

As I soon gathered, the three had been discussing Mama's
recent trial, a conversation not particularly welcome, it seemed,
given Mama's shaking head and galled eyes. They were so exercised, in fact, neither she nor Bernard seemed to notice my
entrance, my presence acknowledged only by Max, who inhaled

deeply while enlarging his eyes as if to express some ongoing, delicate situation. After some listening, I understood that they were discussing the letter Unheim's lawyer, Le Fleuer, had produced, the one supposedly sent from Sandra to ask after Unheim.

"I'm merely asking if you can be sure the letter was falsified," Bernard said. He looked oddly playful as if debating for sport the ending of a forgettable movie.

"Are you kidding?"

"Not at all," he said, sipping from his tumbler of whiskey.

"Her whole life Sandra railed against him, she couldn't stand him," Mama said.

"But isn't it possible that she sent this one letter?" Bernard asked. "That she had one single moment of doubt? You must concede that's possible, no?"

"Really, you have some nerve, you know that. I worked with the woman my whole life. You think you know her better than me?"

"No, not at all. I'm merely saying, it's possible the woman had moments of doubt, of kind feeling for her nephew. That's all." The more upset Mama became (setting her hand on her hip, shaking her head), the more lighthearted Bernard seemed (smiling like a baffled innocent failing to understand why others have taken offense). That same smile was rising on my lips, too, an expression thwarted only by the concerted effort of several facial muscles. *Well, you have been pitying yourself quite a bit, Mama*, I almost blurted out. *After all, I was busy doing only what* you've *wanted me to.* It was happening again: Bernard's attitude finding me.

"You've got some nerve making light of such a matter," Mama said.

"Oh, I would never! No! Never!" He reached across and held her shoulder with his left hand. "Just debating the merits of the case, which don't seem entirely clear to me, that's all." Then he turned to me as if signaling for help in ushering out a pesky caller. And only then did I realize that I had never once in all our correspondence mentioned to Mama the near-drugged sensation my imitations of Bernard induced. "Quite a spirited woman," said Bernard. "Absolutely delightful."

Mama shook her head.

"I know you must curse this Unheim for keeping you away from Giovanni. But I can assure you, not to worry! He's in good hands now." The *now* seemed to be added intentionally. "If you'll excuse me." With a semi-ironic bow, Bernard turned and made his way to the den. Some sort of atonal music was playing there.

Mama watched him leave. "Be careful with that man."

"That man," said Max, "is singlehandedly responsible for every good fucking hallelujah that's happened to us." Seeing Mama unassuaged, he added, "Not the warmest soul in the world, I agree, but harmless, truly."

"Truly," I said, mainly because I knew I should talk and wanted to keep it short. As if dredged up by Bernard, a slew of ghastly thoughts were rising to mind. *(Oh, were you really so, so wronged? Just behave, please. Just be grateful and smile, please. You're here strictly as my guest, understand? I could have you banned. Behave accordingly. Jesse Unheim had a point—you're always meddling in people's business.)* I breathed deep.

"Might we escape to the roof?" Max suggested. "I hear the hors d'oeuvres are a revelation."

In the mild evening air, the roof's garden terrace reeked of tulips and honeysuckle. At that four-story height, the City took on the inviting quiet of a village, and I felt like myself again. Illuminated windows were but yellow patches in the quilt of redbrick. I kept making quick trips to the bar for champagne. Mama, too.

Next to it Marguerite Harris, our host, was holding forth to a group of wary men in suits. I introduced Mama.

"Thanks so much for having us," Mama said.

"Thanks so much for having *him*," Marguerite said, vigorously kissing Mama on both cheeks. "Meet my darlings," she said of the suited men. They were, she explained, homeless, or had been before her intervention. Their cardboard pleas for food or money, scratched with messages like TIRED & HUNGRY or SIK NEED MONY, she had begun to sell at auction.

"You're an artist then?" Mama asked one of them.

The man shrugged and pointed to Marguerite. "I make signs. She sells it like it's art."

"So *edible*," said Marguerite.

"What kind of signs?" I asked.

"Aren't that many types: Go, Stop, Food. Mine was Food."

"Do you find this place strange?" I asked.

"No stranger than anywhere else. I hate places."

"Cut them up with a cookie cutter and *eat* them," said Marguerite.

"You're right," I said. "Places are terrible."

"I'm never right," he corrected me.

Marguerite placed a hand over her heart. "My darlings."

A grave caterer kept appearing with a platter of champagne flutes. Another trailed him to collect the drained glasses. As soon as the first departed, the second appeared, followed again by the first, in an efficient and unending mechanism of inebriation. As if on a ride, Mama and I accepted and returned these flutes and soon found ourselves quite drunk in a corner of the roof. "I hate places,"

I said, "I'm never right." I had been imitating the homeless man we'd talked to, relishing that flat baritone.

"Shh!" Mama giggled. "You're screaming!"

I was having trouble not swaying. "None are the right place," I continued. "You're my only place, Mama."

"My Giovanni."

"I'll miss my Mama!" I said, imitating something, I'm not sure what. The words like hot soup in my mouth.

"You have your Lucy," she said. "That's good."

"But I still can't do her!" I stomped my foot. Heedling— that's who.

"It's the head, I'm telling you." She said, "The tilt of her head."

"Oh, c'mon. Like I haven't tried it."

"Let's see."

I shucked off my shoulders. I took a deep breath. "Giovaaaanni," I said, "you're so creeeeepy." I was going around in a circle by the roof's ledge in that gait of hers, a kind of sped-up lumbering. "Are you kidding me?" I said. "Our show was teeeerrible." I was tilting my head too much. "Geoff keeps fucking up."

"Almost," Mama said. "Walk a little slower."

I slowed down, sped up. I threw my head back. I cackled. I ranged around the roof, lying on my side, hands folded under my head, breathing that slow, deep-sleep breath.

"No, no," Mama said. "Stand up."

Marguerite and the man in the wedding dress had gathered near us like spectators drawn to a foreign ritual.

"Try the head again," Mama said.

I heard my neck crack. "But it iiiiiiiisn't right, Mama," I said. "Giovaaaaanni."

"Tilt it more."

I was groaning.

"No, no, no," Mama said. "The head!"

But I was grunting and moaning. "Oh, Giovanni, oh, oh, yeah!" I was grinding the air with my pelvis. "Oh, Giovanni, oh!"

I could hear Marguerite cackling.

"Giovaaaaanni, you're gonna, you're gonna . . ."

Mama blanched. But I couldn't stop.

". . . you're gonna maaaaake me *cum!*"

There was silence. The man in the wedding dress spoke first. "Bravo, really. Quite something." "How little one needs to understand in order to adore!" Marguerite added. Then I turned and saw Lucy. A tear hung in her eye. I tried to say her name but could only say: "Giovaaaanni!"

I had never seen her cry before, her eyes like blurred pits. "Lucy—" Now that I landed on her name, I could only say it. "Lucy!" But she ran away, and after a frozen moment I chased after her. As I wheeled on to the head of the stairs, a herd of those homeless men was coming up it, thick as the crowds in midtown. "Excuse me," I said. "Please!" I tried to push through, but there were too many men, so many. A familiar voice came crying out behind me: "You must understand. He's just sympathetic, sympathetic to the bone. . . ."

NINE

What I remember of that tour are the phone booths: on street corners, in hotel lobbies and gas stations, those phone booths, which across the country have graffiti keyed into their doors and smell like human palms. The country lay before us like a nude in an oil painting, and I didn't once sneak a peek, burying myself in those booths as into a vertical tomb.

Soon after Marguerite's party word had trickled from Lucy to Bernard, from Bernard to Max, from Max to me, that Lucy had quit the tour. "She doesn't want to see him" is the message I received. It seemed absurd that so many people could *fit* between us. I did all the things: sent flowers and cards, waited outside her apartment, called and called again. I couldn't know if I was doing it correctly, if I was picking the right cards, sending the right flowers, saying the right things.

Mama rang to comfort me. I saw her to the train the day after Marguerite's party in a state of mute despair. "She'll call you," she said on the phone a few days later. "Tomorrow you'll hear from her, I guarantee it, Giovanni, or the day after. And if you don't, well—what you did on the roof—she has to know that's who *you are*."

I said, "Yes."

The tour was clammy hands competing to shake mine. The

vegetable smell of certain stages. Everywhere we went I saw her silhouette: patterns of shade on a suburban lawn, the stars above the desert.

We held a press conference in the lobby of the Bellwether Hotel in Lake City, the crown of the Midwest where we were scheduled for four sold-out nights at the Northern Juke. We sat before a conference table topped with a floral arrangement of microphones. The cameras whirred and cranked. The journalists hovered over their chairs instead of sitting in them.

"How'd you learn to do it?"

"Same way I learned to walk."

"How's that?"

"Who knows?"

Chuckles.

"What do you think about when you're doing it?"

"A choice combination of everything and nothing."

Guffaws.

"What do you think accounts for the popularity of your act?"

"I don't know. But I've never trusted popularity and don't plan to now, just because I'm enjoying some."

Applause.

The quotation marks swaddled me. It was all something I *could* say, something I *could* mean, but the reporters jotted it down as news. One fingered a stray lock, another smirked to himself. I could see them right then hatching their phrases, cherry-picking their quotes to concoct the mystique of Giovanni the Celebrity for their readers, men and women who would happen upon these pieces while waiting for their toaster to spit out their bread or while buckling along on the elevated train, readers who would wonder about this Bernini and so buy a ticket for the tour date nearest them, readers who might, at first, hover by the back of the amphitheater before edging forward to volunteer themselves, readers who would enter the spotlight with circumspection and leave it with merriment—the merriment of having been *verified*—and all of us, in that way, collaborating in a lie.

Touch. This is what Max prescribed. *"Distract* yourself, boy. Goddamnit, that's what life is—food, money, sex. *Sex and money,* Giovanni!" He escorted the faux-coy to the beaded leather booths where we always somehow were.

The sheer pulchritude—I couldn't stomach it. Those buxom brunettes, those doe-eyed blondes, all armed with rehearsed insights and sweet rebukes for the traveling entertainer. "You're like a sculptor," said a redhead with a waist as wide as my hand. "And we're all your marble." "I'm all right," I said, "I'm okay, thank you," and disappeared to claw at Lucy through the phone.

Once—once!—I caught her at the end of the line. I stood in a telephone booth in the lobby of a hotel out west, decorated in melons and pinks. It rang for a long time. Finally I heard, *"Heeello?"*

"Lucy?!"

There was a pause.

"I didn't meeean to pick up. I'm going."

"Please."

"Whaaaat?"

"Oh, please, oh, please." I said, "I love you."

There was the phone-crackle.

"Ugh, I know," she said and hung up.

Those two words—*I know*—buoyed me the last days of the tour. As did that sound she'd made: *ugh,* that grunt of disgust, so nakedly expressed it could only be meant for family. Those two words and that *ugh*—preserved in my brain exactly as Lucy had said them (through the crackling of the line, in a tone of exhausted, motherly forbearance)—steadied my quivering gut, and I returned to the Communiqué that first Sunday I was back.

I caught the last two songs of her set. To watch her sway in that spotlight before a crowd of men in the afternoon dark was to know the blackness of desire. I downed two shots at the bar, waiting until she exited through the wing before opening the side door. I stumbled backstage as through thick undergrowth, tripping, retracing my steps, getting lost again, until I arrived at a small metal table, a replacement for the glass one I'd tripped over months before. Pawing the wall, I located the handle of the door and, with a pause and a wild beating heart, swung it open.

By the glow of the vanity mirror Bernard Apache sat, smoking a cigarette, his brown trousers around his ankles, his moon-white legs spread. A head of long black hair bobbed furiously between his thighs. "Oh," he said, seeing me.

Lucy did not try to right her appearance or dissemble—a futile task anyway, but a kind of expected courtesy—beyond shooting up and rubbing her mouth with the back of her hand, straightening her tousled dress and saying, "Giovanni, oh my G-*ah*-d, Giovanni!" She squeezed and unsqueezed her fists, nervously.

I squeezed mine, too.

"Giovaaanni!" She hopped up and down. "What are you doooing here?"

"Meeee?! What am I doing heeeere?" Like that, I had it! Yes! Her thread. The eyes had been right all along (hurt, wronged, accused, accusing), but I was missing the hands and tantrum feet. This was Lucy. When I would thrust her from behind and she would look back with those horrified, happy eyes, it was to reward me, to announce that she had, for a moment, been *caught. Caught* is what she wanted to be.

"Stooop it," I said to her. "Just—just leave me alooone."

Now that I had it, I could pull away, each strand joining the whole—the tilt of her head, the wild vowels. "Giovaaanni, *please*," I said, squeezing and unsqueezing my fists. The plastic-covered clothes on the rack, the rusty pipes, Apache, who had pulled up his pants but did not move from the chair, lighting a cigarette; Lucy who headed for the door—all of it seemed to be shaking.

"Giovaaaaanni! Nooo!"

A wailing infant on the crosstown bus, a homeless man saying, "Howdy do," an irate black preacher surrounded by bruisers in fezzes notifying Second Avenue that God would be returning in a few days and wouldn't be pleased. "You will be saved or you will be damned!" I yelled back at him. "A decision is required, it is *required!*" until one of those fezzed meatheads shoved me to the curb. "You the lieutenant of the devil," he said. "Be gone, white man."

My ending up at the Ambassador Hotel must have required various darting actions—packing a bag, hailing a cab, surviving the rich, handsome life of the lobby (the perfume shop manned by women who seemed always to pull down the ends of their blouses in a state of vigilant self-maintenance; the ring of armchairs by the window where men with pinky rings and silk cravats spoke in hushed voices)—though I remember only shutting the heavy door to room 3015, entering that sealed chamber ensconced in crimson drapes. It was what I'd come for, that hotel-room silence, thick and expensive (yes, in this fevered state I began to celebrate money and its uses for the first time; it was a means of separating yourself from the noises of the street by thirty stories, to hide away in some tower by the park; I thought of it, physically, as padding that you could stick between yourself and the world).

And yet, after only an hour or so, the silence proved far worse than any street noise. Like outer space, it coaxed a body to explode. I coughed up what voices I knew, but each stung my throat. Pacing, squeezing my neck, I noticed a radio on the nightstand. I flipped it on, undamming the voices. A newscast. A radio play about pilgrims. I mumbled along, like a parishioner. With some relief, I let it play through the night. That way, if I woke up at three a.m., there would be something in the air.

After three days, I tried parting the curtains and stepping out onto the balcony, but that general waft of noise, the honks of trucks and taxis, even at this distance, attached itself to me, and I shut both the curtains and balcony door.

Still, I believed I could conduct my life from that room—or would have believed it, if not for bad dreams, so solid they seemed to inhabit the room. In one, the hotel room was transported to the stage at the Communiqué, where an infinity of faces peered down at me, holding clipboards or winding large watches. Among the faces were all my old classmates in Sea View, Mr. Heedling, Bernard, Marguerite Harris, Mama, and Lucy. There was that man in the wedding dress from Marguerite's party repeating, "Quite good, bravo, really." Later I barged into the greenroom to find Lucy between the knees of a skeleton. Driven by this dream, I one night launched myself out of bed, dropped to my knees on the carpet, and worked my head up and down. "Giovaaanni! No!" I said again, whimpering, an ad for cigarettes playing in the background.

Soon I set up the hotel desk chair, so I could grip its arms as I bobbed my head. After a few beats, I would turn, as if sensing someone behind me. Then I would wipe my mouth with the back of my hand, shift my weight to my left leg, and come to a standing position. "Giovaaaaanni! No!" I would say, stomping my feet. I alternated stomping my right and left feet more quickly, balling and unballing my fists while bringing myself to tears—tears that ended abruptly the moment I started over, kneeling again, and placing my hands on the arms of the chair.

I repeated the act, turning off the radio in order to concentrate fully. With each iteration, I began to place more weight on the arms of the chair, a tweak that helped give more *spring* to the moment when I turned around, wiped my mouth with the back of my hand, and put the weight on my left knee. I had started around three a.m., working straight till eleven a.m., when the crashes and ascents of inspiration flatlined into a kind of airless certainty. My mouth felt wind-bitten from the all the rubs I'd given it with the back of my hand. Peering down at that chair, I understood, in a moment of hopelessness, that no matter how many inches I moved it, no matter how I threw my voice or accelerated my stomping, this chair would not be a person.

I turned on the radio again, my head splitting. And yet just as quickly shut it off. Before I knew it, I was hunting for socks.

I would find him in the office upstairs. "C'mooon, you, we're going to the greeeeenroom!" I'd say, leading him by the hand. Like Lucy herself, I wouldn't care who saw us. And I could picture him laughing as I led him backstage, being *game*. Perhaps he had already done such things before. Perhaps he was, in his inscrutable way, all but encouraging it.

As soon as I stepped into the hallway, though, I ducked back into the room. This time I sat on the chair, sliding my pants down my legs until they pooled about my ankles. I worked my way into that lightly perturbed expression. I sat there for some time, letting it "soak," as Mama used to say. It needed something. I pulled my pants up, and with purposeful strides, entered the life in the elevator and lobby, passing the doormen in broad, brass-buttoned overcoats. With those same strides, all but holding my breath, I made my way to the corner store where I purchased a pack of Blue Arrow cigarettes.

Returning to the safety of my room, I lit a cigarette with matches the cashier had given me. This made it better, except Bernard never used matches, and the falsity of striking one opened a fissure in the act. So I pulled up my jeans and ventured outside again, purchasing a silver-plated lighter at a tobacconist on Amity Street, maintaining what calm I could as I waited, along with two chatty tourists, for the gold-trim elevator doors to part. Then I hustled back to my room where I sat back on the chair and slid my pants down, this time trying the lighter.

It was better, yes. But with this difficulty cleared up, my attention soon scurried to my ankles. Bernard, of course, had been wearing his customary suit, the fabric of which must have felt quite different from my bunched-up jeans. At first I tried to simulate the feeling of his suit by wrapping my legs in a bedsheet. Then I considered my shirt, which was, of course, all wrong. And my bare feet, which were not wearing his cowboy boots. It was like trying to plug holes in a sinking ship, only to have another appear.

The next morning, very early, I went downtown to Bernard's tailor, from whom Max had first rented and later bought our tuxes. (Of course, I could have enlisted the concierge in accomplishing these various tasks, but the idea of explaining any of it to him, even in Max's voice, brought back a terrible sense of panic.) Whenever on the walk my nerves crackled, I smoked a cig.

Marco, a perpetually drunk Greek in suspenders, kept repeating what I said to him. "Same as Mr. Apache?"

"Same, yes," I said.

"Same exact as Apache?" he said.

"Yes, exactly the same."

With a bewildered shake of the head, as if my request represented the latest instance of a larger, dispiriting trend, he reached wanly for his tape measure. "Next Friday," he said after taking my measurements.

That was nearly two weeks.

"No," I said. "I need sooner."

"Next Friday."

"Tomorrow," I said.

"Tomorrow?!" He looked as if I had insulted God.

"I pay double. Double."

"Fastest. Three days. Absolute fastest."

The rest of the morning I looked for the starched white shirt, cowboy boots, and bolo tie. Shopping, what little I did of it, always caused me a certain dread, but this task was easier, for I knew exactly what I wanted, finding the first item easily enough and locating the latter two in the window of a western-themed boutique near the children's park. I rang both the tie and boots up without trying them on.

The following days were spent in stunted and anxious reimagining of the scene as I waited for the suit. I kept sitting in the chair, trying it again, but it would not be right, would not work, until I got the suit. This slow assembling of my costume did seem, however, to favorably alter my dreams. As before, I dreamt that I wended my way through the backstage of the Communiqué to the greenroom, where I found Lucy with another man. This time, however, that man was me.

The morning I was to pick up the suit, the doorbell rang. I had been seated at the chair, trying a new variation, and leapt up at the sound. I tiptoed to the door and, heart loud in my ears, peered through: there appeared a dark convex shape I soon recognized as Max's eye.

Quickly I surveyed the room. The chair, standing in its center, had exerted, it seemed, a magical pull on all nearby furnishings: the bedsheets groping at its legs, the nightstand drawn to its side. On that nightstand sat an ashtray piled high with cigarette stubs along with the silver-plated Zeno lighter, and four more unopened packs, the whole thing like a presentation on the life cycle of a cigarette.

The bell rang again. Hopping from one foot to the other, I yanked off the cowboy boots. I unnoosed the bolo tie and chucked it and the boots in the bathtub, like a drug dealer hiding his stash. Then I drew the shower curtain closed and, with one last organizing breath, swung open the door. "You found me!" I tried to make it sound happy.

Max smiled in a pained, knowing way. With a sigh, he brushed past me, entering the hotel room like a detective with a warrant. A moment later, he paused in front of the chair, taking it in, as he did all the room, with a slow-nod-deep-pout combination. His look seemed to indicate that this chair sculpture was just about exactly what he imagined he'd find here. Continuing past the chair, he walked to the curtains, parting them with a conductor's grand, winging gesture. The midday light poured in. He pulled up the window, too. In came the whining of cars. I went for the cigarettes.

"Smoker now, huh?"

"Oh, not really," I said. He looked at the nightstand with its four packs of cigarettes and burial mound of stubs.

I lit this new one, cupping my free hand around the lighter, a gratuitous gesture given the total lack of wind but helpful in that the act, as a part of the larger process of lighting the cigarette, furnished me with a way of speaking—urgent, no-nonsense—as if the cig itself were talking through me. "In all seriousness, I'm glad you found me."

He sighed, looking around, and then raised his arm and slapped the side of his thigh. He seemed not yet ready to acknowledge me conversationally. "I checked the Communiqué, even Lucy's. The Hotel San Pierre, just in case. I checked the Ambassador, the Belvedere, all the way down to Zephyr House, but then the old wheels started turning." He tapped his temple. "And I thought, well, if the boy's hiding, he certainly wouldn't do it under his own name now, would he? Bernard maybe? Nope, no Apaches. Anthony Vandaline, perhaps? Came up empty. It took several hours, but I got it." He eased into the chair and saluted gravely with his finger. "Mr. Jesse Unheim, I presume."

I opened my arms, trying desperately to attain some levity. "In the flesh."

"Were you planning to come to the Communiqué tonight?"

"What's tonight?"

"I don't know. Our show?"

"Ah." I sat down on the corner of the bed, exaggerating a certain mope in my shoulders.

"Officially you have the flu." He shook his head. "You know your mom's worried out of her skull."

"I appreciate you two exerting such parental concern, but, really, I'm doing okay."

"You look it, this looks great."

"Well, I'm upset, man, yeah. Is that a crime?"

"No, it isn't." He was lightly picking through the contents of the nightstand. Then, as if he'd given me enough of a hard time, added, "I heard what happened."

I continued to play it somber. "You did, huh?"

"Bernard's a bastard." Looking not at him but at the cherry-wood dresser in front of me, I nodded in the jaunty, unserious way of a drug person, that is to say, as if some jazz, audible only to me, were playing in a nearby room. I held the cigarette in a slightly scissoring grip between my index and middle fingers, raising it up to my head. Who was this? Where did these gestures come from? "Your mom thinks you should take a break, go back home for a bit."

Sea View. The words alone turned my gut to fricassee. I pictured a sort of antiparade, pictured myself being dragged through the street before a panorama of inbred scowls; Mama bringing her pointed finger up and down, like a judge's gavel; and only as I began to shake my head saying, "No way, man. Can't do it," did I realize that I had been doing Jesse Unheim, the name on my reservation, ever since Max arrived.

I remembered Jesse's cadence well enough (rushed, muttering) and his voice, too, flinty even by the eighth grade. In what gaps there were I injected the standard hustler's body language, gestures I knew from cinematic visions of light degradation, the kind set in roadside motels and two-bit horse tracks. An alloy like this one (taking parts from one and adding to another) often stirred in me a clenched, wired feeling, like an upper at the tail end of its effect, and I was about ready to jump out of my skin. I was standing up again, pacing. I needed to get Max out of there. Needed to get the suit.

"No, no. I want to work. I've got an idea for a new set."

"Slow down, boy. You seem quite—"

"Excited? Well, I am. Look, Max. I holed up here because I'm working on something, okay? Yes, I'm down. Yes, I'm heartbroken, and I should've told you, but I'm channeling it, or whatever you want to call it. I'm pouring it into this thing. I can't talk about it now, but this is going to be big, Max. *Huge.*"

I saw his skepticism, like some boxing challenger, putting up a fight and being slowly pummeled by his natural enthusiasm. He extended both arms, ostensibly to calm me.

"That sounds potentially exciting."

"It is, I'm telling you. Hell, you're the one who's always saying to catch inspiration while it's in the room. Well, it's in the room, and I'm just trying to catch it!"

"Gotta catch it. Catch it like a little fly. Can't deny that."

"I know I should've called you and my mom—and I will call her—but I just needed some time. A couple days."

"Couple days?" He stood, Max again. "I mean, I'm not going to sit here and tell you that's unreasonable."

"I don't think you should."

"Channeling, yes. Some of the best work can come from sorrow, boy. Intensity—that's what matters! Sometimes I believe the *intensity* trumps the tone of a feeling. Better to be totally devastated than mildly contented, no? I think so, yes!"

"Yes, for the love of God, yes!" I had my hand on his back, ushering him to the door.

Just then he stopped. He seemed to peer through the cracked door of the bathroom. Could he somehow see the boots in a parting of the shower curtain? "I'll give you two days, but tell me something about it. Something to nibble on."

"It will be . . ." I thought of the word as I ushered him out the door. "Total."

Marco unzipped the canvas garment bag, handling the suit with the unsparing intimacy of those in his trade. Physicists describe tiny particles of mammoth density. That's how I felt as he delivered it—so compressed I might burst. Awkwardly I walked in my cowboy boots to the changing room. There it happened, in that small wooden space. As if a trapdoor had opened, and I fell through it, out of this world, leaving behind only this lanky image in the mirror.

"Keep the change," I told him. A bell jingled as I left.

Outside, in the humid afternoon, a mortal fear of rain seemed to grip each passerby. Some furrowed their brows as if already soaked. Others walked with needless pace, upraising their palms every few seconds or patting their heads to check for the first proof of wetness. I purchased a street umbrella and walked west. When the cloudburst came, I opened it, the rain making a great sound against it, like thick grass being cut.

The hall maintained its own internal climate, a zone both airless and bright. Hands scrubbed the copper bar tops, others swept. A concerted, preparatory hour. There was the brushing of brooms, the light knocking of chairs. The empty stage imbued it all with unity and imminence, like some warship prepped before a grave setting off. "Glad to see you're feeling better!" a voice called.

The red velvet steps seemed a material confirmation of the gliding I felt with each movement forward. The knob was just the right shape for my hand. Unlocked.

When I entered, he was pacing behind the desk, the receiver in one hand, the phone nestled against his shoulder. A cigarette hung in the corner of his mouth. Behind him stood an elaborate painted screen depicting a charge of soldiers shouldering their way vertically and left, through clots of gun smoke, toward a pink moated castle.

"I don't disagree, Tom." When he saw me, he opened his mouth and closed it very suddenly. In a low clear voice he said, "Sorry, Tom. I'll have to call you back," hung up the phone, and set it on the desk. He smiled. "Look at you."

"Okay." Before he could offer it, I helped myself to the chair across from him.

As if following my lead, Bernard sat behind the desk. "You come to spook me?" He smiled again in that grand fake way.

"Something like that." Already I was learning so much: The way his eyes changed when he inhaled smoke. How he paused before the last two words of a line, to squeeze the moment. The rain outside was soft and low.

"For the record," he said, "she told me you two had split."

"Guess it's fine then."

He seemed to consider this. "You knew she and I had some times. What's one more?" He exhaled smoke through his nose. "I think the word for that is showbiz."

I said nothing. This alone felt like a revelation—that I was under no obligation to speak.

"She was upset," he said. "Apparently you put on quite a show at Marguerite's."

"Keep talking. You'll find something that sticks."

"Look, you're young. You like Lucy. Guys tend to. Hell, sometimes she even likes them back. Believe me, this gig ain't your last stop, but it's hers."

"All that up to you?" My body felt so pliable, so light—it could tense up or fly away, freed as it was from housing me.

"What can I say?" He made a show of repressing a grin. "The girl likes—how'd you put it? A good dicking?" He did that thing where he revealed the hardness of his eyes without shedding his grin. After a moment, he stood up. My lap began to lift with his, but I tensed, remained seated. "We have some things in common, y'know."

"I think that's why I'm here."

"Is it? I've got an inkling you don't entirely know why you are. Scotch?"

"Sure." I should have said, "Fuck off," or nothing at all.

"You ever think about who our customers are?"

Perhaps it was because he was at the sideboard, out of view. I tried the cigarette.

"Y'know, I think about it a lot. Of course, if I'm gonna keep a shop like this in operation, I need to consider who comes in the door, don't I?"

"Sure you do."

"Well, a customer's someone who buys a ticket to the show, right? We could start there. Grown up around window displays and advertisements and radio programs, our man couldn't help but be born with the dream of becoming one—a customer, I mean. Ask a kid, he'll say he wants to be a doctor or engineer, some new kind of electric fag who'll shock the world. And, hell, he may do it, but he'll also all his life, first and foremost, be a customer just the same way he'll be a citizen." He was pacing, out of view. "So let's say our customer, he meets a nice brunette right out of a glossy mag, and when the time comes, he gets down on one knee because, well, that's what tradition says to do, no? And he buys into tradition. After all, he's a customer, hell, that's the first thing he buys. And he and this little bride, they get a nice apartment on the east side or a split-level out in Woodberry Heights, and they go out to restaurants and drive home with not a helluva lot to say. And he looks out his window at the windows of other customers and wonders what kind of furniture they have and what they look like when they're vacuuming, doesn't he? Maybe he gets bored. Maybe he's sick of watching his pukish little kids do long division, and he decides—well, fuck it, he decides to take out that office girl, the one with the fat ass. The customer's having an adventure now, isn't he? And on any given Tuesday night, after chewing on his girl's cunt for a half hour, he likes to sit on her fire escape and smoke a cig just like that guy in that thing, the handsome one he saw back when he was a customer at the movies. But he's getting older, isn't he? Our customer's getting gray hair! Sundays he sits with the paper and has a good ole time getting as indignant as he can. That's the service the paper provides—indignity all the way home. Yes, he sprays his opinions at it. He's got opinions that are his alone, the customer does; they're precious to him, near holy. Tears come to his eyes when they sing the national anthem at ball games and when he holds his opinions in his mind." Bernard came into view, grinding out the cigarette in the desk's ashtray. "But, alas, he'll forget his opinions. He'll have trouble remembering what the big ones were and why they mattered. Luckily, he socked away some dough. A gravesite, a funeral—these are his last purchases, his last acts as a customer. And they all gather around it—his customer buddies, his customer wife and kids, the girlfriend, whose ass isn't fat anymore—and these mourners cry, because they *buy* that the customer lived a life, don't they? They weep around our customer's grave." He scratched his chin and then waved his hand almost effetely, as if to dismiss all that he had previously said as nonsense. "But what I wonder, as the owner of this outfit, is before he kicks the bucket, why does the customer come to our show?"

I did what I could to make my answer sound flat and rote, like a kid who's heard the same lecture too many times. "Because it makes him feel like less of a customer."

His smile vanished. "I know how it is. You were born, *cursed*, with that urge. To peek behind the curtain. No, the stage can't hold you for long." He added, "I was pleased to see you finally got it right, by the way."

"What's that?"

"Your impression of Lucy backstage. It was finally *whole*."

His smile erupted again. And it was then I realized. The way he acted when he saw me in his office—I was sure he was taken aback, ambushed, but it wasn't that at all. He had been *excited*.

"I don't know how much longer I need to be here," I said, even as I was feeling all the more bolted to my chair and the second chair of my knees and arms. I was back in it. Such a subtle thing, such an infinite difference. The lift of the chin, the tap of a finger. A centimeter between *happening* and tumbling, between having and being had.

"What is it you want?" I asked. But I already knew, it had already started. He was going to make me a spy.

BERNARD

TEN

Once inside the bedroom Bernard with bearlike swipes chased her from the dresser to the mantel to the four-poster bed, at the edge of which the broad-shouldered woman squealed in delight, the belt of her fur-trimmed negligee still somehow staying tied. Earlier she'd performed a perfect B-girl curtsy, turning on white slippers when offering her hand, even doing that thing where she stuck her index finger in her dimple and screwed it in. I understood. It didn't matter how well she pretended, what mattered is that she would never stop.

On all fours on top of the bed she made eyes at me in the armchair as Bernard kissed her neck.

"Am I gonna know your friend, too?" she asked.

"Shut up." He began to insult her body. Each time she emitted gasps as round as quarter notes. It went on like that. Not like he was playing an instrument so much as moving his hands over one of those pianos that play themselves. Buttoning up his shirt, he nodded to me. "You want this?"

"Please," she pleaded as I rose. "Help."

Sauntering toward the bed, I produced a high, whimpering laugh. Around the sheets hung the stench of bad fruit. "Please." Her shoulders were warm and pressed, her hair like steel wool. I pulled it. "Shut up," I told her.

Laughter arose from the beaten armchair the moment it was over. The woman slapped me loosely on the back, her hands slick and warm. "Where'd you find this one, Bernie?"

She had gotten up and was fixing her hair in the mirror. As she did, she bit her lower lip self-consciously and sprayed a lavender bottle around, shaking her head into the mist of it. "Sweet of you to come see us at the Jade House." When she turned to me, her eyes bruised with makeup, I turned away.

She led us back down the dark hallway, holding my hand. In the room lined with green drapes the women positioned themselves not any one too close to another. On the widely opened laps of gap-toothed men. By the bar. Their legs like unsheathed swords. "Come back soon, won't you?" she said. A host of women in negligees joined her in ushering us to the door. In their languid movements only their hips seemed tightly wound. "Thank you," I said again as the door shut. In the canyon below, the lights of the city shimmered a ghostly blue. A hot wind ratted out the palm trees, which were darker, wilder lengths of darkness. My hands trembled as I lit the cig.

"Don't thank them," Bernard said.

Often I didn't know where we were going. "Remember to compliment the teacups," Bernard would say, or, "I hope he doesn't go on and on about that boat," and Frankie or Lou would snicker in the town car's backseat as the pinks of the city oozed down their suits.

Ever since our meeting in his office, my days at the Communiqué felt numbered. For three weeks I continued to perform on Saturday night, a run of awkward and transitional shows during which I appeared in Bernard's getup and, between volunteers, acted in his manner. Max hated it, and I suppose I did, too, but for different reasons. Every facet of the routine bored me, but the ubiquity of touch seemed worst of all. At the bar, after shows, they passed me around like a wind-up toy.

Mostly I kept to the back room with Bernard and his people. I liked to slide the cards to the edge of the table and peek at an inside straight draw. By then I'd gone back to the tailor and had all the duds straightened out—the suit and later the boots, several pairs. One afternoon Frankie found me in the office and, without a word, handed me a heavy crumpled paper bag. A .22, which I kept holstered out of view, like Bernard's. I never once used it. But its heft was crucial, like a sandbag.

All of this helped, of course, with Lucy, the few times I saw her darting around the Communiqué. As Bernard, I viewed her in her totality, like an animal at the zoo, the way everything it does inadvertently contributes to a definition of what it is. The few times we found ourselves alone in a hallway, she made a general show of exasperation, muttering, "Excuuuuse me," as she shouldered past me.

Except it did happen one more time, backstage. Bernard was right: She liked to make people naked. Our bodies started it without us. And once it was happening, it was like staying in a house you used to live in, you know where they keep the gin. She thought it would be like it was. She thought we would frolic and lounge, that I would risk it all to entertain her in that unventilated room. But I got my clothes on quick as I could. "You two fuuucking now?" she shouted, and I walked thirty blocks home trying not to shake.

Mama had written me after the incident with Lucy. Someone had tipped her off. Maybe Max.

Oh, my Giovanni has the heartache. It is a terrible feel-ing, isn't it? I think you ought to come home at once, away from those show-business types. I've got half a mind to go down there myself and scoop you up, put you in my pouch like a kangaroo. I liked Lucy all right, Giovanni, but for her to do this? And don't get me started on Bernard. Really! I have a very bad feeling about that man. Come home. We'll eat fancy foods and see movies and even do some of our old shows, just you and me.

M

She left messages at the Ambassador Hotel. I ignored them. When I wrote, I made it as short as I could.

Mom—

Bernard's not half as bad as you think, and it's all swell, really. As you said, it's done with Lucy, and that's good.

When she wrote and called after that, I didn't respond. At first this made me nervous, but Bernard insisted. He had theories. I don't know if I believed them, but I liked to hear them delivered that way, with the certainty of the vicious. His father also left around the time he was born. "I was deprived all that," he told me once. As I soon discovered, he was as capable of lengthy speech as he was of silence, the latter like a holster from which the former was drawn. "Not the father exactly, but his long decline. Daddy's looking a lit-tle stooped going up the porch stairs. Daddy forgot Aunt Donna's name today. Decline is the real inheritance," he said. "A man with

a father who's present has seen him age and weaken and throughout
the process feels himself edging closer and closer to manhood. But
our fathers are always of immaculate age and strength, and so we
are always boys. It's the principal job of the father to show his son
how to die. You had Max, and he's a serviceable model, but I think
it's time you became your own man."

It may seem ridiculous to claim that I was doing that—
becoming my own man—when I was in every way aping another,
and yet it did feel that way, as if finally, as Bernard, I might tun-
nel my way to freedom. As I'd hoped, the impression sustained
that dreamy sensation, that fog that descended whenever I'd imitated him previously. It was so potent, the feeling, I often woke up
at three a.m. at the Ambassador Hotel not knowing where I was,
or knowing where my body was, but feeling that *I* was distinctly
elsewhere—in the hallway, perhaps, collecting ice or strolling
down a path in the park. When, at the Communiqué, people
gawked at our identical outfits, I didn't care, because I knew they
weren't seeing me, really. That I wasn't there to be seen. In this
sense, no, it didn't feel like becoming Bernard. It felt like entering
a monastery. We wore the same uniform in the way monks don
saffron robes, symbols of the ego's retreat.

In fact, there *was* something Eastern in Bernard's view of the
world. He often described life as a theater or illusion in whose grip
most people lived. "Look at this guy," he'd say sometimes as Clem,
one of his associates, left the table. (The eccentricity of our shared
appearance went over fine among the poker players, largely because
Bernard was the boss and I the star.) "Can you believe this guy?"
he'd say, though the man had done nothing more than cough into
his fist. And yet I knew what he meant, and it took his doing it
several times, with other people, to realize it reminded me above all
of Mama, the way she and I used to hunt for threads in Sea View.

It was Bernard who started bringing up the move out west, the idea of getting into the movies. Each day it waited for us, like a fat chauffeur in a town car. "A star of the screen's the perfect Trojan horse," he said. "You can put anything in it." I cherished that phrase: a *star of the screen*. For a man onscreen can be gawked at and scrutinized, but he cannot be touched.

As the founder and president of Monument Pictures, Nathan J. Sharp possessed a likeness seen widely about town. There was one shot in particular that papered industry rags of the Tinsel Titan, as he was known, striding out of a shiny black limo in coat and tails, like a general taking his first step on conquered ground. It was an image, I discovered, that had little to do with the man bending cautiously over his desk to extract a sip of chicken soup. Every two minutes the phone on his desk would ring, and Sharp would scoop it up and yelp, "Never again," or "Did he mention the carpet?" before hanging it up and gesturing with his arm for Bernard to continue.

Nathan was an old friend of Bernard's. "Old friends," as I soon learned, encompassed a variety of acquaintances, rivals, businessmen, and madams. The phrase functioned, really, as a euphemism for debt, the directionality of which became obvious soon enough. In this case, Nathan seemed to owe Bernard a half hour, no more. In the short breaks between the tending to the phone and his soup, he prodded Bernard with questions about my act back east.

Bernard answered, I smoked. It was the old wind-up toy routine from the Communiqué. Be still. Spring to life. I was not listening is the truth when Bernard tapped me on the shoulder.

"Said I read somewhere you're from Italy," Nathan was saying. He didn't seem much fazed by our getups.

"That's right," I said.

"You tried to scrub it all off. But it's still there." He grinned. "Let me tell you, I came over here with nothing. Nada. Now look at me! They call that *self-made*." He'd started out as a furrier in Poland, he told us, making three cents a day. "My real name? Nathan Sharpovitch. Now I am the famous Nathan Sharp!"

He grew so animated I was moved to share an anecdote about the time I got thrown off a passenger train for imitating a steward with a whistling S. Lying in this way felt like the opposite of effort. Nathan slapped the table viciously and at the end of the meeting pulled me aside to mutter that we foreigners were the ones who invented this country. "You did all right, Bernie," he shouted, mentioning the screen test as we left, like an afterthought.

"Play it low," the director instructed me in the drafty room. "The surface is calm but *underneath's* where we feel it." When he left, I tried a cig. My face, in the bulb-lined mirror, looked thin and colorless. My hands were cold. "Play it low," I thought, walking out.

The lot was vast and dark, the size of a hangar and loud with banging doors. The day of the screen test I got lost inside it, finding myself on a gangplank high above a film shoot in which a blonde stabbed a man to death with a letter opener. Later, I ended up in a hall lined with red doors. When I tried one, a ring of tuba players glared back at me, each wearing a bib. Behind a second, a gray, speckled wolf snored fatly. Another revealed a row of actors in feathered headdresses raising their arms before a firing squad.

Several more of these doors I tried, witnessing a kaleidoscope of increasingly bizarre scenes, before tumbling out into the afternoon.

The lot recalled the backstage of the Communiqué—labyrinthine and black, but blown up to a grotesque size, a backstage swollen to monstrous dimensions so that the actual site of filming, the purported reason for our being there, shrank to a contested detail. Encircled by craning lights, the set provided the sole zone of illumination, like an unexpected fire deep inside a cave. I hurried toward it.

Normally, I would have taken my time. From Bernard I had learned the art of arrival, but the suit, a heavy wool number, broad in the shoulders, ruined it all.

I thought it would be like the screen test. That day, a thin, long-striding man had handed me a sheet of paper with typed lines of dialogue. One line said, "Now you're gonna listen to me." Another: "I'm afraid it's a little more complicated than that." I did it all like Bernard, that is to say, as if pushed by the presence of others into an even greater interiority. Soon the picture was under way: *Everyman*, a spy film about Harry Knott, a master of disguise who through the course of the picture impersonates a slew of characters, among them a Russian diplomat and a British tycoon, to root out a Communist mole inside the government.

But on this, the first day of shooting, I was made to wear this new, double-breasted suit. Then the director ambushed me in the dressing room to discuss my character, Harry, and how he would act "when he's himself." I had thought it was agreed that I would just do Bernard, but the director, an excitable and lanky man with a feral rim of red hair around his otherwise bald head, seemed to have other plans. "Don't use too much wind," he said. "Not too much wind. He feels something *underneath*."

At the set itself I was besieged by attention. The actor Sterling Smith roughhoused my hand, while a chatty makeup artist dabbed my nose. In no time, a long, black microphone materialized inches from my face while someone unseen ordered me to say the words "pepper" and "baby bubble bath," a pair of disembodied hands straightening the shoulders of the suit. "Pepper," I said. "Baby bubble bath." Bernard paced by the police commissioner's desk. "Looking a bit pale," Max said, though I couldn't see his face in the harsh white light.

He sounded worried, as he often did out west. At every opportunity, he encouraged a return to the City, to the stage. Yet it was hard to take these suggestions seriously, as he was so out of place in Fantasma Falls. Months before, we had attended a party at a producer's house above the canyons. Guests (the men in bathing trunks, the women bikinis) draped themselves on deck chairs in postures submissive to the sun. In these loungers' hands every task, whether easing onto a bar stool or waist-deep into the pool, was studiously bleached of pace, a slowness like that of bank tellers in cinematic robberies, who, warned against sudden movements, open the cash register with grinding care.

Among these sun people, Max stuck out, to say the least, wearing a straw hat, knee-length bathing suit, and flip-flops over dress socks. Several times and with no clear destination, he circled the pool, stopping briefly to squat on the end of a deck chair and then rising again to pace along the deep end. At some point in these circumnavigations, he kicked over two martini glasses, then righted them anxiously before speeding back to the pool house, from which he did not emerge for several hours. The whole thing was so strange I later imitated his look (as if the sun were a grandmother pinching his cheek) for Frankie and Lou by the car. With time, it even became a private joke. "Do the body again," they'd say. That's what we called him: "the body," shouting, sweating, bumping into things.

"Just fine," I managed to say.

The director appeared. "You know, as long as it seems natural and right," he was probably saying, given the way he casually waved his hand and then docked it in his trousers' pocket. After one final piece of advice, or a warning, he saluted me and stepped off into the surrounding dark. There was a grating sound, like a giant fishhook scraping the floor. Then quiet.

"Giovanni, door!"

I was meant to go back out through the door in order to reenter. I walked out of the door as well as I could. I could not feel my hands or feet.

"Action!" the director shouted.

I walked through the door into the fake office.

"Harry Knott," the actor said to me in a put-on voice. "That right?" He rested his fists on the desk, apelike. The fake window behind him looked out on absolute darkness. Once you stood in the set, a life-size diorama of a police commissioner's office, you could see only the set. It was like being trapped inside a window display.

"That right?" he said again.

I was supposed to say, "That's me."

"Cut! Everything okay? Try it again," the director might have said. It had the rhythm of something like that.

I walked out again, no blood in my hands.

"Action! Giovanni? Giovanni—"

Later I looked down at the set, maybe twenty feet below, where the director kicked imaginary stones. "Okay, you'll be okay," a voice above me said. Max, I saw. It seemed I was lying limply in his arms, being transported up a set of cast-iron stairs. Bernard was ahead of us.

I was brought up several flights to a door. Bernard opened it, and Max followed. Inside was a high-ceilinged office, the size of a warehouse. A desk occupied the center of the room where Nathan, of all people, held a preposterous leg of lamb to his mouth, like a piccolo. On both sides of the desk, many men, perhaps twenty in all, stood in the same wool suit, fixing their eyes on me with the incomprehension of animals.

Max laid me on the low couch opposite them.

"Victim Two in *Perfume of Shangri-La*?" a man with horn-rimmed glasses asked.

"No, no, he's the, uh, bookkeeper in *Diamonds One*," answered a stooped man with flaking skin.

"The kid's sick!" a third said.

In no time, the word *sick* carried across the room.

There was a pop. A musket. The neigh of a horse. A light cast the men in bloodred. Out of instinct I searched for Bernard, who had established himself behind Nathan's desk. He'd crossed his arms and kicked up his foot, resting it against the window in the posture of a fierce, appraising woman at a cocktail party.

"What's going on here, Bernie?" Nathan asked, not taking his eyes off me.

The door opened and in shuffled Frankie and Lou.

"He fainted." Bernard took his time. "Not an actor, it seems."

"A movie star who doesn't act is the kind of riddle a man in my position can't much afford to contemplate," Nathan said. He wiped his mouth with a napkin imprecisely before embarking upon another bite of the lamb.

Again a lurid red blanketed the studio boss and the men, and

Bernard, too. I understood. The wall behind me was no wall at all, but the back of a movie screen. We were somehow behind it. A voice shrieked, "Mince 'em—to the bone!"

"The boy belongs on a stage," Max said, pacing along the far wall. "As the man who discovered him, I think I'm entitled to some views on the subject."

"Do us a favor, Max," Bernard said. "If you find your mouth is beginning to open, close it, please."

"Break 'em!" the screen shouted. "To bones!"

Suddenly, my mind was full of Lucy's apartment, its warmth in the winter, when the radiator clanged by the soft land of her bed. The couch of Sea View, too, where Mama might have been sitting that very instant, and how greatly I wished to sit on her lap, in the light of the lamp.

"A movie star's the dictionary definition of a man," Nathan said. "This looks like a dog to me. I took a risk on this kid."

"Mince 'em!"

"He doesn't have to act," Bernard said and, with the usual ecstasy of self-control, sauntered over to the side table. There he poured a glass of water and slowly fished something out of his pocket. The men watched Bernard as he decanted the carafe and set it on the bar. He approached me with an extended hand. In his palm lay a green pill.

For the record, I did picture pushing his hand away. I pictured fleeing down the stairs, through the set, out past the lot café where the long-necked women in floppy hats were having their ginger ales; I pictured running past the gate of the studio, past the boulevard to the howl of the interstate, where I would hail a car that would carry me east, back to the City, perhaps, to the Communiqué, where I would step onstage, where I would pick out

the first available volunteer, whoever it was, or even venture farther north, to Sea View, and knock on Mama's door, but in what
suit would I knock? I wondered as I swallowed the pill and was
led, by Bernard, to a nearby closet, where I changed back into my
outfit, that is, one identical to his, at which point the thought of
escape seemed so ridiculous I couldn't believe I'd considered it
at all.

Upon my reentering the room, the men's expressions shifted
subtly but decisively, like figures in a famous painting captured,
as indelibly, moments after breaking their pose. Some cocked
their heads. Others straightened their backs. I lit a cig, bathed in
the blue of the screen.

Bernard said, "I present you Harry Knott, international spy."

"Now why didn't we think of that earlier?" asked Nathan
with a smile, his plate finished.

Mama and I resumed our correspondence some weeks before the
completion of filming. That day I had been running late, heading
out of my bungalow at the Chateau Ravine, a hotel set in a small
hill veiled by Jurassic vegetation. I jogged briefly to the town car
in which Bernard, Frankie, and Lou waited for me. Yet Bernard
was never one to jog, and that harried pace seemed to stick to me,
like a bad thought, once I'd slipped into the backseat. As we drove
along, Frankie told a joke about a black man, and Lou laughed
very hard, and I had a strange premonition that these men were
ferrying me to some abandoned lot, though I only smiled at the
billboards.

That night I wrote to Mama. To my shock, I was able to con-
struct myself on the page.

SEPTEMBER 10

I'm sorry not to have written, Mama. I'm sure you know the story from Max—the movie we're making and all of it. I had a very bad day the first time but otherwise I'm doing well. It is of the utmost importance that I achieve my own person, and this seems to be the way. I grew tired of the Communiqué, of all those volunteers tugging at my sleeve and having to be the man they expected of me. I know you don't care for Bernard, but he is the most unrequiring person I've ever met. If anyone was born for the silent life, it is your son, who has much rock inside him. The world, if it likes, can beat against the rock and make the sound of itself. Please feel free to write. But I think it's best if, for now, you don't visit. Everything I do is for you, Mama.

She wrote back.

SEPTEMBER 16

My Giovanni,

All of it makes me sick, and yes, Max has been giving me sly little updates on all that you're doing. I've been thinking about this Bernard business. I was thinking of when you were a child: Do you remember the day you learned about the guards who stood outside the royal palace all day and never moved once? Remember, they showed you in school? You loved these palace men who barely ever blinked, even with thousands of visitors passing right in front of their eyes, and you decided one day that you were going to be one of these guards. Do you remember, Giovanni? "I was born to be a guard," you told me.

And you stood still for a long time. You were looking out into the distance just as if the queen were behind you! You did it late into the night, but in the morning I woke up and heard the news report going full blast on the radio. It had come on, and you were mimicking it. I said, "I thought you were born to be a guard?" and you said, "I was wrong." Well, it's true—you are not a guard. Remember, there is so much more for you to be in life. I will keep my distance, for now, I'll agree to that, but you must, must write me back.

M

I did, keeping these exchanges secret from Bernard, who would have disapproved, I knew. Yet, he shouldn't have, for these letters, if anything, helped sustain my imitation of him, providing a release, an imaginary realm in which I could once again sound like Giovanni. The two (writing like Giovanni, living like Bernard) aided each other, in fact, as a periscope allows a submarine to dart along, unseen, unharmed. And through this correspondence, all my new adventures, the characters I met, were soon layered with a second, deferred pleasure: that of imagining how I would describe them in my letters to Mama.

So it was the night of the premiere.

Years before a two-hundred-yard desert was built on the Monument lot to satisfy the director Arnold Tolstoy, a by-all-accounts impossible man who considered the set a necessity for the filming of *The Raj*, the three-hour epic that was to make his name. As Tolstoy had just made a killing for Monument Pictures with *The Impossible Tower*, the studio heads happily met his request. Over a period of months, the trucks passed day and night, hauling in two-ton bags of sand marked by the hues (Persian khaki, oasis

yellow) Tolstoy felt necessary to achieve what he called a "heightened verisimilitude" of the Arabian expanse. Union carpenters
spent months shaping dunes of pleasing composition and plausi-
ble distance. An elaborate lighting system was installed to simulate the passage of the desert sun, and its absence, which meant
the stringing up of a vast black tarp wired with a new kind of
scattered electrical light. In the last weeks, hundreds of scarabs
were set loose in the sand. When *The Raj* bombed, ending Tolstoy's career, many wondered what would become of the lot. But
Monument Pictures honored scale above all, whether in catastro-
phe or triumph, and elected to maintain the Desert as an all-
purpose venue for parties and premieres. It was there they held
the event for *Everyman*.

The picture had premiered earlier that night at the Broken
Temple, a theater on Last Hour Boulevard built to seem a half-
century old. Monument Pictures had secured the attendance of its
best actors and actresses as well as other capering types: elegant
figures, mainly, whom I didn't recognize but who carried themselves with the brisk, supple air of the broadly known. They chatted and reached across the soft-cushioned rows to shake a hand or
blow a kiss; some saluted far-off acquaintances or performed some
snappy task in their handbags before turning, at the cue of the
dimming lights, to take their seats, hiking up their pant legs or
sliding their hands cleanly under the seat of their dresses. The
theater went dark. A lively silence. I sat, alert as a rabbit, in the
opera box with Bernard, Max, Frankie, Lou, and Ms. Julie Dark,
the hired woman from the Jade House and my companion for the
evening.

Since my first trip with Bernard, I had returned to the Jade
House several times, beginning to understand it more. Ms. Dark,
I saw, was an exquisitely attuned performer. She could read in the

way a man smoked his cigarette a desire to be punched playfully on the arm or petted on the shoulder. In a moment she could switch from carnivorous desire to motherly concern, and even, at times, performed a sort of *under-self*, in which costume she would, in the longueurs of the late evening, divulge heartrending details about her brother Dennis and his long struggle with leukemia. Not very much of it was convincing, but it didn't have to be. It was the very exaggeration that was of value, like old Greek theater, with its swooning and its masks.

On future occasions I would be provided with different women from the Jade House. Yet each one, whether a broad-shouldered blonde or shy-eyed black girl, went by the name Julie Dark and each, it seemed, had consulted the same well-kept file or card catalogue or whatever organizing system the house used to keep track of notable moments from our previous outings. In this way, each new girl (who said, "So good to see you again," when stepping into the town car or appearing at my door) helped contribute to the illusion of a history, referring with ease to the time the paparazzi chased us outside Town Hall or that oyster night at the Tangiers.

Some of these pretenders, of course, demonstrated more skill than others, and yet I came to enjoy the poorer ones in the way one relishes even amateurish renditions of a familiar song, each, in the vagaries of their difference, pointing to some ur-melody one could never actually hear. Except one girl, a chatty type with bags under her eyes, at the crucial divot in the night when she was to lay her head on my chest and relay the latest episode in the long sufferings of her dear brother Dennis, so mangled the story (making him a *younger* brother and sentencing him to lung cancer instead of leukemia) I immediately, in a strange, high-pitched voice, called for the car to pick her up and, after she left, paced madly around the bed, feeling as I had that first day of shooting. This feverish state of mind might have lasted for several hours if I hadn't swallowed two more of those green pills, a hefty supply of which Lou had given me.

To myself (I never discussed them with others) I referred to these panicked spells as bursting moments and was quite worried, in fact, that I would suffer one the night of the screening. I took a pill before leaving, but when the movie started up in the held silence of that theater, my heart was going hard. There he stood, me, twenty feet tall, peering through the blinds of an office window onto the traffic on Fifty-seventh Ave. A man could be heard shouting from the street, the blinds tinkling under my fingers. Onscreen I raise the cigarette to my mouth as if posing a question. So, deliciously, is presented the life of this character: a man who studies the hieroglyph of traffic from a tenement window. Harry Knott, posing as a private dick hired on the main by desperate men days into their second ulcer. But when a customer comes in, a nervous hat-fiddling man, asking for "a new fabulous raincoat," a code word, we learn the government needs Harry, for Harry is a spy.

We had filmed it on the lot. Rather than a busy avenue, the window looked out on a pile of orange utility cables. But the camera turned that moment into a succulent image, such was the camera's genius. And as the movie went on, I watched myself in a kind of rapture. I watched myself kiss a woman in that way that involves a dip. I shot a man dead at the airport. I could not wait to describe to Mama the dream and statue they had made of her son.

As the red curtains closed, however, my mood seemed to stiffen. I waved too much and smiled weakly to the applauding people below. In the trip from the sidewalk to the waiting car, I walked with a hitched gait, and once inside the Desert had difficulty finding my footing in the sand. I linked my elbow with Julie Dark's, hoping that would help. Attentive as ever, she laid her soft fingers on my arm as we strode into the party, but this made it worse, and I just as quickly released the grip.

Soon I led us to a group of chatting actors, whose company was my favorite. The women held their heads at a soft-focus angle, the men made everything crisp and light. With actors each gesture rose to the level of event. The way they snapped an arm forward and back in order to check the time. The fruitful nodding. I stood around them in my customary silence.

Through the years, I'd tried different strategies, of course. I'd put my faith in politeness first, and later in wit, but silence, I learned, was better still and got you so far, especially in Fantasma Falls, where the point of someone was to not know them. People would descend upon me as tourists would a famous statue, and like a statue, I was charged only with the task of being still. By then, I lived under a haze of rumor: That I acted this way only after the movie came out. That I was "staying in character." That Bernard was imitating me. We were fucking. Uncle and nephew. Crooks. What bits reached me I didn't bother to dispel, and soon, to my delight, words like *mysterious* and *laconic* came to surround my name in the papers, like newsprint bodyguards.

And yet, when the feeling blasted me, as it did that night at the Desert, this armor of rumor, of reputation, did little, and it was best to have Bernard nearby, so that I could draw him live. So while an actor nattered on about the joys of the ninth hole at Trembling Hills, I looked discreetly for Bernard, finding him at last by the five-piece band where he danced in a kind of fever, digging his toe in the sand, twisting his hips, marking this effort with an ugly frown. When I looked up again sometime later, he was standing on his tiptoes to whisper to the band's singer, a statuesque blonde with dark, diving eyebrows. As he seemed to gnaw on her ear, she nodded with slow-dawning comprehension and then shrieked, shoving Bernard to the sand, where he waved his legs and arms in playful arcs, giggling.

Out of the corner of my eye, with Julie at my side, I monitored his raucous passage through the party. Bernard pushed past a bushy-haired waiter, spilling a platter of ruby cocktails. Later he participated in a shouting conversation with a circle of very tall men. At one point he vanished from sight altogether only to appear later on a rafter high above the party, where he crouched like a gargoyle before the fake orange sun.

I'd seen such things before. Once when he was drunk at the Communiqué, he had climbed onto the bar to do a limb-tossing jig, the intended irony of which was difficult to gauge. As it was the time he shushed everyone in the Communiqué's back room to sing a winding, impassioned ballad about sailors who survived the open sea only to perish after visiting the "midnight house" of a lightly mustachioed prostitute named Frangelina. As I remembered it, no one quite knew how to react to these emotive displays, and the few who attempted to muss Bernard's hair or clap him on the back were met with vicious muttered insults.

He seemed to be moving toward us. "Have to go to the restroom," I said to Julie.

"Go to the restroom, darling."

As Bernard moved through the party, I did what I could to push in the opposite direction, hoping, really, to sneak out the back exit, though I soon found myself approaching Nathan Sharp, dressed in his customary premiere-night ensemble. Top hat, tuxedo, white gloves. Seeing me, he raised his arms in triumph. I bent down to receive his hug.

"I got that little feeling in my chest. And it's not angina." He gave me a coquettish look. "It's that sequel feeling."

"There you are!" I turned, and there stood an actress who looked exactly like Mama. The aged version I'd seen in the City. Her drooping cheeks. Hair fully gray. Max stood next to her. The woman smiled in an absent, anxious way.

"Mama."

Her smile filled the Desert, and it was as if all the separating years vanished, like that! In the middle of the Desert, I shrank to the size of a nine-year-old, drowned in an oversize suit and too-big cowboy boots, peering up at my Mama. How many times had I been poked or headlocked or scowled at by some petty parent before Mama arrived, saving everything! And it was as if all the Desert—the peering, braceleted women, the men cocking their heads to airdrop hors d'oeuvres into their mouths—shimmered and then vanished altogether, mere emanations of our play inside the Sea View living room.

"Well?" I said. "What did you think?"

She did not hesitate. "My favorite part was the panhandler. The way you shook the tin—that was my Giovanni, that had the old joy in it."

"Dollar, *sir*. Dollar, please." I couldn't resist, shambling in the sand with that hunched back, my hand raised above my head. I passed Mama, who was already giving me her Look. "Charity helps all, goddamnit!" But as I circled her, planning one more go-around, there appeared before me, somehow, the man in the wedding dress, from Marguerite Harris's party. "Quite something, really," he said before disappearing, an apparition of memory soon replaced by my room at the Ambassador, that den where I had shivered and sweated. The bursting feeling. And I stood up very straight and looked at Max, with Bernard's appraising eye. "Did you arrange this?"

"Well, I did, yes. Call me naïve, but I was hoping you'd listen to *her* and forget all this moviebiz masquerade bullshit."

"I thought we agreed that you wouldn't come," I said to Mama, trying to hold my tone.

"Oh, I know, Giovanni, but I just couldn't resist. The idea of seeing it in Sea View and coming out of the theater all alone—no, I couldn't stand it. I had to surprise you."

"And what a delightful surprise it is," a voice said.

I turned, and there stood Bernard. His hair and face, since his time in the rafters, had somehow become wet. The bolo tie hung around his neck like a towel. "If we knew you were coming, Ms. Bernini, we certainly could've gotten you better seats." He made a vague tsk-tsk gesture in Max's direction and then reached for Mama's hand, which she snatched away.

"But of course, but of course, please, I insist!" Bernard extended his arm toward me with the unctuousness of a maître d'.

"Look at him!" Mama had a fist on her hip and a finger in the air, accusingly. "For a day, fine. For the screen, yes, but not to stay, Giovanni."

"But it seems to be working out?" Bernard said. "It seems everything's been going sort of *perfectly well* since he left home, no?"

"I would never have let you go with Max . . ." she said, ignoring Bernard, who began doing a strange, sort of absentminded pirouette and who, hearing this latest riposte, began to repeat "let you?!" with mock disbelief, with bent knees, and a hand cupped above his waist as if nursing a stab wound. "Thank god, she *let* you," he kept saying until Mama, with whitely pursed lips, stepped through the sand and swatted him with her handbag.

She lit into him, striking him about the head, shoulders, and neck, a look of unholy concentration in her eyes. Bernard, in response to this assault, protected his head with his hands and hopped around in circles, like a tickled chimp, the two of them kindling onlookers' attention until a ring of people had formed, Nathan among them, and Julie, too, who, finding me there amid this chaos, constructed a look of disgust, and then, seeing my own expression, downshifted to concern.

Nathan by then was standing behind Mama, attempting to peer over her shoulder. As he did, however, Mama was winding back to strike Bernard again and whacked the mogul on the nose, sending him recoiling. He back-stepped to the rim of a dune and, before any warning could be given, tumbled down it with a shriek.

"Look at him! Is that who you want to be?" Mama said, waving her arm at Bernard. A lock of her gray hair had come unhinged.

The onlookers gawked at me as they had so many times in Sea View. Nathan's pale, de-hatted forehead was peeking out from the rim of the dune.

"My Giovanni," she said. "You're *sympathetic to the—*"

"I'm not." It came out of me. Harry Knott's voice. The *whoosh* of traffic out my tenement window. "And don't say that I am." I added, "I've never been and never will." My heart beat in my throat, and I turned away.

Bernard by then was stepping into the dune to help Mr. Sharp, the short man brushing sand from his tuxedo pants and yelling in Mama's direction. His shouts called to assembly several turban-wearing enforcer types who gathered close, ushering Mama out, I gathered from her protestations. Each time she called my name, the sound got farther away. Then she was gone.

Ten minutes later, Max returned. They had her thrown out, he said. She's standing outside the lot, he said. "We had an agreement," I said in the right voice. Julie stroked between my shoulder blades.

It was simple enough not to return Mama's calls over the next couple of days. All this entailed was not picking up the phone. Three days later word came that she had flown back to Sea View. But that night, after the energy of the scene had died, and the sun was turned off, and the fist of stars appeared over the Desert with the big auxiliary fan blowing in a hot and idle wind, I snuck out the back door to the part of the lot where they kept the old sets. There was the frontier town, its row of saloons. Past it stood the cardboard façade of a castle, reachable by a metal drawbridge spanning a drained moat. I jumped up and down on the drawbridge, listening to the tested metallic sound it made. I swallowed a green pill. One that I liked to do was pick a cigarette out of the pack. Bernard did it with two taps. After lighting one, I put it out and tried another. Maybe I tried half a pack because a lot of barely smoked cigarettes were strewn about the drawbridge by the time I was pacing, the gun in my hand. I hadn't used it, not once, but it helped now and then to take it out and feel its weight. I threw it up in the air and caught it with both of my hands, laughed. Already I was feeling better.

ELEVEN

"It'll be like a movie without cameras," Bernard said, handing me the speech in the hushed backseat of the town car. Before long we arrived at the fairground where a makeshift stage, festooned with orange bunting, stood before the defunct Ferris wheel. There was an air of frenetic activity behind the stage, a mill of anonymous people excitedly performing tasks.

When the presidential candidate and former senator Rory Stengel finally entered the backstage area, applause traveled swiftly through the crowd. It was a pleasure to watch him smile and greet people and shake his head with warmth and enthusiasm, a head taller than everyone. When he came to me, he held my shoulder and frowned terribly, as if chagrined by gratitude. I don't remember exactly what he said. Something like, "So glad, really, an honor, we're gonna thank you for the yes we're glad." This was my first time meeting a politician, and it surpassed by far the company of actors. A politician, I learned that afternoon, cannot part with a gesture until he's blown it up to maximum size. As Senator Stengel thanked me, his face shining with makeup, I began to understand the event. It didn't matter what my speech said, it mattered only what gestures I made.

The speech itself, as I said, had been written, so, when the time came, all I had to do was stand at the podium and declaim it. Already the crowd thought of me as a kind of hero because of the supposed political undertones of *Everyman* and *No Man's Land*, the second film starring Harry Knott, even more popular than the first. By then I had lived in Fantasma Falls for five years.

I maintained through that time a comprehensive scrapbook larded with articles, profiles, photographs, and puff pieces about Harry Knott. The headlines, in their factuality, pleased me to flip through: THE TOTAL ACTOR, an article about my unflinching commitment, both on film and in life, to the role of Harry Knott; A PATRIOT ONSCREEN AND OFF, a glossy-magazine profile on the extent to which my character's political views mirrored my own; RETIRED MILKMAN CLAIMS TO EYE REAL BERNINI AT LOCAL BOWLING ALLEY, a small item (among many others like it: one week, it was a garbage man spotting me weeping outside Fantasma Falls Hospital; another, a bus driver claiming I, wearing a hula skirt and blue eye shadow, boarded the M30 at midnight and handed him $200 with stern instructions to drive due east), in which a man named Gary Evershed claimed to spot me "violently cursing a gutter ball" at lane four of the Happy Hall bowling alley; WHO IS SHE NOW?, with capsule images of the Julie Darks as they sauntered down the red carpet or emerged from a limousine, along with epithets purporting to describe each woman (*Melanie*, a young actress; *Tabitha*, a nurse and hobby painter); TEN QUESTIONS WITH HARRY KNOTT, a teenybopper questionnaire in which I listed my favorite type of ice cream and the politicians I most admired; THE PRODUCER INSPIRED ENOUGH TO JOIN, a rare profile of Bernard and his choice to imitate the character Harry Knott, moved, as he was, by the character's patriotic actions on film.

That many of these articles were imprecise or wholly fabricated only enhanced their meaning. If anything, I began to see the scrapbook as an act of preservation, aided precisely by these layers of invention. The lies in them helped protect Harry Knott, in the way Knott concealed my imitation of Bernard, in the way my being Bernard, in turn, helped conserve somewhere, however deep or buried, *Giovanni* himself, surviving in the scrapbook's photographs, if nowhere else.

He no longer existed in letters, it's true. Since the incident at the Desert, I had not written to Mama. For a time she regularly sent her own, claiming to be ill. First her lungs, then an infection in her toe lately replaced by a heart palpitation or arrhythmia that "will be the end of me," she swore. "If you want to leave it like this, fine. But I'm close to the end. A body knows these things." I'd called once and knew immediately, from her voice, that she was in fine health, and stopped writing again.

A few days after the episode in the Desert, Bernard had sat me down for a talk at the Chateau Ravine bar. She was trying to sabotage me, he said. However much Mama claimed that she was helping me, that was the exact degree to which she was seeking to *destroy* me.

Sanctioned by repetition, the theory grew more persuasive. For what, really, had been Mama's plan in coming to the City all those years before? (There was a delicacy, a succulence to these speculations, insulated from fear by Bernard's remove.) Why, after all, had she encouraged me to imitate Lucy on Marguerite's roof, knowing that Lucy was herself at the party and might very well come up at any moment? And even if the resulting row had not been Mama's strict intention, why, all along, through letters and in person, had she encouraged the pursuit of Lucy's thread? How could such a search have ended well? And why, really, had she surprised me at the Desert? Was that scene she'd caused with

Nathan and Bernard truly an accident? Why had she gone if not to stir up trouble? To throw my career in jeopardy and lure me back home? After all, what had she been doing all my life if not making me dependent on her and her alone? Why had she trained me to seek threads? If not to yoke me to her and separate us, on an island of two, from every other living soul?

This logic, however, could be easily derailed. Late at night, in the blue-black of four a.m., with Julie Dark fast asleep in bed (one of the worst parts of any evening in her company, for each woman slept differently, some on their back, mouth gapingly open, others on their stomach, creaking like an unclosed door in light wind), I would begin to see Mama anew, as a framed savior. Perhaps she was right, I would think, starting to pace. Perhaps this whole Harry Knott stunt represented a crime against my instincts. Hadn't Bernard *betrayed* me with Lucy? Why should I trust him? Perhaps he, from the beginning, had so relentlessly campaigned against Mama because he knew she represented the sole threat to *his* authority. And so I would go back and forth, these doubts spiraling into my chest, where my heart beat more quickly, my legs, too, speeding up until in my quickened motions the mirror reflected an alien silhouette, a man to my terror, that looked not at all like Harry Knott. The need to call Mama would bolt through me, but then, always, the man in the wedding dress would come to my ear saying, "Quite something, really," and I would need to swallow two green pills to steady myself again.

An hour later, I would lie in bed. Julie would stir or lightly moan, and the bursting moment, now past, would seem the best proof of Bernard's case. After all, if thinking about Mama caused such tumult, imagine what writing her would do?

And in those moments when I ached to call or write her

(moments that grew both less frequent and more extreme), I consulted the scrapbook, which, I knew even then, existed only for her. Each curly-eared article, each tape-mummified photograph awaited *her* fingers. And one day, we would collect in the Sea View living room, where she would dim the lights, and I would present the completed book, and with each page she would giggle and shake her head, relishing this immaculate trick I had pulled on the world.

And what an addition this political speech would make! That day at the fairgrounds, I read each sentence. When I reached the period, the audience applauded. "The Communist threat is still present and will remain present without the vigilance some deem excessive." Applause. "It takes a spy to know one." Applause. Now and then I would look up from the paper to see the concerned, pink-faced men in straw hats holding papers rolled into batons. The women fanned themselves with the same papers, shaking their heads at an indignity I had named. I kept waiting for someone to yell, "Cut!"

As these appearances galloped along, the newspapers, to my shock, reported them as fact. I didn't know which I preferred more: giving the speeches or reading about them a day later in my bungalow at the Chateau Ravine. In truth, it was hard to divide the two, for the event seemed to happen only when it had been written about, or rather, it was only then that it was confirmed to have happened—its *having happened*, its being preserved in the gel of that tense, made it delectable, like hearing of a stranger you happened to be.

On those mornings when I expected a newspaper article, I'd open the door to find the *West News* rolled on the black doormat. Feigning a light curiosity, I'd page through before turning to the Politics section. There I would happen upon the headline, reading the article in a gulp before cutting it out and adding it to the scrapbook.

ACTOR BERNINI ENDORSES SENATOR STENGEL

Former senator Rory Stengel addressed a mixed and boisterous crowd of seven hundred supporters today on the steps of the Old Municipal Tower, marking his third such appearance in Fantasma Falls this month as he, along with his opponents, make their final preparations for the statewide presidential primary on the 21st. While Mr. Stengel has failed to gain a foothold in Fantasma Falls, let alone nationally, his candidacy was bolstered today by the appearance and public support of actor Giovanni Bernini, famous for his role as spy Harry Knott in the films *Everyman* and *No Man's Land*.

Political endorsements from entertainers are nothing new, of course, in this heated primary season. What distinguished this appearance from others was Mr. Bernini's decision to appear as the character Harry Knott, the fictitious spy the actor plays onscreen. Mr. Bernini took to the podium this afternoon in a suit identical to the one worn by Harry Knott, delivering a twenty-minute address praising Mr. Stengel's right-wing positions in a manner indistinguishable from that of the character.

These eccentricities did not appear to faze the energized crowd, however. When this reporter canvassed them after the addresses, many confirmed they had attended solely to see the movie actor. "I'd vote for him if I could," said Carl DeWee, a high school senior. "Have you seen his movies? Now he's taking it into real life." Said Timothy Michaels, a retired engineer, "He hunts pinkos in the pictures, and he'll do it right here, too."

Opponents may well seize upon this appearance as evidence of the former senator's reactionary positions. Given the robust turnout at today's rally, however, it seems a trade the candidate is willing to make. "Mr. Bernini is going to continue to stump with us," a spokesman from the campaign confirmed. "We're delighted to have him."

I campaigned with Rory Stengel for six months, rarely interacting with him backstage and then hugging him or gripping his hand and hoisting it with mine once on it. In this proximity, I learned the strategies. The sanctity of eye contact, for instance. How eruptive a grin can be. Above all, the key was to have said things so many times that when you were delivering the line, whether solemnly or casually, whether to a cigar-chewing reporter or tongue-tied voter, you weren't ever thinking about the words, but about some essential, misdirected thing—the way you touched a man's shoulder, for instance, or seemed to smile unthinkingly to yourself—in the way a magician talks always but never about the palmed ace or hidden thrumming dove.

By the time Stengel was defeated in the election, I had stolen what I could from him. Little time passed, perhaps a month, before my appearances recommenced at political rallies and in convention halls up and down the state, at which events I delivered speeches deviating little from the message I preached with Stengel, the primacy of patriotism, mainly, and the specter of communism. "I am a patriot in the stories I tell and in the life I live," I must have said a thousand times, becoming the master of certain phrases and mottoes, whose syllables I'd run up and down, like melodies. We traveled in a motorcade from event to event, winding our way as far north as Red Rock Shoals.

By that time there had developed a cult of admirers, zealots who attended rallies in my suit and bolo tie and cowboy boots, waving placards and vicious signs. These men seemed to grow in number with each new appearance, and security men often mistook Bernard for one of their lot, checking his passage or giving him a skeptical once-over. "Committed, huh?" a burly organizer once asked him. Bernard answered, "Why, sir, I'm committed to any cause that will awaken this country to the real." After making it past this guard, I expected Bernard to wink, but he looked solemn, if anything, strutting ahead with the bellicose energy of a football player taking the field. During the rallies, I would sometimes spot him in the crowd itself, waving a sign or joining a chant as if electrified, genuinely, by the policies I described. "Meet the most natural politician this country's ever produced," he said when showing me off.

In truth, the content of my speeches mattered little to me. No, what mattered was the *performance*, of which these addresses were but a small part (and the meaning of them hardly relevant at all). How I walked onstage, waving to the peopled bleachers, the style in which I descended stairs—these mattered as much as my rhetoric or tone of voice, and to test these gestures I began to use the mirror every morning.

Previously I had used it sparingly: to verify, say, a look I'd caught on the traffic-scanning face of a jaywalker. I think I saw it as a cheat. But after we announced that I was running for governor, I began to rely on the mirror, to practice in front of it in the morning, usually after reading an article about me, in order to solidify certain details. How I looked flipping the page on the dais, for instance, or sighing.

As I soon discovered, however, the bedroom mirror wasn't big enough. I made the request to Frankie and Lou, and it was taken care of: a larger, multipaneled mirror replaced the length of the wall opposite my bed, so I could examine the full sweep of a gesture. Even this was insufficient, though, and, upon my request, was expanded again. Wrapping around the bed, a semicircular mirror came to be installed, but this, too, disappointed me— seemed to emphasize the lack of mirror elsewhere—and I eventually told Frankie and Lou that I wanted the entire room mirrored, three hundred sixty degrees, and the ceilings, too.

The Chateau Ravine staff, who already considered me a per-
manent resident (informally referring to the property as the
Knott Suite), was happy to oblige. It was achieved with surpris-
ing speed, but my first night in the mirrored room, I could barely
sleep, kicking the sheets, the innumerable Giovannis spitting it
all back so that I had to shut my eyes, the bursting feeling coming
again. I vowed to call Mama first thing in the morning, to book a
flight back to Sea View, when at some hour sunlight nosed the
edge of the curtains, which I parted, flooding the room in angles,
and I understood the mirrors were no mistake at all but a miracle.

For there are innumerable points of view, of course. A man might
choose to see you from a variety of locations in the stands, and it was
best to learn how you might appear to him standing wherever he
was. Soon I had props brought in from the lot: a dais, a set of stairs,
a small desk on wheels. At my request, Julie Dark joined me in that
chamber, part of my effort to be comprehensive. Once she was a tall
Swede with a lightly cruel sense of humor. Another a woman with
black bangs who kept stroking my cheek with her finger. And yet I
soon found that sex itself was too homely an act to bear to watch in
the mirrored room, and I asked Julie to simulate more practical positions, such as shaking my hand or asking me a question at close
range, with that upraised, auditor's tilt of the head.

So when our advertisements began to appear on the radio and
on television, I was not in the least surprised by how I sounded or
looked. When I posed at the desk, I knew how I appeared to the
camera crew, sitting upright, as I was, my hands clasped to con-
note both firmness and fairness. When I rubbed the hair of the
towheaded kid at the library of the kindergarten, I knew how my
slight, seemingly unconscious grin must have charmed the long-
skirted teacher, was in fact *watching myself* as I did it. I perceived
how immersed and engaged I must've seemed reading *The*

Forgotten Cat, an illustrated book, better than any of the actual onlookers did in that school library. Better than that prim teacher, who rested her hands above her knees when bending to scold her students. Better than Frankie or Lou standing against the yellow wall. Better than Max, who sat in an undersized wooden chair, biting his nail with the impatience that ruled him more and more. Better even than Bernard, whose grin seemed the tic of an actor whose films I'd seen too many times.

The mailbox at the end of my block gulped down the letter. I regretted the action instantly, with the kind of trembling regret that occasions a vital risk. The library made me think of her, but it was more than that. I could perform for every soul in the world, and it wouldn't count unless she saw it.

I sent a brief note with clippings. She responded that week.

> *Yes, I've followed this, of course. You know how I feel about this Bernard, you know quite well, and I never thought you one for politics. But I need to see you, Giovanni. I will be quiet as a mouse.*

The day I received this note I gave an address at a soon-to-be-shuttered oil derrick on the outskirts of Palm Haven, a desert town an hour outside of the city. The men wore hard hats and blackened gloves, their expressions yoked together by rage. My voice echoed among the black machinery, the brown-red hills of the desert visible beyond the derrick chuckling with its work like a railroad car. The whole time I was speaking, I was wishing Mama were there, but, no, it wasn't that—it was that I had mistakenly felt her presence, I understood only then. When I raised clasped hands with Senator Stengel, for instance, or leaned in to hear a voter's nervously muttered name, always I felt she was there, her eyes hovering above the events, and only then, at the mouth of the desert, understood that she was not and had never been.

When I returned to the trailer, Lou said I had a visitor. Bernard encouraged these callers as part of our effort to win votes. By then I relied on a playbook of phrases and questions. Depending on what was first said, the conversation, like a game of chess, could branch out to a limited number of topics.

"Guy says he's an old friend," Lou told me.

At that, a tall, rakish figure entered the trailer. He used a cane, wielded for the purposes of style, it was clear. His long face passed in and out of the trailer's slatted shadows, and as he approached, I found that my heart was beating quickly. When he got closer, I saw he was tall and lean, wearing a canary-yellow suit. Soon he settled into the chair. There was a crease, a dissonant ring in his eyes, his features gaunt and time-bitten. I had no old friends.

"Hey, pal," he said and stuck out his hand. "Don't recognize a buddy?"

"I'm afraid I don't."

"Look at you. Damn, just look at you." He smiled. "Big-time politico and all that." He added, "Jesse Unheim. From Sea View."

"Jesse Unheim," I said. This was a technique Bernard used: saying a person's name. I felt myself relax. I was going to relish dismissing him.

"Remember the principal's office? Always you and me stuck down there all but banging our heads for sheer never-ending boredom. God, those were times. Whole time I'm thinking, why they got me down here with this freak. No offense. I mean, now look at you. Heard the speech today. I'm thinking, gee whiz, look at this guy."

"How can I help you?"

"Well, I live out here. Acting a little. Like you. I mean, not like *you*. Trying to. Anyhoo, one day I flip open the paper and what do I see? Giovanni Bernini's giving a big speech right in Palm Haven, my neck of the woods. And I thought, well, how about I pay him a little visit. Have us a parley. I mean, jeez, bud. Haven't seen you in, what, fifteen years?"

"Long time," I said.

"Too long, too long." He scratched his nose with a slightly opened mouth. "So, listen, your mom and I, you mighta heard, had a bit of a dispute. I know you're a busy guy, but this thing—it wasn't quite finished."

"I did hear about that," I said. "As I understand it, you left town before the jury came to a decision."

"Well, my lawyer was on loan, you see, from some interested parties out here. And I could chew your ear off and so on, but my point is—" He exhaled. "See, I just need a little something. A piece. And you and your mom won't hear a peep from me no more."

"Do you think it's my obligation to give it to you?"

"No, no, I don't mean it that way at all. See, your mom, well, she's the one who split up that dough, right? What was rightfully mine. Now, I saw you coming into town and I figure to myself, why not make this simple for all parties involved. Payment won't be felt on your end one bit. I'm talking about eight grand."

"You can talk about it all you want. Just don't do it anywhere near me." I nodded to Frankie and Lou. Soon enough they got him in a grip, hoisting him up like professional movers. It was right out of a Harry Knott film.

"Hey, hey, c'mon." He seemed to be in his natural state, getting thrown out. "Your dad wouldn't approve of this, I'll tell you that."

"What?" Too quick. "My father?"

Looking at each other and then at me, Frankie and Lou understood to release him. Unheim, once seated, made a gloating expression. "Thought that might perk you up." He propped his right foot on his left knee. How he used to sit in detention. "Might a big wheel such as yourself rate it a tale worth paying for?"

"I see you have more to say." It was like being on set: you had to deliver each line slower than you thought. "I don't have my book with me. But you have my word that if you give me accurate information about my father, I will pay you eight thousand dollars."

He nodded, frowned. "See, he was in Dun Harbor when I was coming up. Helped me get in with some of the guys there. He talked about it—how the old lady threw him out after his first bid.

"For some guys, really, it ain't the money at all. It's like the thing food does to a bitch. Lifting someone's wheels. Juicing a candy bar. 'They a-call to me,' he used to say. Smart enough, but he was one of those guys—only one kind of luck, right? First, it was the horse he got caught smuggling in. That's what lost him the gig with the longshoremen. After that, he got wrapped up in an insurance scam at the dock with guys he used to work with. Arson. He torched the office and old storage house like he was supposed to, but two teens were having a time down there, and they got torched with it. Sentenced to thirty years at Dun Harbor."

"The prison?" That dismal building. I pictured a visiting room lined with picnic tables. A handcuffed figure in a tux shuffling through the door.

"Oh yeah," he said. "Stole some fucker's cigs, apparently, fifteen years in. Got his throat cut. I brought you up once. Told him about some of the shit you got into, about detention. He said, 'He even worse than me.'" This bad Italian accent stolen from radio ads for spaghetti sauce—that was as close as I would get to my father's voice. "Check or cash," Unheim said. "Either way."

I made sure not to rush it. "If you think my mother owes you money, you ought to take it up with her. As for me, I think your story's worth about as much as the teller."

Lou and Frankie lifted him again.

"Big head now, I got it. I heard you had to sleep with a muzzle on, that true? You fucking cunt. I heard your mom wore earplugs around you, so she couldn't hear you, cunt." Dragged outside, he continued to yell, his boot heels scraping the ground.

Inside Nathan Sharp's ballroom the fifty guests inspected me over duck and Bordeaux. These fund-raisers required little of me except to seem amused by the donors' jokes or improved by their advice. From the swamps in the southeast and the windy states to the north they had been drawn to this mansion. I stepped out for a smoke and saw their shiny cars in a ring. Behind them the ocean rumbled in the starless night.

Fantasma Falls was a misnomer. There were no known falls yet found in a terrain marked for miles by desert, coastline, and canyon. According to one version, the title was the outright invention of Rutger Smitt, a paper baron, landowner, and amateur versifier from the previous century. Smitt, it was said, scoured the *Dictionary of Geographic Terms*, concocting the most alluring names he could to ease the settling of a land considered mean if not downright uninhabitable. Something of a pioneer in the field of branding, he was rumored to have coined the name Joy Beach, a waterless dump twenty miles north of the city, and Hallowed Hills, a stretch of accursed flatland to the east. Others, though, insisted the name preceded Smitt's arrival and could be traced back to the slaughtered

native population, who twice a year had visited a magical falls
where ghosts were believed to take the shapes of men in order to
reenact the scenes of their death. A committed minority held firmly
to this latter view and were known to go on long hikes and walk-
abouts in the summer, searching for these still-undiscovered falls.

After dinner we retired to Nathan's den, where Bernard had
me do a show. A southerner bravely raised his hand. Next, a real-
estate magnate named Gerald Picaso. The laughter stoked in that
smoky, paneled room, decorated with the murdered heads of bears
and moose, grew like a blaze, the faces of clannish men gathered
around it, grinning and covetous. "This one's *ours!*" a fat man
said to much applause.

After dinner, Max pulled me aside, into an alcove decorated
with paintings of flamingos.

"Do you believe any of it?"

"What's that?" I said.

"All these speeches you give."

"I don't care what I do."

"You know your mom and I talk. She doesn't like this one bit.
Not *one bit!*"

Soon after my encounter with Jesse Unheim I had Frankie
and Lou look into Jesse's claims about my father. A few days later,
Bernard appeared in my room to confirm that a prisoner 8BA94
named Giovanni Bernini had, indeed, been murdered fifteen years
into a thirty-five-year bid for arson and manslaughter at Dun
Harbor Correctional.

"How do you feel?" he'd asked.

"Why, do you care?"

"Don't be sore with me."

"All right. I won't be sore."

"Another instance of her misguided way of protecting you.

Ask me, this is a confirmation that what we've been doing has been right all along."

"And what is it we've been doing?" I raised the cigarette to my lips. To sit at the kitchen table and ask this question while Bernard stood in the partial light of the vertical blinds was to create a poem. One made of time, not words. He liked to look between the blinds at the scrubby little garden, setting one back with his finger, like Harry Knott himself.

"Don't be thick."

"Okay," I said.

"I'm giving you freedom," he said.

"Okay, good," I said with a slight smile.

"That's right, it's good. Freedom from being like your fuckin' daddy, who apparently couldn't keep his hands off another man's cigarettes, that's what I mean."

Perhaps Bernard had filled me with freedom, for in that moment, as he paced in that easeful way, resting his hand in his back pocket (and in so doing slightly opening the flanks of his jacket), preparing, I knew, some diatribe, I experienced no dread. In fact, a kind of serenity—electrically charged—imbued the light tinkling of the blinds, the shard of shadow on the gray couch. Bernard, himself, but another phenomenon.

"Max probably told you I ran for Congress years ago. It wasn't out of vanity. You of all people should know I have none. No, I ran because this country needs people who know the character of our enemies. I wanted it very badly. When people looked at me, they were looking at an idea disguised as a man. Twice I lost. Why? What wasn't working? I asked myself again and again. Then it occurred to me." He threw up his hands. "See, even then it had started. Senators, governors, congressmen. Aldermen, comptrollers, all the way down to the fucking garbage man—everyone, Giovanni, was *an entertainer.* An actor, a comedian, a tambourinist from the county grange.

"So I got into show business—the only business. Every business these days is show business. And it's easy and it's boring and it made me want to do a William Tell with about every last shit that walked into the Communiqué. But then I saw you." He set his hands on his hips. "Now I hope you appreciate what we've all helped to do. What Frankie, Lou, and Nathan have helped me do. I don't mean that you're a movie star. No. Right now, I'm not talking to Giovanni Bernini, the actor, I'm talking to the spy Harry Knott, a man who has stepped out of the screen into the world. And even better, even better, yes! You're *them*"—he flung his arm in the direction of the blinds—"at any moment you could be any voter in the world, and they know it. Don't you see how rare this is? You're both their movie hero and them *at the same time.*" He smiled. "What is it you think we're up to, Giovanni? Why stop at governor? Hell, you're gonna run this country, for, tell me, please, who in the hell can defeat a *make-believe president?*"

He ground out his cigarette, a favorite maneuver of his when approaching the coup de grâce. "About Lucy and me?" He laughed to himself. "Hell, I was hoping you'd hear about it. Really, what interest could I possibly have in a piece of ass like that? No, I was thinking of *you*, Giovanni. I got hard thinking of *you*: how you of all people thought you could have a girlfriend. Really, you think you're gonna find some sweet little piece and sit by a lake and exchange rings? No, the family you've been allotted is the audience, the public, voters, customers—whatever the fuck you wanna call them. They alone preserve you, you understand that? Because *you're imaginary.* Get it?"

"Sounds good."

I stood and emptied the ashtray into the kitchen trash. When ballplayers say of a home run, "I knew as soon as it left the bat"— so I felt after this remark. Bernard tried some things, even patted me on the back. "Anyway, we'll talk more about it," he said as he left. "Absolutely," I answered, with a grin. If his goal had been to make this sound bad, he had failed, for what could be better than becoming fictional?

That night, or one soon after, I wrote a letter to Mama explaining that she was not to visit. Calls followed. Letters. Most I tore up without reading. I knew what they would say. In fact, I almost mailed her a parody of my own, a note riddled with *oh, my boy*s, and *I was only trying to help you*s. That gray prison in Dun Harbor. All those years I'd passed it on my way to the train station, and my father, my namesake, had been there.

At Nathan Sharp's mansion, in that alcove with paintings of flamingos, Max said, "Goddamnit! He's using you, don't you see? He's gonna have you get into office and *use* you."

That was one moment I wished I could have seen on camera (or viewed in the mirror or, for that matter, read about in the paper) because I knew I took the right amount of time. "And what use do *you* have?" I asked. And Max was such an unwitting actor—he huffed, shook a fist, even turned one last time to shake his fist *again* before tramping down the hall, and away, it turned out. Later that night, I did it again in front of the mirror.

From the wings we could hear the herd of reporters: jittery-kneed, pens-at-the-ready, like the old crowds at the Communiqué.

Bernard and Lou waited backstage with me, as did Michael Martet, the owner of the theater. When we first met, Martet had subjected me to his gratitude, squeezing my hand at this rhythm:

down, up, down (held), then a pat on the back, down, up, down
(held), pat on the back. "This sure means a lot, Mr. Bernini," he
said six times. Martet was a head shorter than I was, his face forgettable except for a colorful and bulbous nose. Like a Christmas
ornament on a thin stem, plum-shaped and plum-colored, it lent
to his restless person an availability of spirit. The nose was meant
to be shared. "This sure means a lot" accounted for ninety percent
of what he said to me, and I was pleased when he left me in order
to pace by Lou. For a long time I remembered his nose. Because
of what happened, I remembered and wondered if there had been
signs in it.

I was worried the feeling would come. I worried about this
often. When I had greeted my opponent with a mean vigorous
shake, for instance, equidistant from our podiums before the
moderator, a silhouette from waist to head like a target at a shooting range. Or at the VA hospital when shredded, hopeful men
thanked me as I came around and at the Jade House, where I
knew how everything looked because I had practiced in the mirror taking off my belt and cumming. When admirers outside the
rally in Redwood Park swaddled my back or when they reached
over several rows of people unself-conscious to grab my hand, I
thought then, surely, the bursting feeling would come, and at the
condemned house, too, where the photographers broke their bulbs
over me and the men without jobs smiling. At a fund-raiser in the
hills, when it happened, I pretended it was something I ate. The
pills by then didn't always help. A butler led me to the upstairs
bathroom, where my expression in the mirror looked only slightly
puzzled. Relieved, I lay in the cold hard tub, the murmur of party
guests below. It was this way. Some expressions felt like shotgun
blasts to the nose but weren't really so bad when you took them to
the mirror. Tearing up her letters, for instance. Or waking from a

dream of rattling grates and dumb heads bobbing through slatted shadows. "An inspiration to the conservative majority, if still a mystery to many . . ." the newscaster said in his professional voice. The television made Bernard's grinning face the same blue it made all the hotel suite, lively at the time with balloons and jubilant people whose names I didn't know applauding.

Now we stood at the backstage of the abandoned Jupiter Theater. Bernard had selected it as the site of my first address as governor-elect. A symbol of decay, soon to be resurrected, was the idea. The cobwebs in the rafters were thick. Light bored through the warped paneling. This was not the place I wanted to be: in that musty backstage speared through by light, and yet I could think of no better place. I riffled through all the places I'd been, and none was the right place. More and more this was the feeling. I was not dreading the press conference. If I could dread certain places, like that neglected theater, it would spur me to find the better place, if only as a kind of negative search.

When Bernard and Senator Stengel took the stage, a hubbub broke out in the theater. The two sat at a microphone-laden table. The photographers' bulbs flashed. Stengel was beginning his introductory remarks when Mr. Martet tapped me on the shoulder with news of a phone call.

The short walk to the office, Martet expressed his surprise that the man on the other line could track down the number. On his metal desk sat the heavy receiver.

"I've been trying to reach you all day."

I said nothing.

"It's Ken," the voice said. "Ken Kessman. Your mother's neighbor."

"Go on."

"The police . . . Giovanni, there's been a . . . he tried to rob her . . ."

I said nothing.

"Giovanni—Jesse Unheim—he—"

When I walked onto the stage, the reporters shouted. Their flashbulbs cut me like glass. "You're not supposed to come out yet," Bernard said, looking over his shoulder at me.

"My mother was shot," I told him. "She's dead."

Bernard looked like he might speak when I punched the back of his head. I yanked his hair until his chair toppled over, I shoved his face into the stage, punching it again when the stage broke under us, and we landed in cold dirt. I punched him until my hands were bleeding, and then I reached into my jacket for the gun. Against his forehead I put the nose and cocked the hammer. It clicked. I pulled it again. "A toy," Bernard said, when I was scooped up by the armpits. Lou was holding me, suspended over the crater in the stage, flailing like a swimmer stolen out of the water, while the reporters made the cameras perpendicular to their faces. A sound was coming from inside the hole in the stage: Bernard, on the ground, his teeth pink with blood, like some half-fleshed skeleton. "A toy," he said.

ORPHELS

TWELVE

I woke to two men in white scrubs standing over my cot. "Ready, Mr. Bernini?" the stocky one said.

My body heeded the routine. Without my consent, it followed the men out of the room. They would lead it down the bright hall and stairs to the cafeteria, illuminated, like all of the building, by a floor-to-ceiling window. There it would swallow the pills the men gave it, and be gathered by these pills into a body. When it called to its arm, that arm moved! It could stretch and yawn! But the afternoon would age, and over the body would come a wan and wintry feeling. Fractures would open in its fingers and around its ankles, fissures so small it never failed to surprise the body when these cracks spread to its knees and neck. Soon its legs would shear off at the knee, and the body did its last bad running-up to its room, to its bed, where it could, in privacy, fall apart.

When the pills worked, however, this body—I—could stand to perceive this place. After breakfast, a square-jawed man in white scrubs rounded us up and led us outside to the front lawn, clean and aromatic, where we were organized into rows and exhorted to follow energetic movements he made, doing jumping jacks when he did and squats and jogging in place. It was like he was a volunteer and the twenty of us men and women were slow-footed, self-conscious impersonators. We did push-ups and sit-ups and I did not weep or die, as I feared, and soon we were taken to a side entrance of the building, the men and women separated into different locker rooms.

In the men's room we were each allotted a locker inside of which hung a towel and swimsuit. After changing, we padded across the blue tile to a pool, lined on one side by a bank of Jacuzzis, for what the blond man called Water Therapy. Water Therapy was this: Ten times we walked across the pool, which was long and clean and without a deep end, and then soaked in the Jacuzzis for a half hour. Afterward we were led back to our rooms to shower and change back into our blue scrubs. The same two men came to my door at lunchtime and escorted me again to the mess hall, where I ate untoasted bread, a grapefruit, and some peanuts.

But before dinner there were "Free Hours."

The first day, during this unstructured period, I kept to my room, a taupe square with a cot, bathroom, and closet. In the closet stood a dresser. One drawer held a collection of white ankle socks, the other a pile of neatly folded blue scrubs, identical to the ones I currently wore. On the floor of the closet were three pairs of white sneakers. The medicine cabinet in the bathroom kept an unlabeled tube of toothpaste and a toothbrush. The wall behind the bed was no wall at all, I discovered, but a floor-to-ceiling window covered by a taupe-colored blind that, when raised, faced a sparkling lawn where figures in blue scrubs squatted on stone benches or stumbled, woozily, as though recently struck on the head.

The next day during these Free Hours I explored the house. There was a screening room, commissary, greenhouse, library, and bowling alley, even a squeaky-clean racquetball court. All of this exploration unnerved me, however, and I soon returned to

my room, where I tossed in bed, humming to ward off the silence.
I did nothing that next day (feeling like I might collapse again),
but the following one, during Free Hours, I wandered the grounds.
The house, I saw from the lawn, resembled a venerable prep school
except for those odd architectural choices: the floor-to-ceiling
windows, for example; the marble colonnades on the north and
south sides of the building. The property was vast, encompassing
two lawns, an apple orchard, small pond, and rose garden, all (I
discovered after some cautious exploring through thickets and
pine) enclosed by a high white fence.

That night I learned the story of the place. A man at a nearby
table went on and on, and I eavesdropped zealously. As far as I
could tell, he referred to everyone, himself included, as George. My
back to him, I chewed on a napkin, blocking the escape of his faux-
British accent (at night, as the pills wore off, the old urges surged
back). Given the oscillations of his tone, I could not tell if he was
addressing a lover, child, or himself. "Yes, he had a real *millionaire's name.* Sandy Lewis, I think. An eccentric philanthropist—
watch your sleeve now, come on. Well one day he had an epiphany,
you see. *Walls* cause all the world's misery. So what does Lewis do?
He hires contractors, squadrons of them—with their wrecking
balls and hard hats—orders the men to raze every wall on his
property and replace them with windows, pillars, colonnades. Just
about *anything* that isn't a wall. Will you stop it, really?! Sit still
now, c'mon. Well, then Mr. Lewis extends an invitation to all the
homeless in the area to come in and live here. He gives each of
them a studio and a bicycle. An artist colony for the mad. Except
three years later our millionaire expires. Buried under the stand of
birch trees on the north lawn. They say he had syphilis. Later they
changed it all, of course. Now it's for us *nuts.* Why, of course, yes,
George, they do just *spectacular* business." He switched to a stage

whisper. "That George there, you don't recognize him? He was an archbishop, for heaven's sake. Yes, oh, and that George there was a baseball star, he was, why, of course." I was petrified he would point to me next and say, "This George there was that actor-politician type, wasn't he then?" but he didn't, thank God. And I got up soon after that, all but running to my room.

It's true, no one seemed to recognize me. The beard, I suppose, helped ensure my anonymity. And yet, even if it hadn't, I might not have been disturbed. Among the patients reigned, I soon discovered, a kind of wary discretion, disrupted only rarely by a scene: a shiny-headed man raising his plate in the middle of the cafeteria and then smashing it into pieces on the smooth floor; a woman weeping naked in the middle of the lawn. These transgressors disappeared for a few days, a week sometimes, and then rejoined the buffet line with the same shuffling obedience, the same covetous reaching for breakfast buns.

When I first arrived at No More Walls (if that was its real name), I feared I would make such a scene myself. That I would begin to howl. That when the pills ebbed in their effect, I would steal George's voice. Yet with each passing day, this fear diminished. The medication helped in this, yet so did the routine, whose sheer repetition was its own kind of medicine. I hoped to live like some ball left on the beach, pushed in and out by the ocean—yes, I wanted to be pushed around by the routine. But that day, instead of walking me down to the mess hall my escorts ascended the stairs. "To the doctor," they explained.

The previous day the routine had also been severed. I was told I had a visitor and was led down a gravel path to a picnic table where Max waited.

Maybe I hadn't looked at him in years, for he had aged tre-
mendously, it seemed, magically, as if some painting of Max had
for years been interposed between us, the living man tumbling
out behind it only then. Why did people always age this way?
Purple-black bags hung under his eyes. He had lost weight, and
his face dripped with skin.

Of the days after the incident at the Jupiter Theater I remembered little. My name hollered down a prison hall, the acoustics
like a drained pool's. A country through my porthole. I said,
"You'll have to be the talker." I was thankful for his thumbs
knocking the table, as I was for the breeze raking through the
trees and the birds squeaking above us, all saviors against silence.
The bursting feeling had returned the previous night. It began
with the dream of Jesse Unheim, and then the silence, the first
furniture of every room.

Max attempted a grin. His eyes creased with the effort. "A rep-
utable place, Giovanni. The head psychiatrist, a Doctor Orchfee—
Orgall—Ori*ganief*—a genius. *Experimental*, they say, but
top-notch. I've been in touch with the accountant. He's managing
your funds until you're, um, in a greater position to—well, you
understand." Normally my manager made a religion of looking a
person in the eye—it was the eager salesman inside him—but he
didn't then, squinting, instead, in the direction of the house. "It's
part of the agreement. Legally, I mean. That you spend a little time
here. Bernard's dropped all charges, but the judge insisted. Apparently, they're having a new special election, given the circumstances. You are relieved of all duties as governor-elect, thank the
Lord Jesus Holy Christ Almighty. I've alerted the authorities here
that he's not allowed to visit or call. Not that I think he will, boy.
He knows it's done. Whatever it was in the first place, it's done." He
snickered. "He thinks life's a game, boy. That people don't have

blood in their veins . . ." When Max spoke next, his voice sounded like embers in a fireplace. "I've been in touch with your mother's neighbor in Sea View. He said he'd look after the house and make sure it stays as your mother had it until you're well enough to go there yourself." He said, "I don't know if you want to hear it, but there's word of Jesse Unheim, too."

"Go."

"Owed money to people, apparently. Bookies. The mob. Intended to rob your mother and accidentally shot her. Life in prison, they're saying." He sighed. "The police found him weeping on the floor."

The pills glued me into a person on a bench. Otherwise the wind would have blown through my cracks.

"This will be my last visit, probably. They encouraged us not to come until you're well. It has a *very* good reputation, Giovanni."

"I trust you, Max."

He yawned urgently, or so it seemed. It took me a moment to understand he was crying. "You know what I thought when I first met you," he said, "when we went to my rented room and you sat there on my chair, stiff as a board? I thought, how I would *love* to be this little brat. How he must see people and things! How he must read the world! I saw you onstage and *knew it*. To be Giovanni! Even when you were a mess, a downright mess after Lucy, I thought, how he must be feeling it, the boy who's so sensitive to the world. How *sweet* it must feel, how *deep*! When you were Bernard, too, I felt it. As cold and mean as you were, I thought, this little rascal, he's *experiencing life from the inside*. Me, all the rest of us, what are we in comparison? Even right now, boy, this very moment, looking at you across this picnic table, pale and sick, I can't help but—but *envy* you, you've followed feeling to its very end. Oh, it's terrible, I know. Like the audience, I wanted to feel it *through you*!"

He laid his head on his arm, his arm on the table. He stayed that way for some time, making choked noises and then shot up, like one woken abruptly from a nap. "Really, this Orchelli—he's supposed to be excellent." He repeated that he would write before disappearing past the hedges. For a good half hour I sat there, listening to the birds.

I thought of that visit as they led me up the stairs. The doctor. I was hoping to put it off indefinitely. The previous evening I had heard a very different account of the man while eavesdropping on George. "A very tricky character," he'd said. "Very tricky. Well, no, calm yourself there, please. I think it's fair to use the word *trickster*, yes. Always sending people to the basement."

I was brought to a dark corridor with two benches and a black wall. The nurse knocked on the wall twice until a bar of light appeared at its bottom, a bar that grew in height until the entire wall was transparent, revealing behind it an airy, well-appointed study. I trembled, sure some hideous magic was occurring, the kind where walls vanish and cruel sorcerers are met, but then I realized a curtain was being unrolled from the other side—that the wall was no wall really, but another window. A door had been hewed into it, which the head nurse opened, ushering me forward.

At the front of the room stood two armchairs set at a distance too great to be intimate but too close to be unintentional. There was a crowded bookshelf, a set of diplomas on the wall, and a big desk whose only decoration seemed to be a framed hundred-dollar bill. On the other side of that desk was a floor-to-ceiling window affording a view of the south lawn and, farther away, the blue mountains. The door closed behind me.

"Hello again," a voice said. A man stood in the corner of the room, I saw only then, ratcheting the curtain back down.

"Did Unheim send you? He did, didn't he?!" If it hadn't been for the pills, I would have screamed.

The man was tall, of athletic build, dressed in jeans and a plaid workman's shirt rolled to just above the elbows revealing hirsute and well-muscled arms. He wore his tar-black hair parted down the middle in a European style of an older time and possessed a tremendous Roman nose that skewered his otherwise boyish features like some private joke, or burden, of his ancestry. His front two teeth he kept exposed, perched on his bottom lip in such a fashion as to make him look vulnerable, if not downright imbecilic, yet his eyes were tender and retreated, brown as a bear. He soaked me with them and smiled as a wounded person smiles: that is, with an intensity of expression that is equal to the intensity of its hiding.

"We met once before, but you were severely agitated, and do not, I don't think, remember it. My name is Doctor Josef Orphels," he said. The manner in which he walked toward me—it spoke of a man so confident in the mechanisms of his body that I immediately resented and feared him, backpedaling into one of those burgundy chairs. I was saying a number of things, each word a small bullet against the silence, the silence, which can be shot and shot and lurches on. None of it seemed to perturb or surprise Doctor Josef Orphels. A preternatural calm—the calm of a murderer, I thought—hung about his person. He eased into the other chair.

"Who is Jesse Unheim?" he asked me.

I said nothing.

A few minutes later: "Giovanni, who is Jesse Unheim?"

I had forgotten what surgery questions are, how tiresome and difficult it is to raise an acceptable shield against them. Answers, I mean.

When he asked again, "Who is Jesse Unheim?" I said, "I don't know."

"But you just mentioned him a few minutes ago."

I said nothing.

"Giovanni?"

"I, I think . . . It's hard to know."

"What effect has the medicine had?"

"A good effect," I told him.

"Please contain your enthusiasm."

"*What?*"

"I'm joking," he said, and flashed the kind of wry grin that immediately explains a face. A glint rang in his eyes, and the doctor-veil, that air of seriousness, was lifted, though it returned quite suddenly. "Giovanni, why do you think you're here?"

"Because I've gone crazy, I think."

"Do you remember coming here?"

I had to coax the voice out of me like a cat from under a car. I was still using Richard Nelson's. A tired, failed version of it. "I don't think so."

This Doctor Orphels inquired more about the medication. Side effects and so on. I answered at a stymied pace, favoring economy over veracity, using "yes" and "no" interchangeably. He sat with a regal stiffness, doing without the notepad and pen I was made to believe these doctors used. I wished for him to have them. If he did, perhaps he'd look at the pad now and then and spare me, for a moment, this look of empathy. Worst of all, however, was his comfort in silence.

My longtime ally, my partner all those years in Fantasma Falls, silence had betrayed me. At night, it gathered and swarmed, pulling at my hair, my toes, my fingers until I was sure I would stretch to nothing. And I would hum or clap just to produce noise, like shooting a flare gun against the swallowing dark.

"In combination with the medicine I would like to start regular therapeutic sessions. Do you feel ready?"

"No."

"Why not?"

I thought "no" would speed us sooner to the end of questions. Seeing my mistake, I said, "Yes."

"Yes what, Giovanni?"

"What are you asking?"

"Do you feel ready for a session?"

"Yes, I do."

"But you said no a moment ago."

"I made a mistake with a word."

"But they have opposite meanings."

I said nothing because he hadn't asked a question.

"Do they not?" he said.

"What does it matter what they mean?"

"Isn't that precisely what matters?"

"Yes," I said.

"Why do you think you're here, Giovanni?"

"Here?"

"At the Institute."

"Because I've gone crazy, I think."

"So you've said."

I started clapping, a technique helpful in warding off the silence.

"How do you experience this craziness?"

"It's the, the bursting," I said.

"Giovanni, why are you clapping?"

"Stop it, please!" I wrung my hands like they were someone else's. I bucked and squirmed, wriggled like a man in a strait-jacket. "You *are* him, aren't you?" I said, "Jesse Unheim in disguise!" I said, "Hug me then, brother!"

And this so-called doctor, this impostor so summoned, rose.

With that almost military gait (high knees, all business) as though he himself were a subordinate there to introduce an even greater eminence, he strode toward me, so I knew it was Unheim— Unheim, finally—because no psychiatrist would dare stand a foot away from his patient, as this stranger did now, in jeans and a plaid shirt, casting his eyes at wild me in that burgundy armchair. It was happening, as it had a hundred times in my dream. "An old friend," Lou says. The steps can be heard, and a figure in a tuxedo appears, lumbering through the slatted shadows. A skeleton.

I stood. "Hug me!"

But when I opened my eyes, it was the doctor's face, not a skeleton's, appearing a foot from mine. He had that strong European nose, an altogether European face, which, weighed and blessed as such faces are by real history, carries more consequence than those made here, in our imaginary country. And those teeth, those absurd teeth perched on his lip, like a child who's never learned to close his mouth at the wonders of the world.

"I'm not Jesse Unheim," he said. He studied my eyes one at a time like a lover in a film priming himself for a catastrophic kiss. Then he grinned as he had earlier. That wry grin, it appeared on my face, too.

"I'm not Jesse Unheim," I agreed.

A twinkle came into his eye. He gave my shoulders a fraternal squeeze and returned to his chair. "Feeling better?" he asked once in it.

I looked at my hands, amazed they were connected to my arms. "I believe I am, yes."

"Who's Jesse Unheim?"

The mountains, through the window, looked like a child's cut-out: two blue humps collaged against the sky. A shadow lay over the birch trees. That was the gift of the window. It freed me from the beauty. "I'd rather not say at the moment."

"That's fine," the doctor assured me.

I said, "To your previous question, Doctor, the answer is yes. I am ready for these sessions. I am sure of it."

THIRTEEN

We met the following afternoon, seated at that unnatural distance, our backs rigid against our chairs.

"When can I be released?" I asked.

"You're registered for a hundred days' stay. You've been here for seven. That leaves ninety-three."

"Days that I am *forced* to stay here?"

"I wouldn't use a word like that. But yes."

"This is legal then?"

"Giovanni, you assaulted a man. While the victim agreed to drop the charges, the judge refused to release you without a guarantee of treatment. No More Walls satisfied him as a place for you to receive that treatment. Still, we oughtn't think of it in those terms. Our aims are higher."

"Is the story of this place true?" I asked.

"Which story's that?"

"A man with syphilis knocked down all the walls."

"That it was syphilis has not been proven. It is true he wanted all walls removed."

"And yet walls remain," I said.

"An admirable goal but nearly impossible to execute: a building with *no* walls. When it comes to Mr. Lewis's philosophies, you'll be pleased to know we remain quite faithful. None of our forty occupants are restrained unless it is absolutely necessary. We believe people must be given the freedom, both mental and physical, to explore the breadth of their condition."

"Yet I am *forced* to stay here."

"Giovanni, the purpose of these sessions—"

"Is for you to massage me with questions until I'm lulled into a submissive state and divulge all of my secrets."

"Far from it," he said. "I will be talking to you—asking questions and the like—to find out who you are. Not to correct who that person is."

"How often do we meet?"

"Every afternoon."

"What about you?" I asked.

"What about me?"

"Do you talk, too?"

"Of course."

"I mean, about yourself?"

"We're not here for me, Giovanni."

"So your eyes insist. You have great doctor's eyes. They are probing but not intrusive. You occupy your doctor's chair with a kind of stiffness, so that I, the patient, am to recognize you are fit for your authoritative position without indulging it too much. Your smile reassures me that you are still human despite your duties. Do they teach all this to you in school?"

"I'm a bit confused," he said. "Yesterday you said you were ready for this, that you were sure of it. Now you're being standoffish."

"I am ready, Doctor. Quite. It's just, I'd like to know you a bit before I enter the vise of treatment."

"The degrees are on the wall. Feel free to inspect them. I received my first degree at the City University of Medicine. Thereafter, I received a degree in psychoanalysis from the New-Method Institute."

"A degree admits as much of a person as a gravestone, Doctor."

"Then with my gravestone you must be satisfied," he said. "I wanted to talk about the terrors you mentioned yesterday. Can you describe them for me?"

"Perhaps."

"Might you try?"

"I might," I said. "I might not."

He smiled. "That's very helpful."

"I think you're as guarded as I am."

"Giovanni, every afternoon for the next ninety-three days you will be walked to my office. We can pass these afternoons in a kind of grudge match or we can begin the long process of treatment. The drugs, from what you told me, have helped. What you and I do here can help all the more. It is a long process—one that doesn't always work—but you have clearly suffered. From what I understand you threatened a man with a gun."

"A fake gun."

"Even stranger." He seemed to think for a moment. "What you said about me earlier—about my eyes, my posture in this chair—it's a projection, I think."

"If that's some sort of doctor's term, I don't know it."

"It means you are projecting *your* feelings onto me. You seem to think I am up to something, that I am playing a part, assuming a role, hiding behind some mask—but perhaps *you* are."

My heart quickened. "Is that your specialty, then—is that how you get strangers to open up?!"

"Please. I didn't mean to upset you."

"I'm trying—I'm trying to finally talk and you accuse me of *playing a part*—"

"My father was a psychiatrist, you know," he said.

"What?"

"You wanted to know about me—I'll tell you. My father started the New-Method Institute. The man was an expansive narcissist, a breed that doesn't take to parenting, or rather, takes to it too strongly. A controlling man. A brilliant one, too. Micah Orphels."

"Your father?" I said.

"He emigrated here from Austria, founded the Orphels Psychoanalytic Institute, one of the most influential in the world. Later, he would create the New-Method. Patients traveled across the country, some internationally, to see him. Pilgrimages. He was said to cure the incurable. But these people, they didn't know who my father truly was. That old conundrum of celebrity. His closest friends were his patients, if that says anything. He'd have them over for dinner on Friday night. My mother would cook for all of them, and he'd criticize each one. My father would say, 'Edgar, pass the salt,' and if the man hesitated for *just a second*, he'd say, 'Look at this unconscious hostility. So much deeply repressed anger you can't simply pass the salt?' That was our household. Nothing could be free of reason."

"Oh? So he could be difficult?"

"Quite."

"And . . . and was he that way with you?" I asked.

"Of course. I was his firstborn, Giovanni. The brilliant child. I once finished second in a grade-school chemistry competition. My father sat me down and said, 'Josef, I know you could've gotten first but you're scared to, so you *chose* second. But I'm tell-ing you, it's *okay* to come in first.'"

"He thought you'd done it on purpose?"

"Everything, Giovanni, was *on purpose*."

"But why intentionally lose a chemistry prize?" I asked.

"He told me I was scared to surpass him. 'The consequences of oedipal ambivalence,' he called it. According to my father, I was overly modest, self-effacing. I could outdo him but was scared to."

"Was it true?" I asked.

"Reasons are persuasive. If a child's served them at a young age, he eats them up. Everything that happened in my childhood was that way. My mother received the worst of it. If she was late meeting us, she was trying to undermine him. If she forgot her keys, she was expressing hostility. Everything was a symbol. So, yes, I believed him. What's worse, there was some truth to it. I *was* scared to outdo him."

I smiled. "So did you start getting first place in your chemis-try contests?"

"I did very well in school, yes, but it was complicated. The more my father egged me on—to be what he knew I could be—the more I took it to mean he thought I was secretly incapable, that I *needed* him to nudge me. He developed this exercise in which I would insult him."

"Insult him?"

"After dinner every Sunday night, he and I would go into his dark, cluttered office, in the basement of our brownstone. He would lock the door and lie down on the chaise, where his patients went. I would sit in his chair, where he sat with his patients, and he would force me to insult him."

"And you did?"

"Of course. I was young. Thirteen, fourteen. Too young to rebel. I wanted only his approval. Now to gain it, I had to insult him. I had no idea what to say."

"What did you?"

"He fed me lines."

"Fed them to you?" I asked.

The doctor smiled ironically. "Ah, childhood."

"What were they?"

"'Call me a fraud. Tell me I'm a small man with an overgrown reputation. You will dwarf me. You will outshine me. Say, "You are a shit, Father."'"

"And did you?"

"I couldn't disobey."

"How did it feel, to do that?"

"At first I mumbled, and my father said, 'Speak up, son. Scream it!' He wanted it louder. Eventually, I did. Afterward, every Sunday, I went in my room and cried."

"Did your mother know he was doing this?"

"My mother did whatever Father thought was best. If he believed something was important, she did, too."

"Did you resent her for that?"

"Of course. In childhood one finds time to resent everybody. I don't anymore. I understand. Part of the responsibility of any parent is to provide his child with something to resent. Or else there's a kind of stagnation, an inertia, from generation to generation. Resentment is the language with which parents speak to their children."

I smiled again. "Sounds like something your father might say."

"My father was often right, Giovanni. That was the problem. Nothing, I don't think, is so insidious as the truth. If he had been an abject brute, that would have presented its own challenges, its own traumas, yet it would have been easier, in the end, to rid myself of him. But he wasn't. He was a brilliant and insightful man."

"Who forced you to insult him," I said.

"Worse than that, I'm afraid. By the time I turned seventeen, my father had all but anointed me his confidant. I was his first son, you see, and he interpreted this role with a kind of biblical intensity. He would take me into his office, lie down on the chaise, and confess. This, when I was eighteen. He worried my younger brother was too dull. That he no longer found my mother attractive. In many ways I became *his* psychiatrist, though in truth he orchestrated all that happened in that room. He divulged some very private things to me. Confessed that he'd cheated on my mother. With a patient, no less."

"He told you this?"

"A Russian-Jewish girl, a nineteen-year-old. Her father, a renowned dental surgeon, had brought her in. She suffered from fainting spells, anxiety, and hysterical deafness. After a few months of analysis, though, my father was able to locate the source of her neurosis. The patient's father, you see, had made it his habit to belittle and disparage her and did so terribly during crucial stages of her erotic development. As a result, she felt herself to be worthless. Social settings of any kind created such anxiety in her that she fainted or 'went deaf.' My father uncovered this all fairly quickly. Yet as any analyst knows, naming the problem is simple in comparison with *treating* it. It's in treatment that true ingenuity is required. You may look at a patient—sit across from him day after day—knowing exactly what's wrong with him, what it is precisely that troubles him. But that insight is meaningless if you don't know how to provoke such insight in him." He shifted in his chair. "As it happened, my father tried a number of things: hypnosis, word association, even some Gestalt methods, which he generally considered frivolous, but nothing reached the girl. It was around this time my father was experimenting with his New Method, the one I would eventually study. This New Method—it depended on the concept of transference. Have you heard the term?

"It's a common, indeed inevitable, occurrence in psychoanalytic treatment. When a patient transfers a deep psychic attachment—one usually with the father or mother—onto the analyst. In most schools of thought this transference is considered a kind of spell, one that must be broken. The New Method, however, involved *exploiting* this spell, this transference, very explicitly, so that the doctor—well, let's say, if the patient will inevitably transform the doctor into her father, the doctor, my father believed, must *play the role* of the father, must become the father the patient wished she had. A second, better father. Sometimes this meant he would act domineering, sometimes meek. The character the doctor played would depend on the patient."

"And in this case the better father would *sleep* with his daughter?"

"My father believed the patient needed to *perform* the incest moment so as to free herself from its grip."

"Did any of this *work*?"

"Of course not. She became infatuated with my father. His refusal to sleep with her again she took as a confirmation of her worthlessness. Fun for the night, then in the trash. Daddy's mistress, instead of Daddy's bride. She had a series of hysterical episodes, even told people what my father had done, but no one, not even her own father, believed her word over Micah Orphels's."

"Your father admitted all of this to you?"

"He said, 'I've made many mistakes and will make more. But it is all in the name of science, which is, by its nature, provisional.'"

"And how did *you* take it?" I asked.

"Since I was supposed to act as his analyst, I said, 'Do you really believe sleeping with her was a scientific exercise?' He said, 'It gave me brief physical pleasure, sure. It catered to my ego, yes, but principally it was an experiment in treatment. A failed one, in this case, but I believe I have found a New Method. It needs to be implemented more carefully, but the future lies in transference.'"

"Why deny doing it to the patient's family then?"

"I asked him that exactly. 'They wouldn't understand,' he said, and their misunderstanding would ruin his reputation. Prevent him from helping the patients who depended on him so."

"Did you believe him?"

"No. I was beginning to understand that he was a dangerous narcissist, a master of justification. I hated him and resented my mother for allowing him to run wild. He once asked me to simulate choking him."

"Choking him?"

"'An oedipal pantomime' is what he called it. Part of his New Method. But I began to actually choke him."

"And what happened?"

"I stopped myself, of course. When I did, he began coughing and rubbing his neck, and I was terrified I'd actually hurt him. 'Good job,' he said when he'd caught his breath. 'Excellent!'"

It happened with the doctor's embrace that first session. Like an athlete returned from a long injury, I rediscovered the genius of my limbs, and in the weeks that followed I became, both in and outside of his office—on the benches of the lawn and in my room alone—a second, better Orphels.

An impersonation hadn't fixed me this way since Bernard. I quit my need for cigarettes. Memory of the gun no longer weighed on my hip. When I thought of Fantasma Falls, I felt, if anything, empathy for the people in it—for Nathan, all the Julie Darks, even for Bernard. Toward my fellow patients and the conscientious nurses, for the very birds and bees I brimmed with this same empathy: empathy, which is the surest sign of remove. I was so improved, in fact, it didn't rattle me in the least when word began to spread, and patients began to recognize, through the veil of my beard, the face of Harry Knott. *How did I end up here?* I was asked by a stooped patient with sunken eyes. In Orphels's voice, I told the truth: "I almost killed a man."

Above all I listened greedily. The doctor, I discovered, had fashioned himself into a kind of key, a key of person, unlocking the men and women of the world. On the cushioned perch of a bay window, at tables in the mess hall, I began to conduct impromptu sessions. Underneath an oak tree. In a back carrel of the library, strangers confessed to me. It had to do with my eyes, my smile. A man who couldn't stop chewing his nails told me about the niece he had, in the depths of addiction, prostituted. A curly-haired patient with abstracted blue eyes admitted that he may have killed a man—caught a bum mugging a woman, struck him with a lead pipe, right there on the street, then ran away.

Ideas were striking. A new act. I'd call Max after my release, imminent, I knew, given my rapid convalescence. We'd resurrect our old stage show, with a twist: I would now be Doctor Giovanni Bernini (Max could make up some bunk about a European medical degree). Each volunteer would come onstage and lie on a chaise, and I, Doctor Giovanni Bernini, regal in my chair, would tease out each one's story until the audience—all of us together— had experienced that lurid, healing joy: the airing of another's secrets. "An Experimental Evening with Doctor Giovanni Bernini," we'd call it, or "You, with Doctor Bernini." The first volunteer might be hard to come by, but after that, who wouldn't want their story confirmed before an attentive audience? It was what all of it had been pushing toward: the *insides* of another person.

Of course, the interior I was most attentive to in those weeks was that of Doctor Orphels. That he hadn't yet noticed my stolen speech or upright posture I considered a miracle. I was terrified he'd picked up on it that day he accused me of projection, but there had been no mention of it since. Every day he revealed his innermost experience without the slightest hesitation. No pausing or stuttering, no pocket-digging or side-glancing. The good doctor looked me right in the eyes and confessed, divulging his life story in a voice as airy as his office. There were no walls inside the man. Every question I asked he answered, and in this thoroughgoing manner, like a homeowner showing a burglar around his house, Doctor Orphels opened all the drawers of a forty-year life, handed me his secrets. Like a man confessing directly to a spy.

"All my life it had been my father's plan for me to enroll at City University for premedical studies," the doctor began one afternoon. "And when the time came, I did explicitly that. My parents paid for a studio apartment in midtown with the expectation that I would commit myself to class work. A sensible enough plan, except I was completely unable to focus. Let me say, I have an outspoken unconscious mind. I am thankful for it. For some it's all but disabled: a person might be speeding toward a doomed marriage, an entrapping career, but their unconscious—whether through dreams or sickness or any of its usual emissaries—will keep mum. Mine, however, is, well—let's say, forthright. So it was at school. It—my unconscious, I mean—wouldn't let me focus. For the first time in my life I suffered anxiety attacks, couldn't sleep at all. Soon I stopped attending class altogether. It wasn't so much a decision as a pattern that developed. I didn't tell my parents, of course. On the nights I came home for dinner, I told them school was splendid, though I hadn't been in weeks."

"How did you occupy yourself?" I asked.

"Worrying, as you may know, is a wonderful hobby. It occupied me quite a bit until I discovered something even better. City University is situated in midtown, near the Handelmen Towers, an area flooded with bankers and stock traders. It wasn't long before I befriended some of these people at lunch counters, neighborhood bars. Understand, the world of finance had never interested me. Jews, they say, are divided into two strains: the mercantile and the Talmudic, and I fell comfortably into this latter category. Money was important, certainly, but only as a means to a greater pursuit: of medicine, for instance, the mind, God. These brokers and bankers were the first men I'd met who had devoted their lives to money as an *end unto itself*. Every day they herded into the revolving doors of those midtown skyscrapers, those temples to money—disappeared for ten hours—then came pouring out, each with their slight variation on the same uniform: the fedoras, Italian suits, Swiss watches. Like vestments. The first ones I met were soft-spoken, especially when money itself came up. Real dollar amounts. They had nicknames and code words for it, as if saying the name would be blasphemous. I don't mean this sarcastically: Money for them was a religious object. I started in the mailroom."

"All while telling your parents you were enrolled at school?"

"Yes. As it happened, I found I had a talent for the financial life, the sangfroid for it—that might be the word. In four years, I became a full-fledged trader of stocks. In seven, I had bought a large penthouse apartment uptown."

"Seduced by the high life?"

"Not at all. I've never succeeded in becoming a materialist. I know very well the limits of such consolation. Some of my colleagues may have believed they worked to furnish a certain lifestyle—a word I have never found much use for—to buy their wives diamonds, for instance, or to take lavish trips to Rome, but it's not true. You know what money gives us? Why people worship it?" He smiled. "It's a freedom from reasons. Money is the most efficient way to rid your life of reasons. No one ever questions *why* you want money. Doing something for the money can never be the *wrong reason* to do it. I wanted to eradicate the whole chorus of reason from my life, that life of my father. In this effort, money was a perfect aid."

"Your parents found out, I assume."

"They did, yes. I don't remember exactly when or how. My father, of course, was horrified. For months he wouldn't talk to me. Neither he nor my mother. By abandoning medicine, I'd betrayed them. By choosing the world of finance, doubly so. Keep in mind, he was a European intellectual. All of this was foreign to them, and yet my father's disapproval, which once might have paralyzed me, had no effect now. 'What is it you *do* all day?' he would say. 'What does all this matter? It *means* nothing.' But when he asked me this, I was wearing my finest Italian suit, driving them around in a chauffeured car, so his questions were barely audible, if you know what I mean. You could barely hear them over the shine of my cuff links, my watch. I distinctly remember my father getting smaller."

"Money talks?"

"I think of it this way: My wealth was my moat. I felt it especially with my colleagues, men I had worked with ten hours a day for eight years. I knew their wives, their children, their mistresses, yet we didn't know each other at all. We were all separated by our moats—our suits, our drivers. That's how we wanted it. We were made wonderfully apart, by money."

"I don't quite understand. What happened? How was it you ended up here, as a doctor?"

"My father dropped dead of a heart attack."

"I'm sorry."

"So people say when a stranger dies."

"How did you take it?"

"At the time I took it surprisingly well. I escaped into my work."

"Hadn't you already?"

"Such is the nature of escape: Since one can never truly accomplish it, one goes to further and further lengths trying to. Many nights I slept in the office. I traded day and night. My coworkers were perplexed, I think, and couched their perplexity, as many do, in jokes and nicknames. I was known as a 'horse'—what we admiringly called our hard workers—but never before had I, or anyone at the office, steamed ahead with this kind of urgency: pacing the office day and night, yelling (something I never used to do) at subordinates who bungled my orders. And yet it worked. Watching money accrue in my bank account, watching certain stock prices rally still brought me a near-religious peace, and I thanked God that it could still be so, that money could be my medicine. Once a week I visited my mother, an occasion I very much dreaded, so I dressed in my finest camel-hair coat and treated her to very expensive meals. I gave her gifts: a fur stole, a jeweled pendant, objects she couldn't pretend to want. My father's death had obliterated her. I knew on some level, as everyone does, that I was not entirely well, but I believed that it would pass. A few weeks later the skin ailment appeared."

"What ailment?"

"A rash on my fingertips that soon spread to my palms, up my arms, and down my back. It looked like a second-degree burn. Quite painful."

"Did you go to the doctor?"

"I am a Jew, Giovanni. I went to *many* doctors."

"And what did they say?" I asked.

"It was a food allergy, a rash, a bug infestation. The diagnoses were too diverse to be trusted. Within a month it had spread to my chin. I had to wear a handkerchief over my face. There were fewer handshakes, fewer drinks after work. I had gone from likably eccentric to dangerously so, dressed absurdly in huge wool coats with a bandana around my mouth. It was a panicked time. Some must've thought I was dying. There were moments when I myself did. Alone is when I felt safest. I have never been religious— was not raised to be—but I couldn't help but wonder if I was being punished."

"For?"

"Betraying my father."

"I see," I said. "And how did you find out the cause of it?"

"Accidentally," he said. "I had taken a week off work. Some doctors recommended I do it. The stress of work and of my father's death might, they hypothesized, cause this kind of spectacular nervous reaction. The theory never held much sway with me since my work, no matter how busy, always brought me more peace than anxiety, and yet here I was, away from the office, much improved. In just a few days, the rash receded entirely from my face and back. My fingers were clearing up, too. Imagine how relieved I was. Yet the rash was not eradicated. Indeed, when I paid for groceries or a carton of milk, the peeling worsened in my fingers, my skin itched terribly. So it was that I came to understand."

"Understand what?"

"I was allergic to money. That week away from work, my skin was better at all times, except when I touched hard coin."

"Is such a thing possible? Were you handling so much currency at the office?"

"The allergy, I soon realized, didn't require physical contact with money. If I was making a phone call about a trade, for instance, the receiver irritated my ear. If I was sitting in my office—where stocks were bought and sold—my breath shortened."

"You were allergic to the *idea* of money?" I asked.

"In a way, yes. I was allergic to those objects that through any concatenation of events led me to money. So I came to understand. Of course, it required much trial and error. I now consider it my first diagnosis as a psychoanalyst."

"What then?"

"After much hand-wringing—all too literal, I'm afraid—I decided to visit a psychiatrist. Given my perverse history with the profession, you'll understand my reluctance to do so, but I saw no other option. This was an ailment for the mind—a mental allergy, as it were—so I required a mind-doctor, a shrink, a second father."

"What were you hoping to get out of your analysis?"

"The goal was simple: to rid myself of this skin problem and return, unimpeded, to work. That's what I found so ironic. Mentally, as they say, I had never enjoyed my work more, yet my body was somehow revolting against it. Of course, my analysis changed everything."

"How so?"

"To recapitulate all the reversals, revelations, frustrations, terrors, and insights that occur in successful analysis is to do it a grave disservice. Suffice it to say, I realized I was in the wrong line of work. Often the body cries out on the mind's behalf. Such was the case with me—I told you mine was a forthright unconscious! The more we engaged in analysis, the more my skin cleared, yet the more my skin cleared, the more I loathed and feared my office. My associates, men I had worked with for over fifteen years, men whose company had brought me solace and sturdiness—they looked like cowards to me now, collaborators and liars. They lived in a mode of evasion. That's what money seemed to me now: an exercise in postponement. Watching it accumulate brought me dread. When would I spend all this money? What would spending it *do*? I'll put it this way, though the words only skim the surface of the experience: The moat, the moat of money, protected me *too* much. It cut me off from the kind of human engagement I had so long run away from and now sought again. I realized I could not escape my father. Nor did I want to. My destiny—I use the word intentionally—was to become a psychoanalyst."

"I think I know what you mean," I said.

"Oh?"

"I, too, used a moat."

"Yes? What form did yours take?"

"I played at being someone I wasn't. Someone terrible. I did it for years."

"Who was that?"

I said, "The man I tried to kill."

So it began. As the doctor recounted his father's death or discussed his start in the field of psychiatry, words, unbidden, rose in my chest. "My mother was murdered," I declared. "I used to give these speeches. All of them lies." In Orphels's voice, I would speak. The way it came out, it felt closer to listening than talking. With each name I uttered—Max, Mr. Heedling, Lucy, Bernard—with each anecdote I shared (when I thought I was being booed the first time I performed at the Communiqué, when I first learned to flirt while aping Max at the train station), the more deliciously foreign it sounded. What a rare fellow, I caught myself thinking, this Giovanni the Impressionist.

I wanted a story like the doctor's, one driven by its end, but mine resembled more the first blabberings of a child, when the impulse to speak trumps any ability to do so. My experiences were in a terrible knot, and we depended on the wayward, but thorough, logic of association to untangle them. Often we worked backward, starting, say, with my malfeasance in Fantasma Falls, which led to the sight of Lucy and Bernard backstage, which led, in turn, to my failure to imitate Lucy, which recalled, in the following order, my journey to the City; my encounter with Max; my politeness at the station; my fondness for Mr. Heedling; and last, always, to Mama.

Certain phrases in particular caught his attention. "Sympathetic to the bone," for one.

"Do you feel that you are?" he asked.

"I don't think so, no."

"Why not?"

"I'll explain this way: We used to do an act onstage. Two family members would come up. A mother and son, say. Max would lead the son and me behind a screen at the side of the stage, then the two of us—the volunteer and I—would go backstage for a second and come up with a little speech, one that used the names of the child's parents or some personal details that couldn't be faked. Then we'd hide behind the screen again and deliver our speeches, one at a time, so the mother would have to guess which of us was which. Usually the mothers (and the husbands, and the wives, and the children, for we did all types) were *dead certain* they could pick their son's voice. 'The second one,' they'd say. 'I'd know my Jimmy anywhere.' Lo and behold, after a tense silence, I'd come out from behind the screen. 'Hi, Mommy!' I'd say, and the audience would applaud and this mother, who a moment ago in her heart of hearts *knew* that I was her son, would stare at me, this huckster in a tuxedo—and how did she react? This is why I bring it up. How do you think someone would greet such a surprise?"

"She was happy."

"Have you ever seen a person *embarrassed* by their own good fortune, a person *mortified* by luck? That's how it was. These mothers didn't know what to do with their hands. They blushed, hugged me. The men grabbed my shoulder, they pumped my hand. *Many times* this happened, and yet every time I stepped out from behind the screen, I secretly flinched, sure that the family would see what a charlatan I was, that the audience would join, and I would be stoned."

"That seems extreme," he said.

"The stage, Doctor, knows only extremes."

"Why a charlatan, though? Were you cheating them? Would you pretend to have produced a voice you hadn't?"

"Not at all. Sometimes they *did* guess right, and that was notable, too, for how disappointed the mother or father always was."

"Why a charlatan then?" he asked again.

"Because they thought I was doing something I wasn't. Why else would they react that way?"

"You interpreted their interest in your act as a belief that you were 'sympathetic to the bone.'"

"I suppose so."

"Were you? When you performed your stage act were you being 'sympathetic to the bone'?"

"No. That's what I mean. I knew I wasn't, but I hoped I was."

"How did you *know* you weren't?"

"Because I was so relieved when each volunteer stepped off the stage. After they'd thanked me—hugged me, patted me, shook me—after the applause had died, the volunteer walked down the stairs back into the audience, and a new volunteer emerged, and I was thankful. Because each one—they wanted to talk and share secrets, or do whatever people do to 'get to know each other,' and each, if they didn't have to return to the audience, would have discovered what a fraud I was."

"Fraud, charlatan, huckster. Why? You did exactly what you purported to do: you exhibited a skill and they appreciated it."

"But they believed an insight attended that skill, and it didn't."

"But how do you know that?"

"I appreciate it, Doctor, and I suppose it was thrilling to be imitated, but what I was doing, you see, it concerned the outside of a person. They thought I'd touched *the inside*."

"To the bone."

"Precisely."

"But is there no place where the outside and inside meet?"

"Not that I know of."

"But I think you do," he said. "One of your peculiar phrases. The loose seam that sticks out and, when pulled, unravels a person."

"The thread."

"Let me ask," he said. "Why does one pull it?"

"How do you mean?"

"Why must one—must *you*—pull on it? Couldn't one observe a loose seam without tugging it?"

"I don't know. I suppose it's a malicious act—or it can be—to unravel a person. As a child, it was pure impulse. I couldn't help it. I was impatient."

"Impatient with what?" he asked.

"The theater of things, maybe. I think that was what my politeness was about—my being so polite when I worked at the train station. I was participating in a theater—'Hello, ma'am,' 'A good day to you, sir.' All that false gloss on life. What Bernard called the 'show.' I was entering it."

"It reminds me of the thought you had when you first mimicked Maximilian: that everyone around you was an imitator, too."

"Perhaps. The world was crowded with impressionists, so, I suppose, one had to pull their threads and find out who everyone *really* was."

"There's another word for that," he said. "A projection."

"Not my favorite word."

"Perhaps the *hiding* and *acting* that you ascribed to others was actually your own."

"Perhaps," I said.

"Which begs the question: If you were projecting your own feelings onto others, and as a result pulling those people's threads—well, did you ever wish for someone to pull *your* thread?"

"Perhaps."

"I believe we're hitting on something."

"Why's that?"

"Whenever we hit on something, you say, 'Perhaps.'"

"Perhaps," I said.

"Let me then repeat the reporter's question. The one he asked you that night, for it's an important one, I think: What is your thread, Giovanni?"

"Mine?"

"If someone wanted to impersonate you, how would he?"

"I don't know. I've certainly never been imitated, but I suppose you mean it more abstractly than that. . . . When I discovered Lucy with Bernard, that maybe was close to it."

"The moment of betrayal."

"Yes. It felt like something had been revealed. Like something inside me had been *pulled* out."

"When else?"

"This is strange. It just occurred to me."

"What?"

"When I wrote those letters to my mother, when she wrote hers to me. The writing—I never described or thought of it so— but it felt like that. On the page, I was free to *pretend* to be myself. To pay out my thread, if that makes sense."

"Opposite experiences, it seems to me, and like all opposites, quite similar."

"I don't catch your meaning."

"The two you mentioned," he said. "Writing. And betrayal."

Flooded as I was by the desire to reveal, I had to dam up at times and withhold certain close gems of facts and feeling. Most of all I had to maintain the ruse that I was not impersonating the doctor. This, of all my jeweled secrets, was the one I could not give away. An easy illusion to maintain, it turned out, since Orphels was too engaged in my story to detect the voice with which I told it. Each day he stared into his own wounded eyes, each day listened to his own overenunciated voice, and each day failed to notice. The differences between us were those of dress (he in his jeans and flannel shirts, I in my scrubs), hairstyle (his slick and parted down the middle, mine a cauliflower of black), and facial hair (he clean-shaven, I messily bearded). Early on I hunted around No More Walls for pomade, locating some eventually on a gaunt chin-scratcher named Tony. That night after some modest experimentation I succeeded in parting my hair exactly like Orphels's. For an hour I was delighted, striding about the room. "Money was my moat. It protected me," I said, "Resentment is the language with which parents speak to their children," before realizing, with crashing disappointment, that I would have to wash it out. It brought the resemblance too close. As much as I despised my own hair, it allowed me to maintain the ruse. From then on, I applied the gel only when alone in my room, usually before bed. The sound it made (the faint crinkling against the pillow) functioned as a kind of medicine.

It—my hair—was nagging me the afternoon I narrated to

Doctor Orphels the worst day of my life. I'd failed to wash it the night before. The doctor's, meanwhile, shined and behaved, a black swim cap, except for that thin part in the middle. I envied his jeans and starched flannel shirts, too. Nonetheless, I managed to outline that fateful scene at the theater: the call in the office, the brawl between Bernard and me. "Jesse Unheim killed my mother," I told him and, after the story, confessed that I had never talked about it before.

"How does it feel? To talk about it?" he asked.

"I don't know yet. Good, I suppose. Emptying."

"Emptying?" he asked.

"It's always been that way for me. With my private stories. They're like babies in the womb."

"How do you mean?"

"A pregnant woman wants to deliver the baby, of course, but she is terrified, I'd think, to give birth: to divide with her child. It's like that with these stories."

"You're afraid to separate from them?"

"I suppose."

"This will sound strange: Do believe you were born?"

I looked at my hands. "I think so, yes."

"You said your mother was the one person you never *needed* to impersonate."

"Yes."

"Is that because she was a part of you?" he asked.

"I divided from her pretty violently when I moved out west. For five years we barely spoke."

"Escape is a far cry from separation."

"It sounds wise, Doctor, but you'll need to explain."

"The place or person you're escaping—that is the engine of

your days. If your mother was what you were escaping, then you were quite close to her those years. Too close still. Unseparated."

"Perhaps."

"Is it a betrayal to be born?"

"Abstractly, I suppose."

"Is it a betrayal for the baby to divide with the mother?"

"This is all too abstract, Doctor. You can't talk about life this way. Like it's some math proof."

"Please answer the question."

"But it's the worst kind of shrink question," I said. "Really, it's absurd."

"You're unusually defensive today."

"On the contrary, I've been maximally forthcoming."

"Then be forthcoming again."

"Let's move on to something else: your early days in medicine?"

"Let me in, Giovanni."

"I'm not? I just told you something I've never told another soul in all my life. Is that not *letting you in*?"

"If you refuse to investigate what it means, yes."

"How much does something like that have to *mean*?"

"Please answer my question," he said.

"Fine. Is it a betrayal to be born? Yes."

"Now you're being dismissive."

"When you started in medicine, did you immediately know you'd made the right decision?"

"We're knocking on the door, Giovanni, but you're refusing to enter."

"Was it the refuge you hoped it would be?" I asked.

"I think it's time we moved on."

"Good."

He sighed. "Don't think I haven't noticed, Giovanni, for I myself have encouraged it. After our first session, I knew you would not talk about yourself, would not begin the therapy unless you could do so in another's voice, so I lent you mine. I lent you my voice, my posture, my facial expressions. More than that, I lent you my history. It is the New Method, Giovanni. My father's method. To play the role dictated by transference. Usually one becomes the patient's father or mother or lover, but in your case, the transference has required my taking on the idealized version of the patient himself, of you, Giovanni Bernini, and so I gave you my life story, let you borrow it. I knew some of your story—the death of your mother, the attack on Bernard, whom you had impersonated for years—and shaped my own so that it could better mirror yours. So far it has worked. You've told me quite a lot, and for that I am grateful. And now we're knocking on the door—your betrayal of your mother. But this, Giovanni, this you *must* understand. It is not sufficient for you to surround yourself with yet another moat if you are to be cured. Being me is no different from being Bernard. And so it must be said: You are not me, never have been and never will. Your fingers on the armrests of that chair do not feel the leathery scratch as mine do, your toes do not inhabit your cotton socks as mine do, your thoughts do not move and agitate in the skull as mine do. In fact, these past few weeks, as you've strode in and out of this office in that eerie reproduction of my gait, walked the grounds and, as me, exuded a subtle superiority over the other patients—all the while you have been yourself. When you were Bernard, you were yourself. When you were Heedling and Max, you were. You are yourself right now.

You have always been *yourself*. Behind the moat there you lie, hiding still. We have just been skating on the surface—we've found some words for what ails you, and that's a start, but we need to plumb deeper now. Tell me, Giovanni, is it a betrayal to be born?"

FOURTEEN

A window, too high to look through, let in enough light to tell night from day. Sometimes a shoe appeared in it. A bird. When the nurses came for food and medicine, I did not fight them. I yelled, but I did not fight.

The doctor visited. "You are not me, you never have been and never will," I told him. "Your fingers on the armrests of that chair do not feel the leathery scratch as mine do, your toes do not inhabit your cotton socks as mine do, your thoughts do not move and agitate in the skull as mine do."

He said, "It's true, Giovanni."

I lunged at him. "I lent you my voice, my posture, my facial expressions. More than that, I lent you my history."

"Go on. Please."

"When you were Bernard, you were yourself. When you were Heedling and Max, you were. You are yourself right now. You have always been *yourself*." Tears flew out my eyes like snot. "Behind the moat there you lie, hiding still."

My voice was hoarse, but I couldn't stop speaking, even when alone. "Hell, I was hoping you'd hear about it. Really, what interest could I possibly have in a rotten piece of ass like that? No, when she was on me, I was thinking of *you*." "Boy, the whole point of this—the *revolution* of it—is in imitating the audience. We do celebrities and we're another two-bit nightclub act. But we get *volunteers* and we're *artists*." I tried my old radio voices: Richard Nelson's, Jimmy's. Each one eluded me. In the moment I reached for a voice, it escaped me, like Lucy's in those wanting months, each attempt spurring another failed one until I was pacing, wringing one *finger* at a time. What terrified me most, what caused my heart to throb in my mouth, was to think that it had *always* been this way. That between each of these voices, the voices of my life, and my own, existed this—this *gap*. Always, onstage, in class, onscreen, this *gap*!

Yet I kept talking, babbling, for I dreaded silence more. I hummed, I clapped, anything to cause noise. In silence, I would vanish. I checked my hands, swatted the back of my neck. The fear was so great, I decided to express it to the doctor when he visited, but seeing him there—I had no *voice* to tell him with. "Your fingers on the armrests of that chair do not feel the leathery scratch as mine do," I screamed instead. "Your toes do not inhabit your cotton socks as mine do, your thoughts do not move and agitate in the skull as mine do."

There were new pills. Maroon. Sun-yellow. One gave me the jitters, another migraines. Orphels insisted we were making progress. Dips along the way to recovery. Important to *feel* the process, not just talk about it. I said nothing, except to hum or mutter his speech to me. "I know you can hear me," he said from the other end of that padded room. Eventually I was returned to my room, so someone must have judged me better. It made no difference where they put my body.

———————

I could hear people talking to me. I observed the doctor's arm-chair abiding my weight. The water of the pool cinching around my waist. Every morning, Mama's voice like a radio in my ear.

Spring dulled into summer. Time was passing, I was aware of that, but only distantly, in the way one is aware of a holiday cel-ebrated by foreigners. Time no longer *pertained* to me. I learned that in the basement. A relapse, as it's called by doctors, teaches you this: The condition is more a part of you than the solution will ever be. "You are not me, you never have been and never will," I said to the birds on the lawn.

From the dreams of that period: I am onstage at the Communi-qué. The crowd wolf-whistles, demands an encore. Max, looking as he did the day he visited me at No More Walls, beckons for the next volunteer. "Who will have the gall, the guts, the gumption, to join Giovanni on this grandest stage?" Max shields his eyes to see more clearly the hand in the back. "You, sir. Please come." A hush. The figure ranges in the darkness. He can be heard excusing himself around the tables, takes his first lean steps onto the stage. He is tall and lanky, the volunteer. He is dressed in a tuxedo. The crowd, I see now, is all skeletons, white and shiny, jaws clacking with laughter.

A feeling started inside me: a gut-punching envy. Acute as thirst. I envied the heel of the janitor's hand sweeping crumbs from a table, the liver-spotted cheek of a patient. I walked around with tears in my eyes.

One western in particular I watched over and over in the screening room, envying to death the puggish sidekick. The sidekick leaned over the horse to spit. He wiped his mouth angrily with the back of his hand. I wept at the *perfection* of that sidekick. In no time the film would end, the fluorescent lights would tick on, and the darkened windows would throw out cruel reflections: of me looking bearded, lavishly medicated. All that awaited me was the night and my room, where I hated going, where I was terrified of going, where I was sure—every night, *sure*—that I would vanish. "Your toes do not inhabit your cotton socks as mine do, your thoughts do not move and agitate in the skull as mine do," I muttered in no one's voice.

All I asked from life was to observe it.

It started with one of the custodians, a freckled woman, big-boned. During Free Hours I began to shadow her along the circuit she made to empty the property's garbage cans. Before each wastebasket she'd gird herself like a weightlifter. Then with tensed arms she'd raise the packed can and upend it with a grimace, its contents tumbling, with a clotted rhythm, into a larger bag she'd placed nearby. Setting the can back down, she'd reach into it one last time, stretching for whatever bits of trash remained, her face producing a wonderful, effortful grin.

After the custodian, I followed a sunken-eyed nurse, a security guard. I learned to hide behind bookshelves, to look away at the right moment. These bodies offered a therapy far greater than that of Dr. Orphels, across from whom I sat every day without saying a word. They were my body, these people.

I first noticed her because of the camera. It looked expensive, hanging from a leather strap around her neck. She was always picking it up to take photos, usually of standard objects, like trees and doorknobs, ten or fifteen at a time.

Within the rigidity of the No More Walls schedule, she limited her range even more, sticking to a routine inside the routine. At breakfast she sat alone at a table by the window, consuming a half grapefruit and two hardboiled eggs with the wide-eyed avidity of a child. In the eight a.m. exercise class on the south lawn, she stood without fail in the farthest right row, second to the front, where she jogged in place and stretched with what was either a nervous or very earnest energy. Water Therapy followed where I was treated to a vision of her petite and queenly figure outside the vagueness of her scrubs. She wore the hospital-issued blue one-piece all the women did, and her dish-white legs flashed along the wet blue tiles, her bottom jutting and swinging like some oblivious tail. She had very correct posture, fiddled religiously with her ponytail: stroking it ten times with the right hand, ten with the left. These numbers were precise and repeated, just as she cleaned her fork nine times and walked around the lawn before dinner twice, all the while snapping photos of an oak tree, a wooden bench, a dinner knife. Each day she marched over to the right-most Jacuzzi, tested its waters with her toe three times—always three—then three times up to her knee, before finally sinking in. When she did finally soak, she made a loud expression, as if she'd swallowed hot food.

She could not have been counted among the more social patients, those who chatted in the back of art class or gossiped in the mess hall. Not once had I seen her talk, yet a warmth radiated from her, an availability, despite the cocoon she, like so many of us, wriggled within. Her method of notifying another of her presence—of alerting them, say, that she stood behind them in the hall—was to cup that person's shoulder gently. All in all, she carried herself with the overstatement of a silent-movie actor, frowning, shrugging, darting, her camera always *clipping*, loud as scissors. Behind it, her forehead tense with focus.

During Free Hours she retreated to the small, gummy pond behind the orchard. She liked to sit under the weeping willow. Tree frogs belched and dragonflies, like tiny helicopters, buzzed over the water, but this woman, sealed within herself, didn't seem to notice. Often she chucked pebbles into the pond or ripped out blades of grass. Sometimes she cracked her joints or formed bats with her hands and flew them around. I'm ashamed to say that I, lying on top of the embankment like a scout with a spyglass—I witnessed her do this four or five times before I realized that she was talking to herself. It was sign language.

The next afternoon I discovered the note under my door. A folded piece of paper inscribed with the words *For You*. I recoiled from it as from a rat. The letters were so exact it looked like they had been written with a stencil. I turned on the bedside lamp and opened it.

> *You, Stop following me. I mean this seriously, STOP.*
> *Amelia Stern, Door 12.*

I read the note until it trembled in my hands. A thousand oaths I swore to myself: to knock on her door right then, to hide forever from everyone, and soon I was blathering to the man I trusted least in the world because I had to talk and Doctor Orphels, he was there. My session took place an hour after my discovery of the note, and there I spewed in breathless monologue what little I knew about this Amelia Stern. It was the first time I had spoken to the doctor in months, the first time in months I'd spoken at all (outside of muttering his speech to me), and I was expecting, I think, some theatrical rapprochement—a welcome-back sort of speech, a wry grin, at the very least, but Orphels simply listened, reading her note when I handed it to him. "I know," he said. "I told her to write it."

"Told her?!"

"She's my patient. She noticed your following her and found it discomfiting. I told her she ought to notify you of this feeling. As you rightly observed, she's deaf, so a written note seemed best."

"You knew about this? All this time, you *knew*? Did you, did you *orchestrate* this?"

"But how could I have?" He smiled. "You were the one following her."

"You're just like Bernard. You *use* a person."

"I believe you were the one who had been using me, Giovanni, using my voice, my history. I thought we discussed that."

"You are not me, you never have been and never will." I was scratching my scalp. "Your fingers on the armrests of that chair do not feel the leathery scratch as mine do, your toes do not inhabit your cotton socks as mine do."

"Giovanni, if you had brought up the situation with Amelia sooner, I would have been more than happy to discuss it. You've brought it up, so I've addressed it." He said, "What led you to her?"

"So you can run and tell her?" I was nearly yelling. "I don't want to talk about it."

"Okay."

That's how he was. He picked the best moments to surprise you. He waved her note. "At the least," he said, "you'll have to explain yourself." A few minutes later, the session was over.

That evening I paced the grounds until the sky was black. *You'll have to explain yourself.* I wandered by the birch trees, the mountains going from blue to black to blue again against the sky. *You'll have to explain yourself.* Bats soared and dipped like pieces of night briefly torn free. In low clouds the fireflies rose and evaporated. I wandered into the woods, away from the house, stumbling over roots.

Explain yourself. The words had never sounded so strange.

Soon I was sprinting through the woods. It was like being erased. Smeared in with the trees and ground. An owl was saying, "Whooo?" and the needles crunched under me and just then, without warning, as if God had snapped his fingers, all the intervening years collapsed, and I was thirteen again, being dragged out of the classroom by Heedling. I could *feel* it. The collar tightening around my neck.

Explain yourself.

Then Max slapped my cheek in Dun Harbor. I felt it in the woods: the *slap.* I felt other things, too, *felt* them as though mugged, physically, by memory: felt Mama's arms squeezing my waist, her chin digging into my shoulder. ("Up, up!" she'd said.) The spotlight warming the shoulders of my tuxedo. Lucy's calves scissoring the backs of my thighs. The girls outside Derringer's office, their grins like hobos'. Max's notes in the margins of his papers swarming like ants.

Explain yourself, and before I understood what I was doing I had run back to the house. I found a pen and paper at the commissary and wrote back to this woman, Amelia Stern, *explaining myself,* scribbling in a state of exhilaration:

Amelia Stern,

> *I do not mean to stare. I'm sorry, please know I'm sorry. I'm barely even here these days, so it's medicine to find a person who is. I was invisible, I thought. As loose change gets lost in a couch, that's how I'm lost in my body. You have a superb way of walking, that's all. You have a way of touching people on a shoulder I admire. Of eating soup, etc. My mother was killed. You will not turn and see me following you, I promise. Sometime long ago I was a well-behaved man and will be again. You're sweet medicine, that's all.*

> > *Giovanni Bernini*

I must've entered into some new delirium since before breakfast that morning, after slipping the note under Amelia's door; I visited the library and, with no plan at all, checked out a dictionary of sign language.

Like everything, borrowing the book seemed a frightful ordeal—what with surviving the solicitude of the nurses and the fluorescent lights of the library—but I managed to do it. In my room I practiced, and if it hadn't been for the terror of failing and the terror of succeeding, I could have torn through the book in an hour, so closely did it play to my talents. My hands were two ticklish birds, two anythings. Dancing origami—my knuckles, my meanings. There was a civility involved, a silence, and theatrics.

Awake. Do you know how you say it? You mimic the opening of the eyes. You form two L's with your hands and push them away from your temples.

Freedom. You make fists and cross your arms, then uncross them. Cross, then uncross.

Face. My favorite. With your forefinger, circle your face.

It was like cutting a hole in the air.

As much as it pained me, I kept my promise, switching with the doctor's help to B Schedule, which meant I did everything Amelia did an hour after her. Because her routine was so exact, it was painful but not difficult to avoid her entirely.

My sessions with Orphels those two days were among the least helpful yet. I went on and on about the letter, pecking at him for her reaction.

"Giovanni, you know I can't discuss this."

"I don't know that. I don't know anything about what you're up to. You're like your father, Dr. Orphels. A master of justification."

He grinned. "You distrust me, but that's okay. I would prefer you to be distrustful of me and in possession of your health than the reverse. Please tell me." He said, "How did it feel to write that note?"

I shook my head. "I don't have to say."

"That's true."

A long silence. "As you yourself observed, Amelia suffers from obsessive-compulsive disorder," he said. "Must repeat most actions anywhere from three to forty times. Wash her hands. Open the door. She worked as a newspaper photographer, and this activity, photography, became a way of mitigating the obsession.

Rather than touching a certain hydrangea bush three times, she would take three photos of it."

"Big improvement," I said.

"It was, actually. She's suffered fewer obsessive episodes. There was, however, one lingering problem."

"What's that?"

"She did not like the photos," he said. "Understand, the quality of the photographs was not a problem for me—I thought some of them were quite lovely—but Amelia *hated* them. None of those photos, in her mind, *captured* their subjects. Of course, I suggested many times that such 'capture' was impossible."

"What happened? I still see her out there taking photos."

"A twist." He raised his finger. "She started taking photographs without any film in the camera."

"No film?"

He nodded. "By snapping the photo but not actually committing the moment to record, she was acknowledging that she could never fully 'capture' the object, and yet was able to feel like she had."

"There's no film in that camera?"

He grinned. "It reminded me of you, you know."

I said nothing.

"Maximilian's quotation marks. That the stage is like a pair of quotation marks—everything you do inside them isn't something you're actually doing, but something you *could* be doing. Like taking photos with an empty camera, no?"

"You're up to something here. I can feel it."

"I know you distrust me. You will for a long time. But have I ever withheld anything from you?"

I was trembling.

"Tell me. It's important for me to know. How did it feel to write that letter?"

I was looking off to the side, my hands cupped in front of me. "Crucial. Terrifying. I was trying to *explain myself*. Like you said, Doctor. Writing and betrayal. Writing and betrayal."

I was returning to my room from one of these sessions when I nearly slipped on the note. It was folded primly in half, addressed to me: *Giovanni*. I held it, terrified. I brought it down with me to dinner, unopened, and, after eating, pondered it, folded, for a good half hour in order to savor the moment of knowing it had arrived but not yet knowing how it would disappoint me.

Again it featured those absurdly straight letters.

You're a hell of a lot more charming on paper than you are stalking around with God-knows-what blasting in your head. Don't think I don't recognize you either, even with that bush of a beard. (To your beard I have this to say: <u>Scram</u>!) I covered one of your gigs for City Paper. Just now I shut my eyes and saw the shots from that night. I mean it: on the inside of my eyelids, little dancing movies. There's one of you with a vein, size of a slug, popping out of your forehead. One of you wiping this fake tear from your eye. Digging real <u>hard</u> with your knuckle, like you were trying to fish out a silver dollar.

I swear I've got a museum in my head.

I like you in letters. In the letter you sound like a little boy wanting permission from the world. You've come a long way from that, huh? Perving around with hungover eyes? Write me letters, that's fine. Nothing in person, though. I mean it. I can't stand a man to throw his thoughts on me like that.

Amelia Stern
PS I'm sorry about your mother.

I read the note ten, twenty, thirty times. As I held it, my room took on a doomed and blanched quality, and a great panic fell on my head.

The next day I showed the letter to Doctor Orphels. I could barely sit still. "It's the voice," I said, "the voice inside of her."

"You sound almost religious," he said.

"I want it for myself."

"Want what?"

"That voice! That can't be spoken."

"But you have your own, Giovanni."

"I don't think so, no."

"But look at what she said about *your* letter. She seems to think you did." He said, "You won't tell me what you wrote?"

"Honestly, I was in such a state. It was after our session, when I told you about her note to me, and you told me that I ought to explain myself. Those words had never sounded stranger: *Explain yourself*—I took a long walk at night and all of a sudden I remembered things. That's when I ran back to my room and wrote her." I said, "Why do I suspect you've arranged this all?"

"Tell me about the envy, Giovanni."

"When I was imitating you," I said. "What I envied was the telling—your telling your story. Not just telling it but that it was *complete*, that it made sense. You *explained yourself*."

"Write yours then."

"What?"

"Your story, Giovanni. Write it to her."

Without the benefit of frenzy, the second letter took longer. My fist wouldn't release the right words, but I took solace in knowing when a phrase was right and when it wasn't. Soon I found myself writing, "Sympathetic to the bone," and "Mama's eyes could do things no one else's could." She wrote me back a few days later. Then I told her of the doctor's suggestion. I didn't think I could do it, I wrote, unless she, too, provided me with her own letters. The next day there was a note under my door: "Whatever the doctor thinks."

Since then I've received hundreds of notes from Amelia. Each morning they appear under my door like the most important newspaper in the world.

Here's one:

> *Men always take it upon themselves to pity me, but don't for a minute fucking do it, no. My father's a rich man, Giovanni, the publisher of newspapers. I had maids, a big fat yellow lab, the advantages. Anything for Amelia, that's Dad's philosophy. Here's an image: He used to spread the Sunday issue out on the floor of my bedroom, and the two of us would roll around on it like mutts.*

Her eye is as good as Mama's. Her notes like clues in a treasure hunt. A crack in a tile, a certain chef's frown:

Look at the bark on the first tree in the fourth row of the apple orchard. There's a kind of gray patch on it I really like. The color of an elephant.

Or,

I love the doctor's teeth. The way he just leaves them out. Does it make him more or less trustworthy?

Sometimes she describes old photographs. Like one of a candidate for state assembly:

He had thinning hair. You know how that looks—like a man failing to keep a secret. I climbed up a fucking tree to get it. To get the spots where the scalp showed, pale as a halibut under his wheat-tipped combover.

Or photographs she snapped with the empty camera:

I took a photo today I wish, I wish, I wish I had a copy of. Of a nurse (young, female) and a patient (the one with the gray goatee?) sitting on one of the benches on the south lawn, right at sunset. Both of them with their hands in their laps, hands not clasped, just floating in their laps, both with their shoulders sort of slumped, both with their heads tilted toward the sunset. The same exact pose. You know the way a dog tilts its head up at his owner—that's how the two of them looked at the sun.

Her notes are a physical presence for me, a human company, and without their touch I couldn't have produced this account.

Doctor Orphels saw to it that I was provided with a typewriter. Every night I left a fragment of my life under Amelia's
door, until, writing longer and harder, I would leave a whole sheaf
of papers by her door every couple of weeks, describing the spring
boardwalk in Sea View, for instance, or the pigeons outside the
Stone-Wild Museum. Then I became more serious and asked for
the pages I had given her back so I could revise what I had written, add what was missing, and deliver it when complete. She
agreed, leaving the pages by my door, and I have been earnestly
working since.

Throughout we've maintained our promised distance. Given
Amelia's schedule, this hasn't been as difficult as it might sound.
I've stayed on B Schedule and, in that way, experience the circuit
of No More Walls an hour after she does: I see her residue in the
kitchen, in the front lawn during exercise class. A few times I've
glimpsed her blond ponytail in the commissary or the rose garden
and my heart gasped, like seeing a figure from the other side, like
seeing Mama, and I turned away, terrified. At first I ached to see
her, but I know this is best, the two of us, close neighbors, pen pals.

Or so it had been until recently. At that point I had reached
the moment in my story when I started following Amelia, and I
asked if we could take a walk together to help me better describe
it. The faithfulness of our accounts had taken on a religious seriousness for both of us. Later that day I received a note from her
saying, "East Portico 3pm tomorrow."

I showed up a half hour early, forgetting how bad being early can
be. The night before I had memorized certain remarks in sign language that now crackled in my fingers like static electricity. I
tried to run my hands through my hair, pass them over my face,

but all they wanted was to talk, to talk to Amelia, yet when I looked up and saw her fidgeting before me, one hand on her hip, they fell dead at my side. The dimple in her cheek looked like a play of light.

I said, "Are you early, too?"

She smiled, snapped a photo of me, and motioned with her hand, as if to say, Are we gonna walk or what?

I nodded. "I'm sorry, I'm sorry. After you," but she had already stepped ahead of me and didn't see.

We walked as if chaperoned, maintaining a sort of legal distance, and in that way passed through the bee-haunted orchard and the garden. Amelia stayed a pace ahead of me, starting with the second row of apple trees in the orchard, doing what she always did, even with me trailing her, which I took as a handsome sign. From my week of following her, I knew what would come next: a walk to the garden, where she would snap the blue hydrangea bush four times, lean in, and smell its top flowers twice, circle it once more, and then continue down the embankment to the pond, where she would crouch next to the weeping willow.

All of this she did without once looking back, and I felt like Eurydice in the tale of Orpheus, one of the best and most pitiable from Heedling's class. Watching her head to the embankment, wrapped so firmly in her repetitions, I thought of that myth all over again, and thought I understood it, too. It was that Orpheus loved Eurydice too much to look at her. He had to walk ahead or behind her. But to look at her directly, to see her head-on, the love would become a thing too real to exist. Amelia crouched under the weeping willow, anchored to that patch of earth she trusted. I sat next to her so we could face the same direction and not each other.

We sat for some time. A cloud of gnats hovered over the pond. I kept fearing she might disappear, or had already.

I turned. You just let me know—please let me know—if you ever want to leave.

When she smiled, it was like the world carving joy into her face. I had never seen a person smile like that. You can speak!

A little.

She punched my shoulder. You didn't tell me you were practicing.

My last secret.

I doubt that. I doubt that highly, Mr. Bernini. I'd pin you for a secret machine. *A secret machine*, she repeated for emphasis and dropped her jaw. Then she frowned. A breeze passed and she lifted the camera to her eyes, snapping a photo. You getting all this?

What?

She waved her hand over her face. This. I feel like I'm posing for a portrait. With that, she leaned back, resting her head on her fist. Just as quickly, she snapped back to her previous position. The scrubs made the sound of raked leaves.

I'm getting it. I dared to flash a smile. But by then she was frowning again. Is it a bad feeling? If it's bad, we can stop. Right now we can stop.

I don't know. She shrugged. A new one. I don't like new things usually, but this isn't so bad. She checked over her shoulder. Twice. You really ought to do something about that beard. I don't understand a man's attraction to a beard. It's something yet to be explained to me in any satisfactory way.

Hiding.

She said nothing.

I mimicked the strokes of a razor along the sides of my face. I can shave it.

It's okay, I don't care, really. Just making conversation.

She was sitting cross-legged, tearing out the grass. Each blade made a belching sound. I tapped her on the shoulder again. I'm worried we'll run out of things to say.

Then we'll say nothing. She smiled brusquely and then turned again to the grass. A moment later she looked up. And are you hiding now? With your hands? Is that what this is?

My expression, I realized, was greatly exaggerated: my brow ruffled, lips pursed. No, it's better than that. Everything I'm saying is true, but it feels like, like something I *could say*, a *what if*. The quotation marks—it's like we're inside them.

Ah, Max's famous quotation marks. She smiled wanly and tugged again at the grass.

I tapped her. You okay?

She pursed her lips in such a way that the lower lip hung out more than the upper, nodded, and returned to the grass.

I hope I didn't say anything bad. If I did, please tell me.

But she was facing the ground.

I tapped her. I hope I didn't say anything bad. If I did, please tell me.

She signaled again, and this time I understood. I cried. I covered my face and bawled. I hadn't planned to, but there I was, weeping. It had been a fantasy of mine for years: to cry in front of someone I might love, and the moment, finally come, was like most moments. What I mean is, I wanted to be done with it, hide, and it hit me then how lonely a man I was. The loneliness—all of my life it had been my spine, and I didn't know if I could live without it.

She smiled again, discreetly this time, as if many people were watching.

To the bone, I repeated, and she reached across and rubbed my knee.

We sat in silence. I said, I like speaking this way. It's like writing letters in the air.

Not for me, unfortunately. Just chatting.

But you have a voice, don't you?

She shook her head. Nope. A second later, though, she took my hand and placed it around her throat. I didn't feel it at first. Then it came: a low hum, like the *whoosh* of a furnace. Then she executed a smile I won't soon forget: a smile as vulnerable as it was unshy, a smile I would've killed for in my old days and might have stolen even then if I hadn't been so happy—and frightened— to be the lucky fool for whom it was meant.

She released my hand. She angrily ripped the grass out of the ground, lost in her own thought, and then stood up, wiping the bottom of her scrubs. All in all it took about twenty minutes for her to make it back to the east portico. I was wracking my brain for a proper goodbye when she leapt up and kissed me. The whole thing was very quick and bashful, and felt like language. Like a specific meaning that could only be communicated one way: lips together.

That's all you get till you're done, she said.

Done?

With your story, and with that she opened the door and entered the sunny house.

I've stayed on at No More Walls for two years. It hasn't been a thousand days, but one day lived a thousand times. I see the doctor, eat with the patients, and in every free moment, chip away at this account. That I survived all those years without this typewriter seems a miracle. Yes, the practice of writing, as I've learned, is the best moat there is, or rather, outdoes the apparatus of a moat, a mechanism very literal and clunky compared with the magic of a story. Words, I've come to see, not so much recount experience as replace it, and as I reread this account of the famed impressionist, it is as if he never happened at all or that he is happening only now, here, where he can live as Giovanni the Words.

Doctor Orphels and I have had our moments. Several months ago he accused me of exploiting this story, twisting it into yet another performance—this time, he said, a performance of words. He is right, of course. And I know I've toiled over this account not only to improve it, but also to delay stepping out from behind it, back into the gnashing world, where all the applause and punishment are made. I suffered a relapse while trying to write about my years in Fantasma Falls, and he allowed me to speak sign language with him during that time, when my voice wasn't strong enough. He has read every page I've written, he and Amelia, both. Mama, too, I like to think. Her eyes passing over every word.

Max made good on his promise and sent me a letter stinking of beer and ash. He brought news from Mama's neighbor, Doctor Kessman: how for three months neighbors placed flowers and candles outside Mama's door; how Doctor Kessman will leave everything as is in Mama's house until I return. It is quite respectful of him, but I doubt I can ever enter that place again.

Max lives in the City. "The people here still talk of Giovanni Bernini," he wrote. "Street vendors. Street people, they recognize me still, and they want Bernini. What do I tell them? I tell them the stage is too <u>small</u> for him! And they say, Is that why he went into film? And I said, Films are <u>too small</u> for him. And they say, Politics then? Is he returning to politics? Of course not, I say, <u>Too small</u>, <u>too small</u>. What could possibly be bigger, they ask? And I say, <u>Real Life</u>! He's entering Real Life!"

The other day I shaved my beard. I look tall and anonymous, a man easily unnoticed. I might be the stranger reading the morning paper at the lunch counter, the man clutching the handrail on the subway. When this account is finished, Amelia and I will take a walk together. The prospect makes me tremble, but I can always run back to my room and write it down. Spying on my life in order to live it.

I do my old work, too, sometimes. Early in the morning I tiptoe down the stairs and out onto the lawn, the sky a bruised blue, the land black. At this hour all is for the birds and their homeless kingdom in the trees. A thousand doors opening in nature: squeaking hinges. I crouch under the oak and talk to them: to the blue jays, the thrushes, and cardinals. It's in the tongue, the details of a whistle. Just the other morning a riot of bluebirds lighted upon me. *Come here*, I said. At first they hesitated. But soon they hopped on top of me, tapping me with their curious beaks, amazed that such a creature could be one of them.

ACKNOWLEDGMENTS

I owe a great debt to the following people, places, and institutions: my agent, Jin Auh, for her strength, guidance, advocacy, and editorial help; Jessica Friedman, Jackie Ko, and everyone at the Wylie Agency; my editor, Allison Lorentzen, whose instincts, generosity, and steady hand have been a great mitzvah both for me and for this book; Katherine Marino and Sarah Whitman-Salkin for making introductions; Nick Bromley and everyone at Viking for their hard work; Will Staehle for the killer cover art; Andy Fink for my close-up; those friends who read this manuscript in an earlier form and improved it immensely: Marijeta Bozovic, Alexis Gideon, Leslie Jamison, Taylor Materne, Frank Sisti, Jr., Diana Spechler, Chris Stokes, and Ben Wasserstein; Ruth and Liam Flaherty for my delightful stay at Seventy-ninth Street; Jack, Bo, Ann Pettibone Riccobono, and the Riccobono family for my happy winter in Rock City; Teddy Wayne for his support; Vice Admiral Nick Britell; fellow warrior Nick Louvel; Cameron Kirby, Jesse Schleger, and Ryan Snider, whose visits to Mississippi freed me from my head; Julia Turner, shrewd editor and pal; the New York Society Library and its librarians for fighting the good (quiet) fight; the Jentel Artist Residency Program, a sanctuary; Cormac McCarthy, whose judge said things about fatherhood I stole and gave to the character Bernard Apache; Lan

Samantha Chang, who encouraged me for better or worse; my wise and generous teachers at Ole Miss: Tom Franklin, David Galef, Michael Knight, and Brad Watson; my writer pals from Oxford: Matt Brock, Greg Brownderville, Sean Ennis, Will Gorham, Alex Taylor, and Neal Walsh; Barry Hannah, "the sweetest mother in heaven"; my grandparents Ellie, Ted, Evie, and Sey, providers of love, food, stories, and wisdom; my family and friends, bringers of laughter and luck; my parents, Beverly and Jeffrey, lifelong models of love, care, good humor, and kindness, to whom this book is dedicated (thanks, Mom, too, for the title); and my big sister, Nathania, for everything.